YOU HAD ME AT HELLO WORLD

YOU HAD ME AT HELLO WORLD

RONA WANG

SIMON & SCHUSTER BFYR

NEW YORK   AMSTERDAM/ANTWERP   LONDON
TORONTO   SYDNEY/MELBOURNE   NEW DELHI

SIMON & SCHUSTER BFYR

An imprint of Simon & Schuster Children's Publishing Division
1230 Avenue of the Americas, New York, New York 10020

For more than 100 years, Simon & Schuster has championed authors and the stories they create. By respecting the copyright of an author's intellectual property, you enable Simon & Schuster and the author to continue publishing exceptional books for years to come. We thank you for supporting the author's copyright by purchasing an authorized edition of this book.

No amount of this book may be reproduced or stored in any format, nor may it be uploaded to any website, database, language-learning model, or other repository, retrieval, or artificial intelligence system without express permission. All rights reserved. Inquiries may be directed to Simon & Schuster, 1230 Avenue of the Americas, New York, NY 10020 or permissions@simonandschuster.com.

This book is a work of fiction. Any references to historical events, real people, or real places are used fictitiously. Other names, characters, places, and events are products of the author's imagination, and any resemblance to actual events or places or persons, living or dead, is entirely coincidental.

Text © 2025 by Rona Wang
Jacket illustration © 2025 by Heedayah Lockman
Jacket design by Laura Eckes
All rights reserved, including the right of reproduction in whole or in part in any form.
SIMON & SCHUSTER BOOKS FOR YOUNG READERS and related marks are trademarks of Simon & Schuster, LLC.

For information about special discounts for bulk purchases, please contact Simon & Schuster Special Sales at 1-866-506-1949 or business@simonandschuster.com.

Simon & Schuster strongly believes in freedom of expression and stands against censorship in all its forms. For more information, visit BooksBelong.com.

The Simon & Schuster Speakers Bureau can bring authors to your live event. For more information or to book an event, contact the Simon & Schuster Speakers Bureau at
1-866-248-3049 or visit our website at www.simonspeakers.com.

Interior design by Hilary Zarycky
The text for this book was set in Adobe Garamond Pro.
Manufactured in the United States of America
First Edition
10 9 8 7 6 5 4 3 2 1
Library of Congress Cataloging-in-Publication Data
Names: Wang, Rona, author.
Title: You had me at hello world / Rona Wang.
Description: First edition. | New York : Simon & Schuster and Books for Young Readers, 2025. | Audience term: Teenagers | Audience: Ages 12 and up. | Audience: Grades 7–9. | Summary: "A Chinese American teen navigates a high-stakes coding competition, sabotage, and first love when she is invited to a summer hackathon at MIT" —Provided by publisher.
Identifiers: LCCN 2025010226 (print) | LCCN 2025010227 (ebook)
ISBN 9781534488519 (hardcover) | ISBN 9781534488533 (ebook)
Subjects: CYAC: Programming (Computers)—Fiction. | Contests—Fiction. | Sabotage—Fiction. | First loves—Fiction. | Chinese Americans—Fiction. | LCGFT: Romance fiction. | Novels.
Classification: LCC PZ7.1.W3656 Yo 2025 (print) | LCC PZ7.1.W3656 (ebook)
DDC [Fic—dc23
LC record available at https://lccn.loc.gov/2025010226
LC ebook record available at https://lccn.loc.gov/2025010227

For Chris Hillenbrand

Chapter One

Lola swears this is legit and not like her TikTok "side hustle" that turned out to be a pyramid scheme. She just needs me to float her a hundred bucks.

Even though I'm still sussed out by any scholarship contest with an entry fee, I say yes because, well, she's Lola. And I have enough cash. That's not the problem.

The problem is getting past my stepdad.

Cue the *Mission: Impossible* soundtrack. As soon as the final bell goes off, I rush home. I figure that's my best shot, since both Mom and Michael will be at work.

All my money is squirreled away in the shared bedroom. I kneel down and lift my mattress up with one hand. The manila envelope sits on the bedframe, all innocuous.

I grab the envelope and let the mattress fall back down. I try to shake out only a few bills, but my entire net worth comes clattering onto the floor. Coins spill everywhere. "Jesus fu—"

I cut myself off when I hear footsteps.

My heart drops.

I shove everything back into the envelope, but there's no time to stash the envelope itself before my stepdad, Michael, barges in.

So I'm an idiot, and now I'm trapped with an even bigger idiot. Maybe I could jump out the window. I bet he'd love that.

Michael's still in his pajamas, and his eyes are all bloodshot. He skipped the gel today, so his comb-over is basically a cry for help. I have no idea how Mom finds him attractive. Maybe she makes out with his bald spot.

Nope. Nope. Not devoting any more brain cells to that topic.

Anyway, maybe he's too out of it to notice anything weird.

Okay, here's the new plan: Act normal until he goes away.

"Hi, Michael," I say, but my voice comes out all neon-bright. I want to smack myself. Acting nice is decidedly not acting normal.

He narrows his eyes. "Char, you're home early."

Most afternoons I do homework at the Lucky Panda, the restaurant where my mom works. I get free pot stickers and we haven't had to call the cops on a customer in months, so it's kind of awesome. I shrug. "Shouldn't you be at work?"

Michael has some office job selling overpriced beachfront timeshares. Our town, Chinook Shore, is one of those places that is pleasant to visit for a single week every year and not a day longer.

"Called in sick."

"You don't look that sick."

He scowls. "Phantom pain."

From what I know, phantom pain is like your limb finding new ways to torment you from beyond the grave. Michael lost his left leg in Iraq. There are days when he can't get out of bed. Once, I found him scrunched on the floor, hands groping for flesh and bone that was no longer there.

I'm all caught up in guilt about Michael's bleak existence. Major mistake. Never drop your guard around the enemy.

He snatches the envelope out of my lap before I can even react. "What's this?"

"Nothing." I make a grab for the envelope, but he holds it high. Freaking tall person privilege. We really don't acknowledge it enough.

He peers inside. "Where did you get this? You been stealing from me?"

Nah, the casino's already got that on lock, I want to say, but don't. Instead: "I have a job."

"What job?"

"Just some clerical stuff at school." Okay, this isn't really true—I run the school website—but I don't want to get into it.

Anyway, Michael is way more interested in the money than the job, which is the same energy he's got for his own career. He squints. "How much is in here? A grand?"

It's $2,192, from five hours a week for thirty-two weeks at thirteen-seventy an hour. Not that I'm about to tell him.

Greed flickers over his face as he eyes the cash. "If you've been working, maybe you should be contributing to this household."

There's a sudden glitch in the part of my brain that usually keeps me from, like, walking into traffic. "More like contributing to your gambling fund."

"*Excuse me?*"

"Nothing," I say quickly, but his face is all red and pinchy.

He shoves the envelope into his waistband. "You think you're so much better than me?"

I mumble, "I don't think that," even though I definitely think that.

"Your mama gives me her paychecks and it all goes into one bank account. We share money. We don't keep it to ourselves. If you live under my roof and eat the food I put on the table, you follow the same rules."

And that's when I know he's not giving the money back.

I could totally run for it. Snatch the envelope and shove past him. Bolt out the front door, sprint down the street, and then . . .

And then what? This isn't a Disney show. I can't go, like, live among the squirrels. I'm only sixteen. I'd have to drag myself back here sooner or later.

I have no real choice but to let him win. Like he always does.

After my parents divorced, Mom had a few boyfriends. They didn't stick around for long. Zhao was all sketchy crime-boss vibes and eventually had to leave the country. Noah fell way deep into Buddhism and ran off to some monastery in Vermont.

One night, when my mom was on the evening shift at the Jade Garden, a man came by as I was helping wipe down tables.

"Sorry, we're closed, sir," I said.

He smiled. "You must be Charise." That was when I realized who he was. Mom's new guy.

"Here, let me do that." He grabbed the washcloth and started wiping off the table.

Michael looked like Kristoff from *Frozen*. Hair the color of wheat. Broad shoulders; large, doughy hands. He seemed sturdy and unmovable, like a mountain. Reliable.

After we finished with the tables, Michael said he'd brought me a present. A bag of White Rabbit milk candy.

"*Baobei*, say *xiexie*," Mom chided.

My *thank you* was mostly muffled by the candy in my mouth.

He asked me about how old I was (seven and three-quarters), what happened today at school (our class hamster escaped), and what my favorite subject was (lunch). The same boring questions every boyfriend asked me. My eyes wandered downward. Metal poked out of his pants where his left ankle should've been.

"Are you a cyborg?" My favorite show on Cartoon Network was about these part-human, part-robot superheroes.

Mom cringed. "Char, be polite."

"Quinn, it's okay," he said. *Quinn*? That was the nickname

my mom used with customers instead of her real name, Qinxu. I didn't know she also used it with the guys she dated. Zhao spoke Mandarin, and Noah called her pet names like "pookie" or "honeybun," which made me want to barf.

Anyway, I was more interested in Michael's leg. "Does it have any powers?" On the show, someone had a bionic arm that could beam red lasers.

Michael rolled up his khakis to reveal titanium. "I lost my old leg in an explosion, so the government gave me a new one. But it's boring. It doesn't give me any superpowers."

"Are you going to marry my mama?" I asked. It would be awesome to have a cyborg stepfather.

"*Char!*" My mother's voice was a warning bell.

He let out a whooping, full laugh. Then he knelt down so we were at the same level, and his clear blue eyes were big and sincere as he said, "I hope so, Charise. I hope so."

Four months later, Mom and Michael got married in Portland's city hall. It was a gray, wet morning, the kind where the rain can't make up its mind. I carried the rings and Michael's daughter, Olive, scattered rose petals at our feet.

My mom looked so beautiful that day. She had borrowed a shimmering ivory dress. Her ink-black hair cascaded over her shoulders in ringlets. She was radiant and happy. I hadn't seen her smile like that since my father.

During the vows, I figured that as long as Michael stuck around, he would be better than all the other dudes.

I was so wrong.

Two months after the wedding was the first time Michael blew up. He flipped the table like some Marvel superhero attacking a perfectly innocent dish of three-cup chicken. Mom begged him to calm down. Olive and I hid in our shared bedroom and sat with our backs against the door as he went full Hulk on the plates.

Years later, my mom would explain that Michael was sick with a disease called PTSD, which could bring somebody nightmares even when they were awake. But at age eight, I didn't know that. All I knew was the plates shattering, a bright, clean sound, almost like the song of a wind chime.

Olive slipped her hand into mine. I squeezed my eyes shut and tried to remember the kind man who had wiped restaurant tables and given me White Rabbit candy.

Chapter Two

After Michael leaves with my money, I spend a few minutes figuring out how to kill him. *Sorry, officer, he slipped and fell onto my knife!*

But murdering someone, even someone who deserves it as much as my stepdad, would probably mess up the rest of my junior year. At the very least, I should wait until after AP exams.

So I resort to texting Drew **wyd**.

Drew McVeigh is this senior in third period pre-calc. He's all scruffy-skater vibes: sandy hair, voice like the crackle of dead leaves, and a scar on his chin. You know. The type of cute that inspires girls to comment *I can fix him* on TikTok.

In February we got paired up for a project on parametric equations and we would half-work, half-procrastinate in his bedroom. While we were computing intersection points, he kissed me, and I decided that was fine. We've been fooling around ever since.

He's not the love of my life or whatever. He's not even my boyfriend. But he's heard of deodorant and has his own car—well, access to his dad's girlfriend's car—which puts him squarely in the top ten percent of Chinook Shore High School guys.

Fifteen minutes later, Drew's parked in front of my house. When he sees me, the corners of his lips drag upward, revealing a gap between his front teeth. "Mulan. What is *up*." I've asked him not to call me that, and yet here we are. Maybe I should start calling him Mushu.

He reaches through the driver's window for a high five, which I don't return.

"Don't make me regret texting you," I say.

"Yo, what's wrong with the nickname? Mulan is straight fire. She's a total badass, and she's hot."

"And I'm sure it has nothing to do with the fact that she's also Chinese."

"C'mon, Char, don't be that way." He dangles his hand in the air, still waiting on that high five, and after a beat, I lift my palm to meet his.

Maybe I should give him more crap about the nickname, but it's hard to stay pressed at Drew. It's like being mad at a golden retriever.

When I open the passenger door, the seat is cluttered with empty beer cans.

"My B, lemme fix that." In one fluid motion, he swipes all the cans onto the car floor. Classy.

I sit and click the seat belt buckle into place. "So, your dad's place?" We usually make out in Drew's room.

He drums his fingers on the steering wheel. "Nah, we can't go there today. He's being annoying."

In a burst of recklessness, I say, "Let's go to Osprey's Point."

Osprey's Point is a picnic area near the shore. Benches, sandy gravel, leafy green trees. Gorgeous view of the Pacific Ocean. Like the rest of Oregon, before it was Osprey's Point, it had a different name and it belonged to Indigenous people.

Now it's become an infamous hookup spot for Chinook Shore High School students, exactly as Lewis and Clark intended. Drew has offered to take me before, but I always shot him down. I was scared that saying *yes* was the same thing as agreeing to go all the way. And that was *not* on my junior year bingo card.

But right now I'm choosing chaos.

He cuts his eyes to me. "Serious?"

"Why not?" I try to sound bored, but my heart skips at the thought of losing my virginity. What if it hurts? What if I screw it up somehow? Would it be weird if I find a wikiHow on sex and sex-adjacent topics? That's definitely weird.

After a beat, he nods and twists the ignition to life.

During the drive, Drew puts on a Pink Floyd album, which is fine by me, because my brain is still replaying the incident with Michael. Every time I think about him shoving the envelope into his waistband, how easily he claimed the one thing that was *mine*, bam. New surge of anger. New wave of homicidal bloodlust.

I guess it's good that I'm hanging out with Drew.

When we pull up to Osprey's Point, it's abandoned, although someone must've been here recently—there are seltzer cans littered across the ground. In the sunlight, their tabs gleam like rubies.

He asks, "Do you want something to drink? I have Coronas."

I hate the blunt taste of alcohol, but I find myself nodding anyway.

We find a clean-ish bench facing the water and crack open our bottles. He wraps his arm around me, and I lean into his shoulder.

It's almost romantic. The ocean is humming with sunlight, and there's a soft breeze coming in. A whiff of salt. Somewhere far away, a seagull shrieks. If we wait another hour or two, we could watch the sun dip below the horizon, the same way it does every day.

As we sip our beers, Drew yaps about his older brother David, who recently got out of rehab.

"Dad thinks my brother is this total disaster, but David's still kinda my hero," he says. "He was always so badass. For his senior prank, he and his friends got this cow onto the second floor of the school. They set up all these hay bales. It refused to go back downstairs, so the school had to bring in a farmer to help. It was awesome."

Wait, I saw this on the local news in seventh grade. There was so much mooing. "That was *your brother*? No way."

"Yes way."

I shake my head, amazed. "Has your class decided on a senior prank?"

He smirks. "Wait and see. It's going to be spectacular."

Until right now, I didn't even know David was in rehab. Around here, it's not rare for kids to end up there, but it isn't something that people openly discuss. Drew and I don't really have a relationship like this, where we actually talk about things.

I remind myself that he's leaving in September and I'm not out here trying to be besties with a guy who once joked about me eating his goldendoodle. He did apologize for that one, but still. We don't need to start spilling our guts out to each other.

When I kiss him, he tastes like Corona Light and mint-flavored lip balm.

We do that for a while and I climb into his lap; then his hands start roaming toward my hips. I let them roam. His body is hard and bony beneath mine. When I first started kissing Drew, I thought there would be some hunger clawing through me, some ravenous and obvious *need*—but it's always been more like a mildly interesting science experiment. Maybe I'm not the type to feel anything stronger than that.

I don't know how far he wants to go. I don't know how far *I* want to go. And maybe it's bad to do this here, outside, in plain daylight. But I want him to keep touching me. I want to forget about the rest of my shitty life.

"Char," he mumbles into my mouth.

"Mmm?" I don't really want to talk. It gets in the way of making out.

"Char. Stop." Then he pulls away. "What's wrong?"

"Huh?"

"You're kissing me like you're upset. Like you're trying to get rid of your own feelings."

"I'm not upset." I lean in for another kiss, but he dodges me.

"Uh-huh." He pushes me off his lap, and my butt slides onto the bench. "If we're gonna, um, do it, I wanna be more serious."

I give a faint laugh. "What, like, girlfriend-boyfriend or something?" Why would we define the relationship now? He's going off to college in a few months.

"Not even that. But you never want to talk."

"What? We're talking right now." Which is hardly the best use of our mouths, by the way.

He scrapes a hand through his hair. "Like, you're obviously pissed off. You've been all stiff ever since you got into my car. But you won't even tell me what's wrong."

A small white-and-brown puff of a bird—a sandpiper, I think—lands near our feet.

I point. "Look, a birb."

He doesn't even bother glancing in the direction of my finger. "It's like there's this great wall between you and the rest of the world."

Great wall. He cannot be serious. He's acting like I owe him a peek into the depths of my soul when he says dumb stuff like this. Annoyance flares in me. "You want to talk about something? Let's start with the fact that Mulan is a ridiculously racist nickname."

He blinks in genuine surprise.

"I didn't know that it actually bothered you." When I stare at him, he adds, "Kay, fine, Imma stop calling you Mulan. Happy?"

It doesn't feel like much of an apology. He doesn't get that the problem is bigger than a stupid nickname. "Okay, but what about that time you joked about me stir-frying your *dog*?" Which didn't even make sense. Drew knows I can't cook.

"Stop doing that," he says.

"Doing what?"

He shakes his head. "You're trying so hard to find stuff to complain about when the real problem is that you don't want me to know anything about you."

I throw my hands up. "I'm *fine* with you knowing things about me!" He knows plenty of things. Sure, they're mostly tongue-related things, but still.

"Oh, yeah? Then what happened with your dad?" He raises his eyebrows as if this is a big *gotcha*.

"Drew, that's not some crazy big secret. He's a selfish deadbeat. He cheated on my mom." I haven't seen him in almost a decade.

"Oh." He has the decency to look embarrassed. "I'm sorry."

"Yep."

"So, what's got you so bothered *today*?"

I fall quiet. Talking about my sperm donor is like reminiscing over a sad story that happened to someone else, some past version of Char that no longer exists. Talking about Michael, my current family bullshit . . . that feels different. That feels like handing Drew a knife that he could use to stab me.

The silence stretches between us like a taut rubber band ready to snap.

He nods. "Exactly."

"It's not that interesting," I say.

"I'm sure." He stands up. "Let's just go back. I'll drop you off."

"You don't want to . . . hang out for longer?" My chest tightens at the thought of returning to the house. Michael is there. Michael will *always* be there. I can't avoid him forever.

"Nah, I should get home. And Char?"

"Yeah?"

His face is this mask, and I know what he's going to say before it even comes out of his mouth. "Maybe we shouldn't do this anymore."

Chapter Three

So, yeah. Life is super great. And things don't get much better the next morning.

I find Mom standing in the kitchen. We greet each other in Mandarin Chinese. I'm not really fluent, but we use it when nobody else is around or if we don't want eavesdroppers to know what we're saying. It's kind of like having a secret language, except the secret language is spoken by over a billion people.

Sunshine-yellow scrambled eggs sizzle on the skillet. She's an amazing cook. She should have her own restaurant. Her food is utterly wasted on my stepdad.

"Remember when you used to make those with tomatoes?" I ask. A classic Chinese dish. But Mom hasn't made it in years. Michael has the palate of someone who thinks Applebee's is fine dining.

She smiles. "The most important ingredient is soy sauce."

When's the last time we even had soy sauce in the house?

Anyway, she seems to be in a good mood, so I decide

to ask. "Um, so, did Michael mention anything about my money?" Maybe this isn't a total L. Maybe she can talk to him for me.

Her spatula freezes mid-scrape. "What money?"

I swallow hard. "I had this envelope with cash. He took it yesterday. He stole it."

"How much was in there?"

"About two grand."

Now she looks at me, lips parting in surprise. "Where did you get all that?"

"I have a job at school." Maybe I should've told her. I guess it was just easier not to. I don't know when I stopped talking to her about my life.

She turns back to the stove. "Money is hard lately. Some of Michael's sales didn't go how he wanted."

"Mom." My voice cracks a little. I can't believe she's making excuses for him. Well, no, I can, but I don't *want* to believe it. "It's *my* money. I earned it."

"I know, *baobei*." *Precious baby.* But I don't feel like much of her precious anything.

She slides the eggs onto a plate. "But right now we can't cause trouble. Your stepfather is very stressed. Just until—"

Just until what? Until Michael hits it big at blackjack? Because given how bad he is at gambling, we might as well start buying Bitcoin.

But I don't get the chance to ask before my stepsister

traipses into the kitchen. "Hi, Quinn! Oooh, eggs." She doesn't acknowledge me.

Imagine you're using a public bathroom and then a stranger slides into the stall right next to yours. All you can see are their Converse high-tops, but you're getting a full symphony of toilet-related awkwardness. And after the flush, as they use the sink, you sit and wait for them to dip because you absolutely don't want to put a face to the sounds you just endured.

Yep. That's Olive and me. Two people who happen to be using the bathroom at the same time.

I don't hate Olive or anything. It's more that I don't trust her anymore. When our parents first got hitched, we were total besties. I'd vent to her about how Michael was making Mom cook greasy crap I didn't like or whatever. Then my complaints would magically trickle their way to Michael, and he'd get wasted and take it out on us.

So I learned to stop talking to Olive.

Anyway, if she's up, Michael's probably not far behind, and it's better for everyone if I'm not around by the time he drags himself into the kitchen like a swamp monster. And enlisting Mom's help is a lost cause. So I disappear out the front door.

I get to homeroom early, which means I hear way more tea than normal. Everyone's buzzing about a sophomore named Thayer who got busted for dealing, but nobody is sure about the specific drug. I hear three different versions of this same story before first period. By the time the bell rings, Thayer is apparently a peddler for pot, ecstasy, and something so illegal nobody even knows the name.

Anyway, I have to tell Lola about the money, even though I'd rather step on a Lego. Thank God my morning is AP Chemistry and AP English Language, since she's not in either. Life's looking grim if molecular orbital diagrams are the fun choice.

But I can't procrastinate this convo forever. At lunch, I spot Lola at our usual table.

Quick backstory: Lola Garcia and I became friends in sixth grade, after I walloped her in the face.

My family had just moved to Chinook Shore. Olive and I enrolled in school here, but we had different lunch periods, so I was doomed to the double-whammy friendlessness of being the new kid and the only Asian kid.

In the cafeteria, there was this boy; his name was John or James or something. He moved away years ago. So let's call him John, because who cares.

John's dream was to be like the president. Not to get elected president someday. But to be exactly like the current president, even though he had more in common with a garden slug than with a New York real-estate billionaire.

So John was squawking that Lola's mom, who worked at the school as a custodian, was gonna get deported.

Maybe it's bad, but these days, when people say racist stuff, I don't always call them out. It feels hopeless and overwhelming, like moderating a Reddit community for incels. But at age eleven, I'd just moved from Portland, so I didn't get that blatant racism was accepted here.

So I went up to John and tried to windmill-kick him in the head, but he ducked and my foot connected with only air. (Why did I go for a kick instead of literally anything else? Probably I thought it'd look cool. There is literally no limit to how much a sixth grader will debase herself to look cool.) My arms flailed as I fought to regain balance.

Suddenly Lola clutched at her nose, wailing. I'd struck her with my elbow.

Anyway, even though she went to the nurse's office and I went to the principal's office and John got away scot-free (something he *did* have in common with the president), Lola decided that we were besties after that. I don't know. Eleven-year-olds are weird.

Fast-forward to now. Lola is drawing in her sketchbook with her right hand and shoveling food with her left. Next to her elbow sits the metal tin of Prismacolor pencils I got for her birthday last year.

She's working on her portfolio, the one she's going to submit for the scholarship. Right now she's doing a strapless spring-green slip gown that reminds me of Tinkerbell's dress. Seeing it makes my stomach twist.

For a wild moment, I consider seeking refuge with the other Advanced Placement nerds, who are huddled at the opposite end of the cafeteria. They're these guys from chem that I sometimes check answers with, but I've been avoiding that crowd ever since I overheard them trying to guess my bra size. It wasn't even that they were being gross. It was that their estimations were completely off, which made me seriously question the credibility of their lab results.

Anyway. I'm no coward. I'm not going to flee. I'm going to talk to Lola.

"Hey," I say, plopping down my tray of UFOs (Unidentifiable Food Objects).

She glances up. "Did you get it?"

That's the thing about Lola. No bullshitting around. No *Hi, Char, beloved friend of mine, how are you on this lovely spring day?*

"No. I'm really sorry."

Her pencil stops scritching. "But you said—"

"I know what I said." I fiddle with a loose thread on my sleeve. "Some family stuff. I couldn't get the money." Maybe she'd get it if I explained Michael. But I don't go there with anyone. It feels like letting them read my diary or something.

She's quiet for a sec. Then she sighs. "It's whatever. I'll ask Mari." Lola is the type to call adults—yep, even her mom—by their first names.

"Really?"

"Yeah." She shrugs. "I didn't want to because, ya know, with everything going on with her treatments and the medical bills . . . And I didn't want to tell her about the scholarship and, like, make it a thing."

"I'm so sorry, Lo."

"Stop apologizing. Mari's always saying I should let her help me anyway."

I nod, not knowing what else to say. There's this awkward silence, which Lola always hates.

"Okay! Change of topic. Lookie there. Why's your man hitting up your stepsister?"

She jabs in a vague direction with Prismacolor Premier Colored Pencil in Spring Green, and I follow with my eyes. By the vending machines, Drew is all up in Olive's space. Every so often, he throws his head back and guffaws. There's no way my stepsister is that funny. She's the kind of person who says "LOL" instead of actually laughing.

I shrug. "He can do what he wants."

Lola slaps a hand over her mouth in exaggerated surprise. "Did you break up?"

"Kinda?" I don't know if there was anything *to* break up. "He said he doesn't want to make out anymore."

"You can't be *that* bad of a kisser."

I stick my tongue out at her. "That's not why. He asked to get *more serious*, whatever that means, and I complained about his casual racism."

She kisses her teeth. "Rookie mistake, darlin'. You can't accuse white people of being racist."

"Lola, he called me Mulan." And I guess I sat there and took it.

"Mulan *is* the best Disney Princess," she says. "Well, after

Lesbian Elsa. And the Little Mermaid. Okay, she's top five."

"You rank Ariel over Mulan?" I shake my head. "Ariel loses her voice *for a man*. Mulan saves all of China!"

"Yeah, but consider." And then Lola launches into a rendition of "Part of Your World" in her rich alto voice. When people begin to turn and stare, I kick her in the shin.

"Oww!" She clutches her leg in mock pain. "But I get you. Did I ever tell you why I broke up with Sarah?"

"Because she kept posting Bible verses about homosexuality on her Instagram story?"

"No, that was Church Sarah. This is Hot Sarah."

"Oh. Then no." I try to recall Hot Sarah's face, but I'm pretty sure my brain's just defaulting to Sadie Sink.

"She wanted me to speak Spanish while hooking up. I don't know if she had a Latina fetish or she was too lazy for Duolingo or what. I tried to go along with it, because she was so absurdly hot. Case in point: she was a natural redhead. And she was obsessed with yoga, so her butt looked—"

"Lo," I say.

"Okay, sorry. The last straw was when she asked me to recite Pablo Neruda poems in bed. Girlie, I'm not even doing the required reading for English class, you think I'm gonna read something with line breaks *for fun*? So I had to end things."

"Tragic." Personally, I might've tried to stick it out with someone hot enough to earn the nickname *Hot Sarah*. But Lola has more self-respect than I do.

We watch Drew's fingers graze Olive's bare shoulder. She giggles and flips her blond ponytail. I imagine a nature documentary voiceover: *Here, we observe two American teenagers in their natural habitat, engaging in a primitive mating ritual.*

Lola scoffs. "That dude is. Pa-the-tic." She punctuates each syllable with a tap of her fork against her plastic lunch tray. "He's probably doing this to make you jealous."

"Probably," I say, more to placate her than out of any real anger.

Drew shifts, and I catch a glimpse of his face. He's got this dazed, dopey look.

I force my eyes away. Maybe I should be heartbroken. Like, I was fully ready to lose my virginity to this guy yesterday, and now he's trying to slide on my stepsister. That's messed up, right? So shouldn't this hurt more? Maybe something is wrong with me. Maybe I'm a heartless bitch.

But then I remember my mom, and how my dad broke her heart cleanly in two, and how my stepdad now chips away at whatever remains. Bit by bit, day by day. Maybe it's better to be a heartless bitch.

Chapter Four

After school, I drop by my guidance counselor's office. Mrs. Lombardi waves me in. She's rocking this fuchsia blazer with a chunky gold necklace. For an old person, her drip is always on point.

"Charise!" She gestures at the chair across her desk. "How can I help you?"

Here we go.

I sit down. "I want to quit the webmaster job."

Her eyebrows rocket up so fast I think they might escape her forehead entirely.

"But you've been doing great! Mr. Horowitz has spoken about how helpful you were in getting rid of that virus he downloaded."

Mr. Horowitz, our librarian, gets scammed by these pop-up ads that claim there are "sexy singles in your area." An obvious lie, since we live in Chinook Shore.

"I think, um, my family . . ." I trail off, because it isn't like Michael straight-up told me to quit. But working feels pointless now. All those hours, all that cash, just *poof*, gone. And now that Michael knows about the job, I'd have to fork over whatever I earn. But I don't want to get into this with my guidance counselor. "I'm just busy."

She nods. "Everything okay at home?"

"Splendid," I lie. I don't even know where that comes from. It's probably the first time in my life I've said that word out loud.

A pause. I can't tell if she believes me.

"Charise, it's April of your junior year. You got a perfect score on your PSAT, a first in our school's history, and you have straight A's," she says. "Have you given any thought to college?"

College isn't the obvious path forward for Chinook Shore kids. Lots of people end up in farm or factory jobs, since our county has a major agricultural presence. Others go into timber. Some of the overachievers head off to a four-year university like Oregon State, and a few years ago the valedictorian—his name was Zach or Zane—went to a fancy school on a full ride.

"I was probably going to apply to some local places," I say.

"Why don't you consider going out of state?"

I shrug. It's not that I don't want to make out with an entire frat house or drink until I piss myself or whatever it is you're supposed to do in college. I'm not actually sure what people do there. I've heard they also attend classes and learn things, but that might be a myth.

But I don't see how I could afford elsewhere. "I don't want to take out loans." I don't want to owe anybody anything. My mom took out student loans for grad school and look where that got her.

"Did you know that private universities often offer financial assistance? Especially for families like yours."

Families like yours. I try not to wince at the subtle diss.

"I don't think I'm scholarship material."

"You never know until you try." Mrs. Lombardi rummages in her desk drawers, then slides a pamphlet over. "We got this in the mail. You should apply. The deadline's tonight."

I pick up the pamphlet. In blocky print, it says, *Alpha Fellows: An all-expenses paid, highly selective summer program for high school students. Building the next generation of tech leaders.* I've heard of it before. Some of Silicon Valley's top founders and engineers attended as teens.

An incredulous laugh escapes from my mouth. "I'm not going to get in."

When I was in ninth grade, I stumbled upon this forum, College Confidential, where these teenagers masturbate to their own SAT scores. They write unhinged rants about how they won't get into Harvard unless they cure cancer or solve world hunger or sleep with the admissions committee. And, of course, they have endless amounts of money for stuff like trombone lessons and mission trips to Bolivia. These are the kids who are attending a program like Alpha Fellows.

Mrs. Lombardi doesn't seem to be the type who lurks College Confidential, and I don't know how to break all this down for her. So instead, I say, "I barely know how to code."

"Char. You helped the administration so much last year with that cheating situation."

Last year, someone blasted an anonymous email to the entire school with test answers stolen from the AP Chemistry teacher's desk. Colossally stupid way to cheat. The principal asked me to bust them, so I built a script that, once downloaded by the anonymous person, used browser fingerprinting to identify their ass.

"That was a simple script. Their security was really bad."

"And you're the webmaster for our school?"

Webmaster is a pretentious way to say I get paid minimum wage to maintain our school's website. "It's just static JavaScript. Almost all client-side. There isn't even a database . . ." I stop talking because Mrs. Lombardi's eyes are glazing over.

I pivot tactics. "Besides, I don't even want to go. I have summer plans already."

I'm supposed to work at the Lucky Panda with my mom. Mother-daughter duo. We even wear matching qipaos. Tourists eat that shit up.

Plus, Lola is convinced that Taylor Swift is going to drop a new album sometime in June. Something about Mercury being in retrograde.

So, you know. Big plans.

Mr. Lombardi picks up the pamphlet and shakes it. Actually shakes it, like I'm a puppy and she's teasing me with a bag of treats. "Let's make a deal. Get this application in tonight. Put me down as a recommender, and I'll write about everything you've done for our school. I'll mention that we don't offer any computer science courses. This could be a big opportunity for you."

Ugh. "I have a first draft due tomorrow for AP Lang..." Four hundred words left to write about Jay Gatsby and his hard-on for a green light. Spoiler alert, Gatsby dies because he gets too ambitious and tries to overcome his poor, small-town origins. Seems relevant.

My excuse withers on my lips when I see that Mrs. Lombardi's eyes are brimming. Whoa, okay. I didn't think she felt that strongly about my English essay.

"Char, your stepfather is Michael Saunders, right?"

I nod, still freaked out by her tears.

"Did I ever tell you that I taught him?"

Wow, plot twist. I know I called her an "old person" earlier, but I meant like regular-old, not old-old. I do some quick math in my head. Maybe Mrs. Lombardi has an incredible skincare routine?

"I was a student teacher," she explains, as if she knows what I'm thinking. "I was, I dunno, twenty-two or twenty-three, and he was in the geometry class I was shadowing. He was one of the brightest students."

Michael was smart once? Yikes, wonder what happened to that.

"Then I joined the staff for real and I taught him calculus, too, his senior year. He was on the honor roll, great kid. Instead of college, he went to the army like a lot of his classmates did. The military recruiters would come to our school and make all these promises to teenage boys who were mad as hell—sorry, *heck*—about 9/11 and Al-Qaeda and didn't have anywhere to put that rage."

I nod, even though I already know the TL;DR of this story.

"Well, he suffered a lot during the war, and you know how he is now—" She purses her lips. "Char, you're too smart to waste your life."

"Um. Thanks?"

"Promise me you'll try for this program."

It doesn't actually matter. It's not like Alpha Fellows will admit me. I'll just rush through the application in an hour or two, then forget about it.

I grab the pamphlet and stand up. "Fine. Yeah."

"Forward me the confirmation email when you're done."

"Sure." I'm dying to bounce.

Only a few minutes later, as I'm walking out of the building, does it hit me. I totally failed to quit my job.

Chapter Five

The Alpha Fellows application is decently straightforward, which is kind of disappointing. Like, hi, I expected at least one question to be written in binary or hidden in the page source code.

One of the short-answer questions goes like, *Tell us about your first experience programming*. I respond with this sappy paragraph about writing Hello World at age six and how it felt like magic. I don't mention that my father was the one who taught me how to program. That it was the last time I ever saw him.

During Mom's pregnancy, Baba got a job in Shenzhen, China. He moved there while my mother stayed behind in America—they wanted me to get citizenship here. After I was born, he visited every few months, and when he came for my sixth birthday, he brought me a laptop. It was made by the company he worked at, Huawei. It was sleek and silver. I thought it was the most beautiful thing I'd ever touched.

"Tang Yijun." Mom said his full name like that only when she reprimanded him. "How much did this cost?"

"Relax, Qinxu," he said. "The boss is going to give me a big bonus this year. I can smell it." He even sniffed the air for dramatic effect.

"She's too young," Mom said. "What does a child need a computer for?"

"It's the future. Don't you want her to be part of the future? Isn't that why we decided to raise her in America?"

He smiled with dimples. My mother once told me that those dimples were dangerous; he could use them to get anybody to do anything.

She sighed. "Don't show her those video games you play."

He nodded vigorously. "Of course not. Educational purposes only."

After dinner, he showed me how to turn on the laptop, set up a username and password, and access the Web through Internet Explorer (which was still a thing back then). We created a Gmail account for me. I thought the computer was awesome, but I was happier to have an excuse to spend time with him.

"You have to be careful on the internet," he said. "There are a lot of bad people. A lot of lies."

I pointed at a banner ad with a voluptuous blonde, the words *Sexy singles are waiting to meet you!* plastered beneath her photo. "So that's a lie?"

My dad coughed. "Yes, don't click on any of those. Actually, let's install Adblock for you."

He wanted me to learn how to code. He demonstrated how

to make the computer print *Hello world!* in Python. He signed me up for the Art of Problem Solving, a website that had programming exercises for kids. Together, we worked through the easiest problems.

While I was puzzling over the concept of a *boolean* (which sounded like a good name for a stuffed animal), Mom screamed from the kitchen. "Tang Yijun! What the hell is this?" I flinched.

Dad swallowed hard. "I'm going to help your mother," he says. "Keep going. If you get stuck, you can click on the hints." So I did.

When my parents argued, it was like a volcano (my mom) fighting a glacier (my dad). The volcano would spew more and more fire, and the glacier would simply evaporate into steam, which of course would anger the volcano further. This analogy only works if you forget everything you know about geoscience.

Whatever the fight was about, it seemed to have been fixed by the day Dad had to leave. We drove him to the airport, and before he disappeared into the security line, he squatted down such that our eyes met. "Make sure you do the exercises while I'm gone, okay? I'll be checking the leaderboard for your username."

I nodded.

My father's next visit was scheduled for around Christmas. It was hard for him to get away from Huawei.

Every day after school, I would complete as many problems as I could. I daydreamed about how proud he'd be when he saw how far I had gotten. Maybe it would even make him want to stay in America for longer.

The day before he was supposed to fly in, my mother sat me down. "Your father won't be able to come tomorrow. He got busy at work." She had this horrible, creepy wrinkle in her lips. I think she was trying to smile.

"When can he come?"

"I don't know yet." Which was not a satisfying answer to a six-year-old.

So every night, for maybe a week, I asked her the same question. And every night my mother would toss out the same nonanswer.

Finally one evening, she snapped. "Stop asking, Char! Stop. He isn't coming. He has a new family now. He has a new daughter. Understand?"

I started crying because her voice was so harsh and mean. I couldn't even process her words. I didn't get what it meant to "have a new family" or how Dad could have a new daughter if my mother hadn't been pregnant.

Mom's face softened. "Oh, *baobei*. We will be fine without him."

She held me as I dissolved into tears. Later, she boiled a bag of frozen dumplings (chives and pork, my favorite) and we watched *Journey to the West*, the nineties animated series about the monkey king Sun Wukong. I think she assumed those things would make me feel better, but after that night, they were forever stained by the memory of Dad abandoning us.

And week after week, for years, I kept going back to the Art of Problem Solving. He said he'd be watching the leaderboards. He'd said that right before he left. Maybe he'd notice my rising score.

It's so stupid. It's so cringe. But deep down, I believed that if I got good enough, maybe he'd come back.

Chapter Six

Three weeks after I apply for Alpha Fellows, Lola and I catch a dine-and-dasher at my mom's restaurant.

When tourists stop by the Lucky Panda, they're expecting Chinatown in microcosm: red and gold banners dripping from the ceiling, ink paintings of bamboo and plum blossoms pinned on every wall. Oil-glistened platters of duck and rabbit gliding through the air.

As some Yelp reviewers so helpfully point out, the real Lucky Panda is not that glamorous. The table surfaces are wood-grain laminate. There's always at least one burned-out bulb among the ceiling lights. Peeling off-white paint on the walls, the forever scent of peanut oil clinging to the carpet.

Today, Lola and I do homework in an empty booth, munching on pot stickers while my mother prepares for the evening shift. Or rather, I'm wrapping up my final report on *The Great Gatsby* while Lola scrolls through Shein's prom dress collection, even though she doesn't have the money to buy anything new.

Prom is early May, and only seniors and their plus-ones get

tickets. Lola's situationship Rachel invited her. Apparently it's to make Rachel's ex-girlfriend Meredith jealous, but Meredith is going with some sophomore named Esperanza who used to have a crush on Choir Kelly (not to be confused with Stoner Kelly) whom Rachel hooked up with behind the bleachers during homecoming last year. Unless Meredith is actually going with Choir Kelly? Honestly, I had some trouble following the saga, although I was still riveted while Lola spilled all the tea. Cue that Marie Kondo screencap: *I love mess.*

"Do you think I can pull off a sweetheart neckline?" my best friend says. "Do I have the boobs for it?"

"Your boobs are fine," I say without looking up.

"I don't want fine. I want spectacular. Scrumptious. Succulent."

"Please don't describe your boobs as succulent." The English language was a mistake, truly.

"I want, like, Sydney Sweeney cleavage."

How did I end up in this conversation and how can I get out of it? "YOUR BOOBS ARE FANTASTIC, LO." I say this too loud, and my mom looks over from the table she's setting. Wonderful, now she's walking in this direction.

Lola tilts back in her chair. "Quinn! Love the new earrings."

My mom gingerly touches the hoops swinging from her earlobes. "Present from Michael." What she doesn't mention is that Michael won them in a poker game from this recent divorcée. "How is your mama?"

"Mari's been wearing this cold cap to prevent hair loss from chemo. Wanna see? She's the only person I know who can pull it off." Lola unlocks her phone and shows us a photo of her mom, who's wearing a navy blue helmet with a matching sweater. Somehow, she still looks like a J.Crew model.

"Mari always pretty," my mom says.

"Quinn, I'm not paying you to chitchat," the restaurant manager calls, and my mom stiffens.

"Sorry!" she calls in her lilting customer service voice. She excuses herself and hurries away. I frown. The manager can be such an ass. He once made Mom cover a dine-and-dasher out of her own paycheck.

The evening starts off low-key. A regular couple comes in and flash around photos of their fat-cheeked grandchild at a tulip farm. Some college kids, sun-dazed, collapse in a booth and linger for hours. A boisterous toddler spills a bottle of Kikkoman less sodium soy sauce and his embarrassed parents tip two twenties.

An hour passes. I write a concluding paragraph about how striving for the American Dream is totally pointless. Lola looks at more prom dresses she will never buy.

"Char." She pushes her laptop screen toward me. "You'd serve so hard in this." The dress is emerald green, with rhinestones sewn into the bodice. My eyes fall to the price—eighty dollars, but hey, at least there's free shipping.

Jesus. Isn't Shein supposed to be cheap? Isn't that the point of their human rights violations? Even if I were going to prom,

I'm not going to drop six hours of minimum wage on something I'll wear once.

I shrug. "Lo, nobody is taking me to prom." I'm not a girl who boys want to rent a tux for. They don't want to gasp after seeing me all glammed up, they don't want to slip a corsage on my wrist, they don't want to awkwardly sway to John Legend with me. And that's fine. That stuff seems like more trouble than it's worth. John Legend is overrated anyway.

"Darlin', forget Drew," she says, as if I haven't already forgotten him. "Hey, I know. Wyatt Callahan is going alone. You could be his date."

"Wyatt Callahan, the dude who got caught masturbating in a supply closet last year?"

"I mean, he's probably washed his hands by now." But after Lola sees my scrunched-up nose, she relents. "Okay, okay. I can ask Rachel if she knows any other seniors without dates."

"Nah, don't bother. We can go together next year when we're actually seniors."

She flattens her lips into a slash. "Char, I need to tell you something."

But before she can say more, my attention is diverted by a commotion several tables away.

A scowling man—a boy, really, he doesn't look that much older than me—towers over my mother. "I don't understand."

"So sorry, sir, but your card declined," my mom says. The corner of her mouth wobbles, which is how I know she's frightened.

"Try it again."

A crease appears between her eyebrows. "Maybe you have other form of payment?"

He tries to sidestep her, but she shuffles her body closer so he can't leave. Then he shoves my mother hard enough that she stumbles back. He bolts for the exit.

Both Lola and I jump up. My feet bring me out the door, with my best friend right behind.

The coastal wind ices my throat. It feels like my rib cage is shrinking around my lungs. In gym class, I run an eleven-minute mile. The guy is already so far ahead, it's going to be impossible to catch up.

But Lola is on the track team, and she sprints ahead. When he stumbles over a crack on the sidewalk, that gives her enough time to catch up. She launches herself at him, and they both fall to the ground. With a renewed burst of energy, I propel myself forward and sit on his legs. Quick, shallow gasps force themselves out of my throat. Now that my body finally has permission to stop, it wants to complain about pain everywhere. I can barely collect my thoughts.

Lola sits on his torso.

"Crazy bitches," the guy mumbles.

For the first time, I see him up close. His glasses rest askew upon his hooked nose. His face is gaunt, his cheeks mottled by ice pick scars. He looks familiar.

My phone rings, but I decline the call.

"Torres?" Lola spits out.

I try to place the name. Torres. Zach Torres. A senior when we were freshmen. Teacher's aide in my study hall, which meant he played *League of Legends* while the actual teacher on duty indulged his hairnet fetish by sneaking off with the lunch lady.

Wasn't Zach valedictorian? I thought he got a scholarship to a private school. Notre Dame or Vanderbilt or somewhere. I guess they must've been impressed by his Bronze 2 rating in League.

"Aren't you supposed to be in college?" I blurt out.

"How's that your business?"

For someone who's pinned on the sidewalk, he sure has a lot of sass. I shift my weight on his legs. "Well, given that you just dined-and-dashed on my mom, we can call the cops and make it their business instead."

His mouth twists unhappily. "Vandy put me on academic probation."

"What's that?" One of my mom's coworkers is on probation for a DUI. But that had very little to do with academics and a lot to do with three too many beers.

"I failed some classes. They asked me to leave for a semester."

Lola frowns. "But weren't ya, like, good at school?"

He lets out a bitter laugh. "Acing Chinook Shore is completely different from acing college. At least at a top private school like Vanderbilt."

"Is Vanderbilt a top private school?" Lola asks. "I haven't even heard of it. It's not Harvard."

Zach scowls. "As if you could even get into Vanderbilt."

My best friend looks like she's ready to rearrange his teeth, so I cut in. "Torres, can you just go back to the restaurant and pay your bill?"

He finally has the decency to look ashamed. "I wasn't trying to steal."

That's about as believable as a YouTuber apology video. I scoff.

"Serious! That's not me. I just . . . I got an email from Bank of America saying my debit card's been overdrafted, and I didn't have enough cash, and I panicked." Now he looks like he might cry. "I didn't think I'd end up back here, you know? I was supposed to be the one who made it out."

God save me. I really don't need to hear about his crash-out. If his lip starts quivering, I truly may barf. "It's Chinook Shore, not federal prison."

Ugh, now his eyes are weirdly shiny. I hate this. I don't want to feel bad for him. Really, if there is any victim in this situation, it's my butt, which is starting to go numb from prolonged contact with his knobby knees.

My phone rings again.

"Char, are you sure you don't need to get that call?" Lola asks.

"Nah, I'll check my voicemail later. It's probably a friend."

She squints. "You don't have any friends besides me." I open my mouth, but before I can protest, she adds, "The Advanced Placement nerds don't count. Half of them are just using you for homework help. The other half are hoping you'll let them touch your boobs one day."

Damn. She just obliterated me.

"Get the call," she says. "I'll figure things out with this dumbass."

"You know I can hear you, right?" Zach says.

We both ignore him.

My knees squeak as I stand. I press my phone to my ear. "Hello?"

"I'm looking for Charise Tang?" The male voice on the other end pronounces my name like the syllables are jagged metal.

"Um, yeah, that's me."

I cast another glance at Lola, who is still perched on Zach's chest. She mouths *Go,* and I take a few steps away from them.

"My name is Edvin Nilsen," he says. "Is this a good time?"

Chapter Seven

Edvin Nilsen. Founder of Alpha Fellows. CEO of Nexus, a data analytics company specializing in defense. I don't really know what Nexus does—since they work with the government, they keep everything hush-hush.

"Uh," I say, like an idiot. It feels like someone is pumping air into my skull. My feet start moving by themselves, taking me farther and farther away from Lola and Zach.

"The committee was wowed by your application," he says. "We wanted to extend you an invite to our summer program."

"Uh," I say again. This single syllable may demolish whatever impression Edvin Nilsen has of my intelligence.

He launches into what sounds like a prewritten script about logistics. The program is in Cambridge, Massachusetts, on the MIT campus. It runs eight weeks long, from mid-June to mid-August. All expenses are covered, including flights and lodging. The main component of the program is a hackathon, a competition where students team up to build technical projects—video games, mobile apps, hardware devices, sentient AI, whatever. One team will be awarded a hundred thousand dollars and considered for early admission to MIT.

He talks like all of this comes so easy. Like he lives in a universe where the most abundant element is not hydrogen, but money.

When I applied to Alpha Fellows, I saw that Edvin is a *Forbes* billionaire. A billion has nine zeroes. Three commas. Even in binary representation, it only takes thirty digits to represent a billion. Written out, it doesn't look like a particularly big number.

But it might as well span an entire galaxy between Edvin Nilsen and me.

"So, can you confirm your participation?" he asks.

The answer should be obvious, but suddenly I picture my mom, all alone, stuck in Chinook Shore. "I don't know."

"You don't *know*?" There's this edge in his voice. I can tell that he's not somebody who is used to being told *no*.

"Sorry, this is, um, a lot to process."

"I don't think you understand," he says. "This is one of the most prestigious summer programs in the country. You're the only student from Oregon we're admitting this year."

Wow. How is this even real? I'm tempted to ask if he's sure he got the right Charise Tang, but I don't want to be annoying. "I, uh. I need some time to think it through. Sorry . . ."

Edvin's voice is crisp. "Okay, let us know. There are plenty of students on the waitlist. You have until tomorrow to decide."

Tomorrow? That's, like, zero time. "Wai—"

But he hangs up, and then I'm listening to dead air for a few seconds.

I turn around, but Lola and Zach are gone. She probably dragged him back to the restaurant. Might as well go meet them.

I walk toward the Lucky Panda. The street is wide and empty and sad in its emptiness. It's close enough to the sea for the salt to gnaw away at the buildings, but not quite close enough for Airbnb vultures to start circling. I pass by abandoned storefronts, sidestep bottle-green glass shards on the sidewalk that nobody bothered to sweep up. Chinook Shore. The whole town feels like a sigh.

Lola is leaning against the brick wall of the Lucky Panda exterior, beneath a lamp that pins her in an orange pool of light. She brings a vape to her lips.

"Those things are liquid cancer," I say, even though I'm not one hundred percent sure that's true. Maybe I'm thinking of cigarettes. I'm probably thinking of cigarettes.

She exhales a thin, white wisp. "Darlin', at least my cancer will be strawberry flavored."

I don't say anything else, because Lola and I have argued about her vaping before, and I lose the argument every time. Really, I would've thought her mom going through chemo would've made Lola quit, but if anything, she's only gotten worse.

We all have our ways of coping. Hers is a Juul. Mine is—well, was—a cute guy who feels me up in his dad's girlfriend's car.

"What happened to Zach?"

"Begged the manager not to call the cops. You shoulda seen the blubbering. Snot and everything. He's washing dishes for a month." She pushes off the wall and starts walking toward the parking lot. "Quinn said we should clear out. I'll drive ya. I put your stuff in the trunk already."

At least Mom is fine. "Thanks."

We climb into her car. But Lola doesn't reach for the ignition. She's staring through the windshield at the restaurant door, her mouth a thin line.

I shift in my seat. "Soooo . . . Should we go?"

Suddenly she smacks the steering wheel. "God-freakin'-dammit! Just . . . Why would he do that? Duh, college ain't easy. Tough shit. But he ruined it. Why would he ruin it?"

"It sounded like maybe he didn't have a choice," I say.

She stares at me incredulously. "There is *always* a choice. *Always*."

I don't know why she thinks that, given that our entire lives seem to be written by other people, but I'm not in the mood to argue about the existence of free will. This isn't sad philosopher hour. So I repeat, "Should we go?"

"Mmm-yeah," she mumbles, and then we're finally moving.

As we roll down the street, she asks, "What was your phone call about, anyway?"

I explain about Mrs. Lombardi, Alpha Fellows, and Edvin Nilsen.

"That's amazing, Char." We stop at a red light, and she takes the chance to give me a quick side-hug. "So when are you leaving?"

I keep my eyes fixed on the road. "I haven't decided yet if I'm going."

Lola swerves around a pothole. "What is there to think about? Isn't it all expenses paid?"

For some reason, my brain decides to remind me of Zach's face. How defeated he looked. *I was supposed to be the one who made it out.* It pissed me off when he said that. Like he thought he was so much better than the rest of us. But he's the loser who ran out on a thirty-dollar restaurant bill.

I don't know why I'm thinking about Zach.

"Weren't we going to spend the summer together? Go to the county fair? Try every ice cream flavor at Scoops? Flirt with tourists?" I wanted us to live our best lives. Channel all the main character energy.

But Lola's not smiling, so I add, "Didn't you say Taylor Swift has a new album coming out? Mercury's in Gatorade."

"Retrograde, dummy," she says. "Char, I got something to say."

"Oh, right, you mentioned before. What's up?" Maybe something happened with her not-girlfriend Rachel. Lola hates how Rachel abuses the gritted-teeth emoji. She says it's so boomer.

We turn onto my street and my house comes into view.

Lola silently pulls up to the curb by my front door. She grips the steering wheel tighter. "I'm graduating this June. I've been taking classes online to get the credits."

What.

My mind pinwheels. Our final year we were supposed to have together, just . . . deleted. No more lip-syncing to Chappell Roan, no more hate-watching *The Kardashians*. No more sneaking leftover scallion pancakes from the Lucky Panda. No more senior prom. No more signing yearbooks, decorating graduation caps, fretting over The Future™.

There's so much I want to say, but all that comes out is, "Why?"

"I'm enlisting right after my birthday." She turns eighteen in July.

"Why the fuck would you do that?" The question comes out louder than I meant for it to.

At school, there are free sign-ups for the ASVAB, a standardized test for joining the military. Every fall, recruiters set up tables right outside the cafeteria and chat with whoever will listen. Each year, there are a handful of kids who end up in the army or Air Force. But Lola's always dreamed of being a fashion designer. She wants to serve looks, not our country.

"Char, chill."

I lower my voice. "You think camo print is a crime against humanity."

"It is. But my recruiter said Mari could get her green card and good health insurance."

Right. Lola's mom doesn't have citizenship. Mine does; when I was thirteen, I helped her study for the naturalization test. She snagged a green card through marriage. I've wondered if that's why she was in such a rush to lock a guy down after my father left.

But there are other options for Lola and her mother. There have to be.

"What about the scholarship contest?"

She blinks fast. "I didn't win."

My heart squeezes.

"I'm sorry," I say. The words seem so freaking inadequate, but I don't know what else to say. "Why didn't you tell me sooner?"

"Felt stupid, I guess."

"Not winning isn't stupid."

"Not because I didn't win. But I was delulu to ever think I could. I stalked the winner on Instagram. She goes to a bougie art academy in Chicago and her mother is this famous fashion designer whose clothes Billie Eilish wore to the Met Gala."

"So she didn't even need the scholarship money?" Like, I know this random girl has the right to apply for whatever scholarship she wants. But this makes me angrier than it should.

"The rich get richer. What else is new?"

She tries to smile, but the left corner of her mouth quivers, and then droops like it gave up on propping itself skyward.

God. I lean across the gearshift and envelope her into a hug.

As she cries, I think about Michael, who also grew up in this town. Mrs. Lombardi mentioned him. I've seen a photo of him at age seventeen, smiling at graduation. He has this awful mullet that looks like a roadkill squirrel, but otherwise, he could be any classmate of mine. Who would that seventeen-year-old have become if he hadn't shipped off to Iraq? If he hadn't watched his friends die in combat, if he hadn't lost his leg in a convoy ambush?

Even now, he has nightmares, nightmares that he tries to drown with liquor. He has rage and shame and loss, all these different hues of pain. The war never left him, not really. It leaks out of my stepdad and the rest of us become collateral damage.

I don't want Lola to return haunted, but I don't know how to save her.

A few minutes later, she breaks away, leaving my shirt damp in the spot where her face pressed against my shoulder.

"Char, look at me." Her voice is watery.

I meet her glistening eyes.

"You have to take this opportunity. You have to. You don't get how lucky you are that somebody decided to give you a chance."

"Okay," I say. "Okay."

She sniffles. "And you better not squander it the way Zach did. If you screw up, I'll come back from boot camp just to kick your ass, I really will."

Chapter Eight

May breezes in quietly. The first wave of summer tourists floats in, buoyed by the ocean wind. Meanwhile, Olive posts photos of her and Drew at prom. He's in a rented tuxedo.

For Advanced Placement exams, thirty of us get bussed to a different school forty minutes away. Psych and English Lang are fine. Chemistry is a dumpster fire, which is entirely expected. Our original teacher got fired last December for cooking drugs, which, in my opinion, was at least proof that he was good at his subject. Since then, it's been a string of substitutes who reply *gesundheit* whenever somebody utters the word "stoichiometry."

I want to get in extra Lola time before she ships off, but that's pretty much impossible between her mom's doctor's appointments and her online classes.

So instead I prep for camp. I teach myself mobile development on Swift, the programming language for iOS. I google all the instructors and study their lives—their professional accomplishments, their academic achievements. I even revisit College

Confidential for tips on how to win hackathons and avoid the posts from kids jerking off to their own SAT scores.

Meanwhile, I don't mention Alpha Fellows to Mom. I know, I'm the freaking worst. I'm her only daughter. We're supposed to be at the Lucky Panda together this summer. I'm about to dip for eight weeks. I could give her a heads-up.

But what if she says no? Worse, what if she rats me out to Michael? Let's be real. After that mess with the money, I don't really trust her anymore.

Every day, I think, *Maybe I'll tell her*. And every single day, I say nothing.

Then suddenly, June catches me by surprise, and it's too late.

Saturday. When my alarm vibrates, dawn is seeping through the window blinds. So this is it. It's five a.m., and I'm jetting off to Boston today. It still doesn't quite feel real.

Across the room, Olive is knocked out cold. Probably hammered from one of those end-of-year ragers that seniors throw. And Michael is off doing his usual casino nonsense, so he won't be back until Sunday night or until his paycheck is gone. Whichever hits first.

So that means the only person I have to be careful about is Mom.

Maybe I should wake her up. Tell her that I'm dipping so we can do a proper goodbye moment. She'll be happy for me. I think. Or mega pissed, which is valid. I think I forged her signature on the Alpha Fellows forms.

My phone flashes with a text from Lola. It says one word: *Here!*

Okay, so no time for Mom. Maybe a good thing, honestly. Even if she didn't kill me for, you know, committing identity theft, it would've been a super-awkward conversation.

I crack open the bedroom door and then freeze.

On the floor, there's a yellow rhombus cast by the refrigerator light. Somebody is in the kitchen. From the heavy movements and grunts, I'm guessing it's Michael, or maybe a walrus.

Probably he lost big. That's the only reason he ever comes back this early.

If he blew through all his money, he's going to be in the worst mood. The last time this happened, he put his fist through our living room wall. I wanted to hang a picture frame around the hole, like it was modern art. *Untitled, Michael Saunders. Materials: Drywall and toxic masculinity.* Mom didn't find the idea funny.

Anyway. Maybe I could wait in my room until he passes out. But who the hell knows when that'll be? The plane might be above Montana by then.

So I have to risk it. I lift my suitcase up so the wheels avoid the ground. It'll be quieter like this. Carefully, I pick my way down the stairs and tiptoe past the living room. Now all I have to do is—

"Where you goin'?"

Fuuuuck.

Slowly, I turn around. "Nowhere." Which is the stupidest lie ever. I'm literally dragging a suitcase.

"You think this is a hotel? You come and go however you want?" Michael throws the living room's light switch. I blink rapidly, my eyes stinging at the sudden brightness.

He squints. "What's in the suitcase?"

"A dead body."

He doesn't laugh.

"I know where she's going." It's Olive. She pops out onto the second floor, looking totally sober and awake. God, why isn't she drunk off her ass? What's even the point of dating a senior guy if you're not getting absolutely wasted at graduation parties? "I saw the pamphlet in our room. It's that summer program. Alpha Fellowship. It's funded by some billionaire."

"Why didn't you say something?" Michael asks. Wait, actually, that's a legit question. I've been side-eyeing my stepsister for being a snitch. But she didn't snitch on me.

Olive is silent for a beat, then says, "I didn't think she'd actually get in." Which. Okay. Thanks for the vote of confidence, I guess.

"Char?" It's my mother in her nightgown, rubbing the sleep from her eyes. Fucking awesome, now it's a full-blown family reunion. Maybe we should invite my dad and his mistress too. "Why do you have a suitcase?"

"She's going to some fancy summer camp," Michael sneers. "For rich kids."

This conversation is destroying what few remaining brain cells I have, and Lola is waiting outside. "It's not for rich kids. It's for smart kids."

I turn to leave, but Michael's hand clamps down on my left forearm. "Hang on, missy, where do you think you're going?"

"I have a flight to catch." I try to shake him off, but he's too strong.

His voice is poisonous and low. "What, you think you can just up and leave? Without telling anyone? You think you're too good for us?"

"Let go of me." I squirm, trying to twist out of his grasp, but his nails dig in deep, like knives. "Let go, dude! You're hurting me."

"If you leave, you can't come back. Got that?" His grip tightens, and I bite back a cry of pain.

My eyes land on my mother. She's hunched near the wall. Her shoulders are trembling. She's doing nothing to help me. She sees exactly what's going down right now, and she's doing nothing. And somehow my mother's mousy inaction is more infuriating than anything Michael could do.

With a supernova of rage, I knee my stepfather in the groin and wrench my arm out of his clutches as he doubles over in pain.

"Have a nice life," I spit out. I'm not sure if I'm saying it to only Michael or to all of them.

I grab my suitcase and bolt for the door. Without looking back, I pound down the steps and jump into Lola's waiting car, shoving my suitcase in next to my knees.

"Drive, drive," I yell.

My best friend frowns, glancing over my shoulder. "Hey, what—"

"Just *drive!*"

"Okay, okay." She slams her foot down on the gas and we tear off into the ink-blue dawn.

As we drive, I take in deep gulps of air. My entire body is on red alert, as if it doesn't know that it's safe now. It's like I'm on the verge of a panic attack.

But once a few more minutes pass and nobody tries to kill me again, my heart stops trying to launch itself into orbit.

Once we're cruising down US 26, Lola finally clears her throat. "Soo . . . How did your family take the news?"

"My stepdad was a flaming bag of dicks. My mom was a coward. Olive was that Michael-Jackson-eating-popcorn GIF. Exactly what I expected."

Lola's gaze falls onto my forearm, red and puffy from Michael's grip. It's going to bruise, I can just tell. Even though it's a balmy June morning, I fish my Pikachu sweater out of my backpack and shrug into it. Best to hide the damage.

To Lola's credit, she doesn't comment on the injury. Instead, all she says is, "It's pronounced *jif*. Like the peanut butter."

"Sorry?"

"You said *gif*. It's *jif*."

I frown. "But GIF is short for Graphics Interchange Format..." Before I can begin reciting all the Wikipedia facts I know about this topic, Lola shushes me.

"It's okay, darlin'. Just accept that you're wrong. Nobody is perfect." She pauses. "Like, remember that time you wanted to make our yearbook into an NFT?"

"Okay, I still think that would've been a more effective fundraiser than the cheerleaders' bake sale."

Lola shakes her head. "That bake sale had so much wasted potential. All they had to do was lace the brownies with pot..."

We spend the rest of the drive yapping and laughing about our time in high school. We don't even bother with Spotify.

But even though I'm hyped for the upcoming summer, when the highway sign indicates that PDX is the next exit, this cold dread washes over me.

I'm not ready to say goodbye to my best friend.

She pulls up to Departures. "I guess this is it."

This is it.

There's this lump in my throat. She's shipping off to the army before I get back to Chinook Shore. I won't see her again, at least for a long while.

"Yeah. Thank you so much for driving me." The words feel so boring. They don't come close to expressing what she means to me. She's in, like, every single good memory I have of Chinook Shore. I don't even know where to begin.

Computers are so much easier to talk to. That one movie about a guy falling in love with Siri . . . I sort of get it.

I cough. "Um, let me know how much I owe you for gas money—"

"Char, shut up." Suddenly she's swallowed me in a bear hug. "Kick those boys' asses, okay?"

Chapter Nine

When the plane tilts down, I press my face to the window, hungrily absorbing every detail. Massachusetts rushes toward me. Lush fields edged by suburban rooftops. In the afternoon sunlight, colorful cars in parking lots glisten like these fistfuls of hard candy. The rolling green slowly melts into meandering asphalt roads, and oh, look, there're skyscrapers now, yawning upward in glass and steel. White sailboats float lazily in the blue harbor. Freaking gorgeous. There are adventures strewn everywhere. All I need to do is reach down and seize the right one.

The landing is rough—I don't think planes are supposed to bounce like that. As soon as the cabin lights flicker on, people push into the aisle like they're rushing for Taylor Swift concert tickets.

I turn off airplane mode and scroll the notifications I missed.

From Lola, a TikTok of a raccoon washing cotton candy and being confused when the cotton candy disappears into the water. Mood. I'm the clueless raccoon and my cotton candy is, like, my entire life. I reply with the crying-profusely emoji before I remember she also thinks that one is for boomers.

Nothing from Olive or Michael, not that I expect or want them to contact me. I have several missed calls and texts from Mom, but I don't open the messages or listen to the voicemails or dial her number.

I don't know. I'm not ready to deal with her yet. Maybe I never will be.

Once I'm off the plane, I follow the signs for baggage claim. People from my flight are already crowded around carousel number four. I recognize some of the passengers, like the screaming baby from seat 17A and the snoring dude who reclined his seat directly onto my kneecaps.

The bags spew out of a metal mouth and settle onto the conveyor belt. People rush to grab their luggage, and the throng around me thins. I wait.

After I watch the carousel circle several more times, I have to admit the obvious. My luggage isn't here.

There's a customer support desk nearby, manned by a middle-aged woman with white skunk stripes in her otherwise dark hair. When I get closer, I see that she's watching a steamy clip from *Bridgerton*. Actually, she's watching it on loop. Not that I can blame her. Everyone in *Bridgerton* is so pretty it should be illegal.

I clear my throat several times before she looks up.

"I'm looking for my suitcase," I say. "It's red."

It was a present from my dad. *For when you visit me in China,* he had said, like the total liar that he is. I never had the chance to use it until now. And now it's gone. Vanished into nothing, like cotton candy dissolving into a river.

It's not that I'm emotionally attached to the suitcase. Honestly? It's a reminder of my dad's broken promises. But I need my clothes. My toiletries. My graphing calculator, just in case I have to compute parametric equations or something. It's a hackathon. Who knows what kind of emergency math I'll need to do.

"Did you just come in from Portland?" she asks. "Your suitcase might be delayed. Your flight was full, so some of the luggage was moved to a later one."

"But what about my things?" I can't hide the frustration in my voice. Suddenly I imagine myself exactly as she might see me—a skinny, five-foot-two unaccompanied minor wearing a Pikachu sweater, whining about her lost stuff. Like a brat, and not in the lime-green Charli XCX way.

"I wouldn't worry too much. This happens all the time on every airline." That doesn't make me feel better. Mostly it makes me lose faith in the commercial aviation industry. "We'll let you know if it turns up. In the meantime, fill out this insurance form and itemize everything that was in your luggage."

I bite back a groan.

It's nearly six thirty by the time I finish with customer service, and the next shuttle to MIT isn't until eight p.m. But I don't want to miss dinner. One of my goals in life is to maximize opportunities for free food. So I hop onto the silver line.

When I step out of the subway station at Kendall Square, everybody's in a hurry. Cars lunge. Joggers and their eager dogs whiz by. A cyclist nearly runs me over and doesn't bother to say sorry.

It makes me giddy. This city is alive with kinetic energy. There's something about it that makes me feel like I have lightning in my veins. Like I'm finally someplace bigger than myself.

Anyway, I'm happy for about two minutes until some jerk splashes his iced coffee all over the front of my sweater.

It takes me a second to process what just happened. A cold shock on my torso, and a shriek that my brain sluggishly registers as my own.

There's an Asian boy about my age clutching a plastic cup half-filled with iced coffee. He's apologizing very fast and dabbing at my general boob area with a napkin. Maybe this is his usual perv move that he pulls as an excuse to grope girls. Maybe I should tell him to stop touching me, but I'm too annoyed to care.

"Why did you do that?" The words surprise me with how pointy they sound. "That was my one top with long sleeves." My other hoodies and sweaters are in my suitcase, which is currently floating somewhere over Cleveland.

There's a pinch behind my eyes, and suddenly this sadness floods through me, like something has finally broken. It's not really about the sweater. It's about this entire day.

"Hey, it's okay. I'm Khoi, by the way." Suddenly his hand is at my cheek, wiping away my tears, and somehow this scrap of kindness from a stranger only makes me cry harder. It's mortifying. Like, I'm not even the weepy type. I barely teared up when Bambi's mom died, so Lola thinks I might secretly be a robot.

"Myoclonic seizure." His ears redden as he says it.

"Sorry?" I sniffle.

"You asked why I did that. I have epilepsy. Sometimes I get these spasms. They're called myoclonic seizures. That's why I spilled my coffee on you." He says this all in one rush, like it's a confession.

Now I feel bad for being rude. "It's okay."

"I'll buy you another sweater."

That's too much. I shake my head no.

There's something so casual in how he throws out the offer—*I'll buy you another sweater*—that makes me think he's not concerned about money. For the first time, I actually look at him, trying to figure out how wealthy he is.

He has limbs that seem a little too long for his body, like he doesn't know what to do with them. Lush eyelashes, a scattering of freckles across his cheeks. He's wearing an unzipped jacket, a shirt that reads THERE ARE 10 TYPES OF PEOPLE IN THE WORLD: THOSE WHO KNOW BINARY AND THOSE WHO DON'T, and lemon-yellow Crocs with fuzzy socks. I don't recognize the brand of his backpack.

So. Nothing obviously expensive, although that could mean he's *rich*-rich.

In Chinook Shore, people do whatever they can to brag about their money, even money they don't have. *Especially* money they don't have. The tourists drip out in counterfeit Louis Vuitton and Gucci. My neighbors go into debt for new four-wheelers. But I've learned teeth are the universal billboard for "my family is loaded."

I can't see Khoi's teeth right now, but I have a feeling his smile is dazzling and pearly white and perfectly straight.

He unzips his backpack. "Here, I have a spare T-shirt."

"It has to have long sleeves," I say without thinking.

He cocks his head. "Why?"

Ugh. Why did I say that?

Well, Khoi isn't holding a suitcase, so he's not here for Alpha Fellows. I wouldn't usually do this, but hey, I'm never going to see this kid again, so I wordlessly roll up my left sleeve and show him the bruises on my forearm, the angry purple apostrophes that Michael indented into my skin.

I don't know. Maybe I just want sympathy from a kind, soft-eyed stranger. I want someone to acknowledge that my existence is a total dumpster fire.

He inhales sharply. "Who did this? Are you okay? Do we need to call the police?"

"I'm fine," I say, ignoring his other questions.

"Seriously, what—"

I try a quip. "You should see the other guy."

"Why?"

"Because I totally beat his ass . . ." I stop when his eyes widen with shock. He's clearly not getting the joke. "Never mind."

"If somebody is hurting you, there is help out there." He rattles off the words like he memorized a health class pamphlet. He probably did memorize some health class pamphlet. Laminated, with cute illustrations of multicultural families holding hands.

This kid doesn't seem to have any real-world experience with this kind of thing, so I don't need his advice.

"Forget it." I check my phone. It's already seven thirty. "I need to go."

"No, wait. You can have this." He removes his jacket and hands it to me.

"Thanks." I reach to peel off my sweater. I guess my shirt lifts up with it, because suddenly he starts coughing.

"Don't you, um, want to get changed in the restroom?" he asks in a strangled voice.

Oops. I ignore him and yank down my shirt with one hand while tugging my sweater over my head with the other. When I glance at his face, he's blushing furiously, and I swallow a giggle at how scandalized he looks. He's probably sixteen or seventeen. Is this really the first time he's ever caught a glimpse of a girl's bra? Back home, most people start hooking up before they learn the quadratic formula. I mean, given our public education system, I'm not sure they ever actually learn the quadratic formula, so maybe that's not saying much.

I wad up my sweater—poor Pikachu's face is now mottled brown, like he has that skin condition, vitiligo—and shove it into my backpack. "Nah. I don't have time to find a restroom. I'm already late for my thing."

"What's your thing?"

"Um, it's in Simmons Hall? Do you know where that is?"

He looks too young to be a college student, but maybe he's the son of a faculty member here. He seems like a sheltered kid who would have professor parents.

Well, Khoi isn't holding a suitcase, so he's not here for Alpha Fellows. I never thought somebody's face could become the ^_^ emoji, but there's no other way to describe Khoi's expression. "No way, I'm going there too! For Alpha Fellows? Serendipity!"

"Serendipity," I echo, even though I'm not one hundred percent sure what that word means.

It's like somebody just slapped me across the face. How did I not see this coming?

Now I regret showing him the bruise.

Chapter Ten

Khoi, of course, knows exactly how to get to the dorm.

Unfortunately, he also has this insanely frustrating habit of *meandering*. He strolls like he thinks we're an elderly couple on the beach. Sometimes he even pauses to check out various posters papering the infinitely long corridor. By the time he tears off a tab from some flyer looking for volunteers, I'm ready to ditch his ass. At this rate, we're going to be eligible for senior discounts by the time we get to Simmons.

We pass a tourist group posing for photos. For no reason, my brain goes, *They look like me*. But I push that thought away. They don't look like me. They're just Asian. So actually, maybe that makes *me* racist?

But I guess I've hardly ever seen so many Asians together in one place before.

As we finally reach the end of the hallway and pass through a sun-drenched lobby, I have a stroke of genius. Which is rare for me. "Wanna play a game?"

"I love games!"

I reach to push the door, but it glides open on its own. We step outside into the crisp evening. Majestic ivory columns tower above us, stark against the deepening sky. I recognize those columns. They're on all the MIT marketing materials.

For a moment, I forget about whatever I was saying. I'm here. Actually here. Standing on the same steps where so many geniuses (genii?) have laughed and cried and dreamed. What even.

Khoi's staring at me.

Right. The game. "Let's race to the dorm." I'm totally going to lose—he has longer legs than me and my lungs malfunction at speeds faster than five miles an hour—but at least this way we can hustle faster.

He gauges the distance, then gives me a once-over. "Loser owes the other a boba."

I haven't had boba in years. The Lucky Panda sells it, but it's a cheap white-people imitation made from powder, and they call it "bubble tea." And it's chocolate-flavored.

"Fine. We'll start after we cross this road." We shake on it. His grasp is surprisingly firm. It's nice when someone has a good handshake. I hate it when it feels like I'm grabbing a floppy, dead fish.

We descend the steps and wait in front of the intersection as cars soar past. The lights change, and the crowd surges onto the crosswalk.

He counts down. "Three . . . two . . ." Before he gets to one, I kick off and propel forward.

"Hey, that's cheating!" he yells, but he doesn't sound very mad.

I ignore him and weave around a pack of tourists wearing Harvard sweaters—yikes, hope they're not too lost. I dodge a wayward drone, but behind me, Khoi yelps.

My legs are flying and blood roars in my ears. There's a stitch stabbing into my side. But soon he's caught up to me anyway. I hate tall people privilege. Actually, he's not even that tall. I'm just short. "Oolong, lychee jelly, one hundred and fifty percent sugar, no ice," he calls over his shoulder as he passes by.

"What?" I huff. I can barely get the word out.

"My boba order."

Which is just an unhinged amount of sugar. I may have unwittingly gotten mixed up with an actual sociopath. But I can't think too hard about that when my lungs are on the verge of collapse.

Once we cut across to Vassar Street, the dorm finally comes into view. It looks like a sponge. A futuristic sponge. It's a colossal silver block with thousands of tiny square windows.

When I finally reach Simmons, Khoi is leaning against the building, arms crossed, grinning.

I double over, hands on my knees, heart in overdrive. My mouth desperately seizes for air like I'm a goldfish.

"Stop doing that," I force out between gasps.

"I'm not doing anything!"

Before I can answer that, I focus on not dying. Charise Tang is fully in her being-alive era.

Once my body feels more like it got hit with a grenade than a nuclear bomb, I straighten up. "Your face. It's too smug."

"That's just my face!" He unlocks his phone camera and peers at himself. As if he needs to check that his face is still his face. "Wow, what a fine-looking young lad."

I mean. I'm not even going to dignify that with a response.

At check-in, an Asian girl with square glasses and a *HellomynameisBrenda* name tag hands us tote bags and reads us the rules. There's curfew at eleven. No alcohol, no drugs. No sex in the ball pit (apparently there's a ball pit). No torrenting, no hacking, no crypto scamming, no normal scamming, no threatening national security.

"Okay, but what if there's like an Edward Snowden situation where it's in the general public's best interest—" Khoi yelps when I elbow him in the ribs.

As we wait for the elevator, Khoi riffles through his tote bag. "Hey, they gave us info on our roommates." He reads his paper slip out loud. "'Obi Udechukwu.' Is that Nigerian? From Santa Clara, California. His fun fact is that he once won a jujitsu tournament against Mark Zuckerberg." He whistles. "I'm gonna stay on Obi's good side."

I fish out my paper. "'Aisha Chadha, Boston, Massachusetts.'

Oh, she's local. Her fun fact is that she's danced at the White House?"

"Oh, Aisha! I've known her forever."

"How?"

"She goes to Phillips Andover, a boarding school about an hour from here. We do the same local STEM competitions. She's also . . . We're . . ." He seems to be on the verge of saying more, but then he shakes his head. "Nothing."

Ugh. Of course all the smart kids know one another. I'm manifesting that I'll find some decent friends. At least Khoi seems nice. Well. Maybe I should keep my guard up. He has that sociopathic boba order, after all.

When we get to our floor, Khoi follows me so he can say hi to Aisha. The door to my room is ajar.

"Just in case," a woman is saying. "For emergencies."

"*Ammi*, when am I going to need *bear spray*? The only wild animals here are the tech bros."

Even though I haven't even seen her, I already vibe with my roommate.

I push my way inside. There's a South Asian girl, dressed head-to-toe in Lululemon, standing in front of an overflowing suitcase. She has a ballerina's build, tall and lean, with lethal-looking shoulder blades. An older man and woman are hovering about. They must be her parents.

I open my mouth to greet them, but before I say anything, Khoi strides over and slings his arm around her shoulder. "Hey, babe."

Babe?

They're *dating*? Like. Khoi could've *mentioned* my roommate was his girlfriend.

She pecks him on the cheek. "Baaaabe."

And I get the sense that their tongues are not going to remain inside their own mouths, so before things get gross, I start looking at anywhere else but them. Like suddenly these concrete walls are fascinating. So awesomely solid and gray. It's giving prison minimalism.

I'm surprised, honestly. It's not so much that I'm shocked that Aisha is his girlfriend. I don't even know her. It's more that Khoi didn't seem like the type who would have a girlfriend at all. He exudes major hopeless dork aura. I'm not trying to be mean. It's cute. But I'm just saying, I clocked him for someone who would, like, bring a TI-84 calculator to prom instead of a date.

Anyway, to my eternal relief, they don't start making out, maybe because Aisha's parents are in the room.

Aisha's father smiles. "Are your aunt and uncle here too?"

Khoi shakes his head. "Sharon and Graham meant to drive over here with me, but there was a performance at Symphony Hall tonight they really wanted to see, so I took public transit."

"Ah, yes, the Shostakovich string quartet?"

Khoi snaps his fingers. "Yes! With that famous cellist Graham likes. Gosh, what's her name . . . ?"

The rest of this conversation becomes rather confusing and string-instrument-flavored.

While her boyfriend and dad are geeking out, Aisha looks at me. "Are you my roomie? The one who . . . " She fishes a paper slip out of her sports bra. ". . . memorized the lyrics to every single Olivia Rodrigo song? Cute! I love 'driver's license'."

Even though she sounds sincere, I flush. I guess it's not dancing at the White House or beating the Zuck in jujitsu. When I submitted the fun fact, I didn't realize it was supposed to be a humblebrag. "Charise Tang, but you can call me Char." I cross the room to shake her hand, but she's a total hugger. Her perfume is vanilla and cinnamon.

Her parents introduce themselves, then turn their attention to Khoi, whose arm is still around Aisha. "Have you decided where you're going to apply early? Our daughter is doing Harvard."

"Sounds like Harvard for me, then." He grins. "So we can stay together."

They're adorable and it's almost nauseating.

"There goes our daughter's chance of getting in." Mr. Chadha says it in a light tone, but I don't think he's one hundred percent joking.

"Are you kidding? Aisha is way smarter than me. I'm scared of her!"

Mr. Chadha doesn't respond to that, just turns to me. "And what about you?"

Damn, I wasn't expecting to get interrogated too. "I haven't . . . I haven't thought about it."

"We can help you brainstorm," Mrs. Chadha says. "I volunteer as a college coach. I got Aisha's older brother into Princeton."

Aisha groans. "*Ammi*, Char doesn't want—"

"What did you get on the SAT? That'll give you an idea on what caliber of universities you should target."

"Uh, I haven't taken the SAT yet." Chinook Shore only administers it once a year, in October. If you want to take it some other time, you better haul ass to the next county. And that's, like, way too much effort.

Mr. Chadha gasps as if I just fessed up to murdering puppies.

"You can sit for the SAT this summer," Mrs. Chadha says. "It's too late to register for the June exam, but there's one in August. Plenty of places in Boston you can take it."

I do this half laugh, half shrug, noncommittal thing. I'm kind of scared she's going to actually have an aneurysm if I say anything else.

"*Ammi*," Aisha repeats in this annoyed way. She gives me a sheepish look.

Khoi excuses himself to drop his backpack off in his room—he mentions his aunt and uncle are coming by later with the rest of his things. I duck outside to use the restroom.

When I come back, I'm about to push the door open when Mrs. Chadha's voice makes me halt.

"*Ladli*, we like Khoi, but he shouldn't apply to Harvard on your account. It's a big decision."

Aisha now. "Maybe he just wants to go to Harvard anyway. I've heard it's a decent school."

"No need for sarcasm, young lady."

"Sorry," Aisha says, not sounding sorry at all.

Mr. Chadha: "He's a lovely boy, but you can't get too serious. You know you can't marry him."

Aisha's voice is full of derision. "Yeah, yeah, because he's not brown."

"Don't act that way," Ms. Chadha says in a tone that tells me Aisha's spot-on.

"I'm not going to marry Khoi. We're seventeen. It's not going to get serious. 'Kay? So you don't have to worry."

Oof. Does Khoi realize he's just another extracurricular to Aisha? Should I warn him? Nope, not my place to get involved. I hardly know either of them. I've already heard too much. I sort of wish I could unhear it.

I nudge the door open.

As soon as she sees me, Aisha's expression shifts from annoyance to relief.

"Char!" She grins. "Let's go down for dinner?"

Chapter Eleven

The dining hall is nothing like my high school cafeteria. For one thing, the food is actually edible. There's a make-your-own poke bowl station and a salad bar bursting with fresh vegetables grown on a campus farm. But it's the gelato machine that truly steals my heart: it has flavors like lavender honey and dark chocolate sea salt and white chocolate matcha swirl.

"What if I have *just* ice cream for dinner?" I ask Aisha.

She laughs. "It's your life, babe. Our parents aren't here."

After we fill up our trays, we survey the tables. There are maybe a hundred students. Probably three-quarters of them are dudes. The few other girls are easy to spot, like 1s in an ocean of 0s.

The classic problem of where to sit. At school, everybody kind of knew how to clump together: the mediocre athletes, the actually good athletes, the theater kids (who got absorbed by the band kids after budget cuts), the aspiring criminals, the current criminals, and so forth. Lola and I had one goal: stay out of the firing range of any faction that was known to mistake chicken nuggets for ammunition.

Here, it feels like the factions haven't formed yet. Everyone is still jostling for a spot in the social hierarchy. I wonder how clout works at Alpha Fellows. Back home, it was this uncrackable formula involving Instagram followers, Friday night party invites, and whether you owned the latest iPhone. But here, maybe it's about how many programming languages you know or something.

Some girls who appear to know Aisha wave her over. There's only one empty seat at their table.

She looks at me guiltily. "Oh, um, those are my school friends . . ."

"You should go sit with them. Don't worry about me." I spot Khoi several tables away, surrounded by guys. There are plenty of open chairs there. "I'll find somewhere else."

As I head over toward Khoi, something strikes me. Shouldn't he and Aisha be sitting together? At school, the couples are all over each other every possible spare moment. Honestly, it's like softcore porn in the Chinook Shore cafeteria. The administration is totally chill with that, but God forbid a girl wear spaghetti straps.

Maybe Khoi and Aisha want to catch up with their separate friends. It is the first day. And it's really none of my business. Mentally, I hit delete on this sitch.

"Char! Long time no see." Khoi is gouging his corn on the

cob by taking random bites out of the cob, in no discernible pattern. Inwardly, I shudder. You can tell a lot about a person by how they eat corn on the cob. Khoi is obviously somebody who wants to see the world burn.

"Is your roommate here?" I ask.

"Obi found a concurrency bug in his code and started muttering to himself. Said he won't eat until he fixes it or until Java releases a better threading model, whichever comes first. So . . . he's probably going to starve."

The other guys do intros. There are identical twins, Austin and Dallas, who demo themselves solving Rubik's Cubes in sync. Haru, who I immediately clock as a stoner—the lazy speech and bloodshot eyes are dead giveaways—and who has also played cello at Carnegie Hall. Diego, who boasts half a million followers for his competitive programming TikToks.

With each introduction, I want to sink lower into my chair. They've all done so much even though they're the same age as me. No, Austin and Dallas are even younger; they just finished ninth grade. Ninth grade. When I was in ninth grade, my biggest achievement was convincing the cafeteria lady to sneak me extra tater tots.

When it's my turn, I say, "I'm Char, short for Charise. From Oregon."

Dallas (or maybe Austin) belches. "What kinda name is that?"

"I think my mom picked it randomly?"

My biological father was supposed to fly to America for my

birth, but I arrived two weeks early, so at the hospital, Mom was drugged-up and alone. She chose something that sounded pretty out of this baby name book. I used to hate how unique it was. I went by Char, hoping people would assume it was short for something normal like Charlotte.

"Oregon is a cool state," Haru says. For a split second, I'm relieved that at least someone is impressed by my background, until he adds, "They were the first one to decriminalize cannabis possession."

"It's irrelevant in tech, though," Diego says. "Sandwiched by Seattle, which has Microsoft and Amazon, and San Francisco and Silicon Valley, which has everything else that's important."

I want to defend my home state, but I don't know what to say. Somehow I doubt Diego is going to be interested in our thriving lumber business. He probably thinks "logging" is something you only do to debug code.

"So Char must've worked even harder to get here," Khoi says. I know he's trying to help, but somehow it makes me feel worse, because it isn't true. I didn't work *that* hard, and I'm not as accomplished as these dudes, so what am I even doing here? Maybe Edvin Nilsen really did get the wrong Charise Tang.

"Oregon, what's like, your schtick?" Austin (or maybe Dallas) asks.

I fiddle with my silverware. "My . . . schtick?"

"Like, everybody here has a schtick. My schtick is cubing. Haru's schtick is celloing."

"Not a word," Haru mumbles.

Austin-or-Dallas barrels on. "Diego's schtick is influencing. Khoi's—"

Diego seems offended. "I'm not an *influencer*. The only thing I promote on TikTok is C++. Which is superior to Rust!"

"Oh." I don't even know what Rust is. "I don't have anything like that."

"It's fine. It's easier for girls to get in anyway." Diego smiles benevolently, as if he invented affirmative action just for me.

"Please stop talking," Khoi says.

"What? I'm not saying she doesn't *deserve* to be here." He looks me square in the eye. "Like, Oregon, I'm sure you're smart."

"Um, thanks?" Also, how do I get him to not call me that? I really don't want to commit to that nickname for the next eight weeks.

"All I'm sayin' is, I know someone who works on the admissions committee for Alpha Fellows. She said that they were tryna improve the gender ratio this year. So like, two thousand guys applied and eighty-five got in. But two hundred girls applied and twenty got in. That's an admission rate of four percent vs. ten percent. Simple stats." Diego lounges back with his fingers laced behind his head.

It sounds more like, for whatever reason, not enough girls are applying to this program, but before I can point this out, Austin-or-Dallas glances up from his Rubik's Cube. "Wait, for real? That blows. Our cousin Houston got rejected this year."

Dallas-or-Austin turns to Diego. "If what you're saying is true, that means that one of the girls here might've taken his spot." He tosses me an accusatory look, like I personally dragged his cousin off the flight that would've brought him here.

I want to argue back, but before I can think of anything to say, Khoi pipes up. "No, it means that your cousin wasn't good enough to get in."

"You don't even know Houston," Austin says. "He was the national AP scholar for Arizona, meaning he got the most fives on the most exams out of anyone in the state. Just because he's not like you—"

"Oh heyo, look who it is!" Khoi says a little too quickly. He stands up to side-hug a girl who's walked over.

She reminds me of Sabrina Carpenter—petite, piles of brushed gold hair, heart-shaped face. Freckles dot her collarbone like constellations. Mini lime slices dangle from her ears.

The other guys fall silent when they see her. Behind my palm, I hide a smile. I bet that suddenly none of them care that she might've *taken a spot* from a more deserving boy.

She swivels her hand. "I'm Jenni, with an i."

Dallas-or-Austin scoots over to make space at the table. "How do you know Khoi?"

"We met at nationals for Science Bowl."

"Jenni is a botany goddess," Khoi says. "She destroyed us on those questions."

Even her laugh is pretty—it's like wind chimes. "Don't glaze me. I'm just a plant nerd."

She settles into an empty seat. Haru starts peppering her with questions about how to genetically modify marijuana seeds, and whether it'd be feasible to do it in a small indoor space that gets poor sunlight, such as a dorm room (hypothetically, of course).

There's this twinge of disappointment. It takes me a sec to realize why. Because Jenni-with-an-i is a girl and looks like the human equivalent of golden hour, a subconscious part of me hoped she'd also be less accomplished. That she'd prove Diego right, and I wouldn't be the only one at this table with nothing going for her. Which is so messed up.

I look down at my melted gelato and realize I've lost my appetite. I push away from the table and stand.

"Char, where are you going?" Khoi asks. The others barely glance over.

"Bed. I had a long flight."

"Oregon, if you're not going to finish your pizza, can I have it?" Haru asks. Yep, classic stoner munchies. Wordlessly, I slide my slice onto his plate.

Chapter Twelve

Sunday morning, when I wake up for the opening ceremony, Aisha's bed is empty. Her absence reminds me of Olive's, like she's avoiding me. I scour my brain for anything I might've done wrong. What if she thinks I'm a hillbilly loser for not doing the SAT? Maybe she doesn't want to associate with me, this scoreless freak, when she could be with her glamorous boarding school friends.

I'm probably being ridiculous. Probably. But just to be safe, I go to the College Board website and sign up for the August SAT at some nearby location. Luckily, they still have my information from the AP exams—*why* does College Board own everything? They're like the Elon Musk of teenage stress dreams—so my fee waiver gets added automatically.

By the time I'm done, it's already too late for breakfast—maybe for the best, considering how dinner went last night. Now for the fun part: getting ready while my suitcase is still MIA. At least my toothbrush made it into my backpack. But clean underwear? Socks? Forget it. When I shower I lather myself with the bathroom's chalky pink hand soap. Eau de Desperation.

God, I hope my luggage turns up soon. I sure can't afford to replace everything.

Across the expanse of green grass, Kresge auditorium is an elegant one-eighth of a sphere, sliced by sheer glass walls. It's lit from within, a shimmering arc of white fluorescence. It looks clean and futuristic, and it doesn't look like somewhere I belong. I'm tempted to go hide out in my dorm room with the leftover Fritos from my plane ride.

But if I can't handle a mere opening ceremony, how am I going to get through the entire summer? It's not like I have any other options. I can't fly back to Oregon. I just can't. I'd rather go live in a dumpster.

I force myself to head in.

Once I'm inside, I scan the half-filled seats. Everyone is chattering away like they've known one another forever. Nobody casts a glance in my direction. No sign of Aisha, either . . .

I find Khoi next to a Black teenager clutching a metal rectangular box. He introduces himself as Obi, Khoi's roommate. Right, the kid who ditched dinner to cozy up with a concurrency bug.

"Do you know where Aisha is?" I ask.

"Oh. That . . . uh . . ." Khoi's face goes blank. "No idea. She does her own thing."

Yeah, okay. Between Aisha saying she isn't serious about him and Khoi's completely *whatever* attitude, I feel like someone should just throw the kill switch on this relationship.

But I'm not about to comment. Like, I'm too much of a broke bitch to be giving away my two cents nobody asked for. I turn to Obi.

"What are you holding?"

He tightens his bear hug around the box, as if he's scared I'm going to nick it. "It's an Nvidia A100."

Sounds like a spaceship. "What now?"

"It's a GPU."

"Sorry?"

He stares at me like I just asked how to add two plus two. "A graphics processing unit. For doing big computations."

"Okayyyy." I don't ask for more details, not wanting to give him another chance to make me feel stupid. "But why did you have to bring it here?"

"Obi's GPU is very important to him," Khoi says.

"Didn't want it to get stolen. It's worth fifteen grand." Obi cuts his eyes to Khoi. "Not like this guy would understand. He doesn't need to care about money."

"Wait, why not?"

"Don't you know? Last year he—"

"Wow, the architecture of this auditorium is fascinating," Khoi interjects. "It's one-eighth of a sphere. You know that's called an octant?"

For some incomprehensible reason, that distracts Obi. "Whoa. What other geometry facts do you know?"

"Are you familiar with Ptolemy's theorem?"

Khoi pulls out an iPad and draws the math proof, which is actually sort of interesting, but not interesting enough to make me forget that there was something Obi was about to say that Khoi didn't want me to know.

Then the program director, a smiley woman with a HellomynameisCourtney name tag, steps out onto the luminous stage, and everybody falls silent.

She has some speech about how it's an honor to be here and how Edvin Nilsen, the billionaire founder of Alpha Fellows, is sorry he couldn't deliver the keynote. He got tied up with some *last-minute business meetings*.

Obi whispers, "Heard his company has been catching strays."

I glance over. "Nexus? For what?"

But before he can answer, a girl turns around and does a very aggressive *shush* at us.

HellomynameisCourtney mentions some of the program alumni. Photos of famous tech bros flash on the screen. They even include a picture of this *Forbes* 30 Under 30 crypto founder who went to prison recently, which leads to some muttering.

"Why are they flexing about him?" someone mumbles from behind us. "He's a horrible person!"

"Anybody who ever believed in crypto deserves to lose their money," Obi shoots back. "Remember the FTX scandal? Or Pegasus? And NFTs are the most brain-dead invention of the twenty-first century."

Khoi starts coughing.

HellomynameisCourtney glances up at the presentation and flushes. "Ah, sorry . . . I thought we updated this slide. But, uh, let this be a life lesson: technology is powerful, but humans are the ones who decide how to wield it. Being good is more important than being brilliant."

Someone boos, and there's another ripple of laughter. And I snicker, too, until I notice Khoi staring at me, almost like he's disappointed.

Which, okay. He can think whatever he wants. It was just a silly moment, and everybody else was laughing too. It's not like I actually believe in using tech for evil. I'm not about to build a drone that assassinates kittens.

Still, it gives me this pang of guilt, like I've let him down somehow, even though we barely know each other.

I forget all about that once the prizes are announced. A current of energy zips through the audience. There are some sponsor-based awards—I've heard that in previous years, internships at companies like Apple or Amazon were up for grabs—but the grand prize is $100,000 and "consideration for admission to MIT," whatever that means.

I never thought about what it would be like to attend a school like MIT. I kind of assumed that stuff was for other kids. The College Confidential kids.

When the room has finally quieted down, HellomynameisCourtney explains the structure of the program.

There are three checkpoints. The first is two weeks from now, a written exam based on optional coursework. The second, a project proposal, is a week after that. And the last one, a final presentation and project submission, is at the end of the program. During each checkpoint, we'll be ranked publicly, like a Hunger Games for nerds.

But hey, even if I completely flop, they won't feed me to robot dogs. Hopefully.

Before the first checkpoint, we'll get college-level classes that teach us computer science. That's good, since I definitely need to play catch-up. After the written exam, the program will be more unstructured, and we'll spend most of our time working toward the second and third checkpoints with our team members.

The first checkpoint is individual; the other two are judged per team. Our results on all three will be weighed as part of final judging. Teams can be comprised of one to four people, but the prize money is split among everyone. My heart sinks when she says we choose our own teams. I was kind of banking on those being assigned for us.

I mean, even in my head it's a little pathetic. Like I need my teacher to help me find friends.

Kids are gesturing to each other in that *yeah?/yeah* way that people in middle school do when picking dodgeball teams for gym, except now it's not about who can fling a ball hardest—it's about who wrote their first Hello World in the womb. Of course people are going to choose their buddies or whoever won the latest genius prize.

Whatever. Yeah. I can work alone. Totally in my solo era. And I won't even have to split the prize money.

But there won't be any prize money at all if I don't win. If I don't win, I'll be crawling back to Chinook Shore with nothing but disappointment and a backpack stuffed with dirty laundry, and everything will be exactly the same as it always has been. Scratch that. It'll be even worse. Because now Michael hates me even more than before.

To win, I need to find teammates. I'm not deluded enough to think I can win by myself.

So it's time to rizz people up.

Chapter Thirteen

But rizzing people up is hard.

The rest of the day is devoted to fun, since, as we all know, scheduled fun is the best kind of fun. They split us up. Khoi and Obi get assigned to other groups, and I quickly lose track of them.

Mom and Michael sent Olive and me to overnight summer camp one year, so I recognize the classic bonding games: human knot, get-to-know-you bingo and such. But the rock-paper-scissors tournament spirals into an argument about whether the game needs blockchain integration, and two truths and a lie quickly becomes a circlejerk where everyone is humblebragging about their prestigious internships. *Two truths and a lie: I worked at Google, I worked at Amazon, I worked at Microsoft!* (The lie is Microsoft.)

I try talking to different people at each activity. I meet a brother-sister pair from Illinois who speak only in chess moves, a purple-haired girl who tries to recruit me into her crypto cult, and a guy who spends ten minutes explaining his theory about how having multiple girlfriends is actually the best approach to dating. Honestly, I'm shocked he could even get *one* girlfriend.

By the time we get to the trust fall exercise, I'm seriously considering just letting myself hit the ground. Then someone taps my shoulder. I turn to see an Asian girl with auburn hair, a faint sunburn on her cheeks, and a frilly pink sundress.

"Hiya, I'm Stella from Texas," she says. She has a slight drawl. "You're Aisha's roommate, right? We go to the same boarding school."

"Char," I say, surprised that she knows. That means Aisha must've mentioned me to other people. Maybe she's not actually trying to avoid me.

She grins, revealing these lime-green gel braces. "Want to risk potential concussions together?"

Stella turns out to be shockingly normal: she doesn't mention her IQ or grill me on my GitHub commits, and she has decent opinions on the latest season of *White Lotus*. We end up doing the rest of the activities together. The last event of the night is a yacht party with some Alpha Fellows sponsors. My social battery is super drained, and I'm tempted to retreat back to my room and maybe FaceTime Lola. When Stella hears that, she gasps in mock disbelief. "Girlie, it's a yacht! You have to go."

"I've been on a yacht before," I protest. Okay, it was last summer when I was picking up shifts at the Lucky Panda. We were hired to cater a wedding reception, which ended abruptly before dessert because the groom got caught with a bridesmaid in the bathroom. But still.

"Char, it'll be fun. We'll dance together." She pauses. "Well, my boyfriend will probably also want to dance."

Third-wheeling isn't my idea of fun, but I want her to like me, so I agree.

As soon as we get on the boat, I'm tempted to belly-flop into the Atlantic. Lights flash hot pink, then orange, then lime green. It's hot and loud and crowded. Even the ice sculpture—is that supposed to be Edvin Nilsen's head?—is half melted. The music is screechy. Newton's Second Law states that the more obnoxious a song is, the louder it must be played.

Stella and I exchange looks.

"We could go find your boyfriend?" I venture.

She squints. "Don't see him right now. Let's go get something to drink."

We try to weave through the crush, but there's a huge swarm of people around the bar area. There's barely enough room to breathe.

"Baby!" A scrawny guy wearing a knit beanie (in the summer?) appears out of nowhere. He clamps his mouth onto Stella's, and I watch them do mouth-to-mouth resuscitation for a good minute.

In my head, the *National Geographic* baritone voiceover returns. *We observe two adolescent humans pressing their food-intake orifices together. The evolutionary purpose of this display is unclear.*

When they finally break apart, she looks like a fish gasping for air. "Hiya, Lucas," she manages. "This is Char from Oregon. Char, Lucas. Lucas, Char."

"Hmm," he says, barely looking at me.

"We're trying to get something to drink, but the line for the bar is ridiculous," she continues.

"Here. I have something." He hands Stella his Hydro Flask water bottle. After she takes a swig, she passes it to me. I take a large, grateful gulp.

The liquid goes down with a fire that makes my eyes sting. It's the worst thing I've ever tasted. I immediately spit out whatever didn't invade my throat. Oh my God. They're trying to poison me!

Both Stella and Lucas burst out laughing.

I sputter, "What the hell?"

"Did you think that was water? It's vodka." He turns to Stella. "Baby. The venture capitalists are here."

As I cough and cough, she asks, "Even Reynolds?"

"*Especially* Reynolds."

"He didn't get back to me about writing a recommendation letter," Stella says. "You think I can go and ask him?"

"Maybe in a bit. All of them are swarming that kid. The dorky one with the Crocs. Khoi."

Khoi?

Stella shrugs. "Let's dance." And then they walk away as if I'm not even there. Cool.

I trail them onto the dance floor and try to vibe with the

music. Most people here don't seem to know how to dance. There are a few girls bringing the TikTok moves, and a couple of guys who don't seem to care what anybody else thinks. But the vast majority of people on the dance floor are sort of bouncing up and down on the balls of their feet. It's awkward city out here.

The DJ is blasting something that sounds like pots and pans being thrown down a flight of stairs, when a wave of seasickness sweeps over me.

It's a fluttering in my stomach, but not like butterflies. More like bumblebees, their tiny stingers pricking my insides. I stumble.

"Excuse me," I say to nobody in particular. Maybe I should head to the bathroom. There better be a bathroom, right? Do all yachts have bathrooms? I mean, they must. Where else would people hook up?

But it's too loud and too stuffy and too much. I need to get out of here ASAP.

The evening sea breeze kisses my face as I stagger out of the boat interior and find a spot near the railing. I take greedy slurps of salted air. Yachts are terrible. Completely terrible. I don't get why rich people are so hyped about them. They could be hyped about something else, like solving world hunger.

As I pray for the bees' nest in my stomach to die, my phone buzzes with a text. It's the airline, letting me know that my luggage has been located and it'll be available at BOS tomorrow morning for pickup. Thank God. No more desperation showers with the bathroom hand soap. I set an alarm to retrieve it before class.

My mood is suddenly way brighter. I want to tell somebody about this, even though nobody cares besides me. Maybe Stella. Nah, she's too wrapped up with her obnoxious boyfriend. Maybe Khoi?

Back on the dance floor, I bump into Obi first. "Char!" he yells over the music. "Whadupppp."

If he's here, Khoi can't be far away. "Where's your roommate?" I ask.

"Whaaa?"

"WHERE'S KHOI?"

"Oh!" Obi jabs a finger in a vague direction. "Good luck getting to Mr. Popular, though."

I spot Khoi in the corner, surrounded by actual adults. He's talking to all of them, and he seems mildly terrified. It looks like a seven-on-one fight club for people wearing Patagonia.

"What's he doing?"

"Schmoozing with the sponsors. They probably want to know what he's building next. If they can write a check for his round. They're like vultures." He does this weird growl-clawing combo that tells me he's never seen a vulture in his entire life.

"Why do they care about what a random teenager is building?"

Obi frowns. "Khoi's not a rando teenager." But before I can ask what he means, a Kendrick Lamar song comes on, and he whoops. "Sorry, can't chat! This is the anthem of my *soul*." He shuts his eyes and starts swaying to the beat. I don't bother asking why a diss track is the anthem of his soul.

I wander toward Khoi. As I get closer, I spot Lucas and Stella huddled together instead of dancing. They keep shooting glares in the direction of Khoi and the suits.

"—so selfish," Lucas is saying. "He doesn't even need a rec letter. He's going to get in everywhere."

"What's going on?" I ask.

"Nothing," Stella says quickly.

Lucas narrows his eyes at me. "Wait, you're friends with Astor, right? Can you tell him to stop hogging all the attention?"

"Why are they talking to him?" I ask.

"*Imposter Syndrome*," Stella says. "The video game? *His* video game?"

Everybody knows *Imposter Syndrome*. It went viral last year. Gameplay is simple: There are six to ten people, and one or two are randomly assigned to be imposters. The imposters have to kill everyone else while avoiding being found out. I never really got into it. Mostly because I was bad at surviving past the first round.

"Like, he worked on it?"

"Like, he made it by himself? Or so he claims. He sold it to some private equity suits for almost a million dollars." Lucas leans in closer. His breath has a familiar boozy stench. I resist the urge to slap a hand over my nose. "There's something sus about his story, though."

"What's sus?"

"Guy is full Vietnamese, so why's his last name Astor? I thought maybe he was a nepo baby, but there's no info online about his family. Something is off. A teenager doesn't just pop off like that unless he has connections."

I should defend Khoi, but I don't want to screw up my shot at teaming with Stella. She's the only somewhat normal person I met today. And . . . what if Lucas is right? What if Khoi is some industry plant? I just met the kid, after all. What do I really know about him?

Lucas continues. "And he's so weird! I talked to him the other day, and I swear to God he's re—"

"Baby, you're not allowed to *use* that word!" Stella says in a way that tells me he's casually dropped this slur too many times before.

"Fine, he's autistic. Is that politically correct enough for you?"

"Lucas, stoppp! You're being mean," Stella says, but she's laughing.

Suddenly, the bees in my stomach are back. No, they're wasps now. Poisonous and evil.

"Sorry, feeling sick," I mumble.

I shove past random partygoers and bolt out into the fresh air. The pinprick of wind doesn't fix whatever is wrong inside of me.

Something burns in my chest, and it takes a moment to identify the emotion. Shame.

At dinner yesterday, Khoi said *Char must've worked even harder to get here* when Diego implied I got accepted only because of my background. He defended me. And I couldn't do the same for him today, right now. I so easily listened to Lucas's garbage, even though the dude's obviously seething with jealousy.

I spend the rest of the night leaning over the side of the yacht trying not to vomit.

Chapter Fourteen

On Monday morning, after a subway ride featuring a dude who is determined to sit next to me despite the many other empty seats available, I'm back on campus with my rescued suitcase. There's no time for breakfast, so after dropping my luggage off in my room, I head straight to Stata, where most camp activities will take place. The building looks like the architectural version of an existential crisis, with metallic panels that jut out at impossible angles.

The first class of the day is Software Studio, taught by this computer science professor named Dr. Kaminski. Before camp, I stalked him online. He writes these op-eds railing against AI. He thinks it's going to get too advanced and enslave all humans or something.

When I walk into class, half the seats are filled. Lucas and Stella are near the back and she waves at me, but I pretend not to see. I can't bring myself to join them, not after what they said about Khoi. Not after I didn't defend him.

Soooo I guess I won't be teaming up with Stella. Back to square zero.

Obi has an empty desk next to him. When I sit down, he's deep in it with someone else. They're chatting about transformers, and it takes me a few secs to figure out that this is some machine-learning thing, not the sci-fi movie franchise. I want to jump in with an interesting contribution, but I don't know anything about the topic.

Khoi is nowhere to be found. Probably skipping class, since it *is* optional. And even though some part of me is disappointed he's not here, I'm also kind of relieved because I feel weird about what went down on the yacht.

As Dr. Kaminski paces, his wire-rimmed glasses catch the fluorescent overhead light. "Who here writes test suites before implementing their code?"

A few hands shoot up. Obi's arm is practically kissing the ceiling.

"Tsk, only five people? God, AI coding software is really destroying your brains." A few nervous laughs that quickly peter out when it becomes obvious he's not kidding.

As the professor launches into a TED Talk about test-driven development, I try to focus. But my mind drifts. Who actually tests their code before writing it? Makes zero sense. Like writing an essay outline after you've finished the paper . . .

"Listen up!" He claps his hands. "Laptops out. You have twenty minutes to build a React countdown website. Users should be able to input a deadline. You can use the internet, but no AI assistance. That's for lazy bums."

My stomach folds over. Twenty minutes? I've never coded that fast in my life. And it's not like I've done this kind of thing before. Back home, our school website is basically a digital poster. It doesn't take any user input.

The rest of the classroom fades away as I furiously comb through React docs like they might explain the meaning of life. Sure, I could make this countdown in Python, but JavaScript? My brain's throwing an error.

A hand slams down on my desk. I jump.

Dr. Kaminski's face looms. "I said close your laptops."

"Sorry," I squeak.

At the end of class, our autograded scores get posted, and I bite back a groan. At the bottom in angry red is my name: CHARISE TANG: 0 TESTS PASSED. I'm the only one who didn't pass anything. Obi is near the top. So is Jenni-with-an-i.

A few snickers float my way. I don't want to care—c'mon, it's so immature to laugh at someone for failing a test—but my neck still heats up.

"Diversity admit," somebody coughs.

Unfortunately the other classes don't go much better. In Computer Systems, we have to read this paper on how IP addresses work, and while I'm struggling through the first page, I overhear people complaining about how "baby" the material is. In Data

Structures and Algorithms, I can't solve a single graph theory problem before time's up—meanwhile, Obi breezes through the entire set in thirty minutes and spends the rest of class playing *Imposter Syndrome*. At least he gets murdered every round, judging from the groans he periodically emits.

Thank God lunch isn't graded, because I'd get an F in that, too. I sit with Obi and Diego, and they spend the entire hour arguing about whether *P* equals *NP*. When I try asking what *P* and *NP* stand for, they ignore me.

After class, most of the cohort peels off for a camp-organized tour of the Freedom Trail around Boston. I should probably go. I've never even been on the East Coast, and it's a cool opportunity to see more of the city and the history behind it. Hear some fun tidbits like *Here is the harbor where Paul Revere took a piss*!

But I feel emptied out, like someone reached inside of me with a long silver spoon and scooped away my guts. All I want to do is crawl into bed and cry.

Sullenly, I walk back to Simmons. My room is empty. For once I'm grateful for Aisha's commitment to being anywhere but here.

I want to talk to someone. Someone who won't make me feel shitty for everything I don't know, which disqualifies almost everyone within a five-mile radius of MIT. Maybe I could FaceTime Lola? I check her location on Find My Friends; she's at the diner where she waitresses. Probably shouldn't bother her while she's scrounging for tips from tourists.

So for some reason, I call my mother. Aside from a quick "still have all my vital organs" update, I haven't spoken to her since I got here, even though she's called and texted multiple times. When I first landed in Boston, part of me thought I would never speak to her again. Which is also what I thought when I was five and she wouldn't let me go to kindergarten with my stuff in a shopping cart, like the homeless guy outside her restaurant. But I'm not five anymore.

Still, it's been several days, and though the anger remains, it doesn't have such a jagged edge to it. I can think around it.

She picks up on the second ring.

"*Baobei*?" Mom says. "It's so good to finally hear from you. How are you?"

The naked relief makes me wince. Like. It is so, so obvious that she cares about me. Which means that I have to reconcile this version of her with the version who stood by and did nothing as her husband raged. It was easier to think of her as cartoonishly evil when we weren't speaking.

"I'm . . ." I wanted to speak to someone about my sadness, but now that she's actually here, the words die on my lips. I don't want her to worry. I want her to think that I made it out, that I'm okay.

But I feel so behind. It isn't even like I'm running some race and the other competitors kicked off long before the *bang* of the starter pistol reached my ears. It's like I showed up expecting to compete on foot only to discover everyone else driving Formula One cars.

Somehow it feels frivolous to say all this when she's in Chinook Shore, trapped in a hopeless marriage.

It's scary how easy it is to get caught up in the pressures of Alpha Fellows and forget about what my life used to be like. It's like I've already lost the password to an old email account.

Why did I even call her? It's not like she'll understand any of the details. At most she'll tell me to work hard, keep my chin up, keep my eyes on my own paper, or some other aphorism. Maybe she'll say to *zhuajin*, which translates literally into "grab tight" but means to "save time," as if time is a bolt of silk that I could cling to for dear life.

"I'm okay," I say. "Things are pretty busy; I should go. But I wanted to let you know that I'm doing fine."

The distance between us feels like this tangible thing.

After we hang up, I start on homework. There's a paper on DNS to read by tomorrow for Computer Systems, and I prop the printout on my lap. But my mind keeps wandering.

What will life be like if I don't win?

Will Michael even let me back into the house? He told me to never return. The bruises he left on my arm haven't faded yet.

Maybe Lola's mom would let me crash in Lola's old room so I can finish out senior year. I could work part-time at the Lucky Panda. Mrs. Lombardi probably has some pamphlet on colleges that might give me a full ride based on my stats . . .

I don't realize I'm crying until tears splash onto the paper.

Ever since I stumbled upon College Confidential years ago,

I always knew things were different outside of Chinook Shore, but it's hard to actually be here. Surrounded by kids like Aisha and Khoi and Stella. If they don't win this competition it'll be a disappointment, a loss of a shiny gold star for their college apps, but let's be real. They'll survive. If I don't win, I don't know where I'll go in September.

There's a knock.

"Yeah?" I call, swiping at my eyes.

"Char?" It's Khoi.

I swing my legs off my bed and open the door.

"I was looking for Aisha?"

"Haven't seen her all day." She wasn't in class, either. She's evaporated. "Have you tried texting her?"

"She doesn't—" Khoi pauses. "Uh, it's fine. Why aren't you at the tour with everyone else?"

I shrug. I don't want to explain how awful I feel. "Why aren't you?"

"My family is from Boston, so I've walked the Freedom Trail before." He peers at my face, which is still sticky with drying tears. "Are you okay?"

"Yeah, fine." It's my default answer.

"Are you sure?"

I'm about to brush off his question, but then I pause. What's so bad about confiding in Khoi? He's been nothing but super nice. I'm the one who failed to defend him when other kids were talking shit. He deserves some honesty.

He'll judge you for your struggles, a small, nasty voice whispers. *Look at how accomplished he is. In comparison, you've done jack shit. You really want to give him more reason to look down on you?*

But Khoi seems too wholesome. He isn't like the other students here. He's in another stratosphere, so maybe he doesn't need to resort to the same petty insecurities that fuel the toxicity and competitiveness of my classmates.

And I really, really need a friend right now.

"Let's get boba first," I say. "Don't I still owe you for that race you won?"

Chapter Fifteen

We end up in a boba shop near Harvard Square, nursing our drinks as I spill my soul to him. I don't tell him everything. I skip the Chinook Shore backstory. But I give what I'm sure is a riveting recap of all my classes today and how difficult they were, and how overwhelmed I am, and how stupid Lucas's knit beanie is.

"I'm sorry," he says when I've finally finished rambling. "There are a lot of kids here whose parents have always paid for the best schools, the best after-school programs, the best tutors. Like in that movie *Parasite*."

I take a sip of my boba. It tastes like a liquified rose. "Wasn't the tutor in *Parasite* actually a fraud?"

"Maybe? It's been a few years. Also, I saw it on a plane and the baby behind me was wailing its lungs out, so I wasn't really focused."

"I'm pretty sure that the tutor being fake is, like, a big part of the plot."

"Okay, my point is that other students *are* coming into this thing with privilege you didn't have. And it sucks. But Char..." He chews on his bottom lip. "Feeling sorry for yourself isn't going to help you win."

The bluntness of his words surprises me. Honestly, Khoi always seemed so sunshine-y. I didn't think he had this side to him.

Then I'm irritated. Wow. So helpful. As if I didn't already know. Why did I even bother confiding in him? "Easy for you to say. You made a viral video game that you sold for a million dollars. You didn't even bother going to class today."

He raises his palms up. "Don't lash out at me."

"Sorry."

"All good." He slurps a few tapioca pearls. "You know, I could help you."

I blink. "You would do that?"

"Why not? I have plenty of time. Perks of cutting class."

Why not?

The answer arrives easily. Because I'm freaking terrified.

I'm scared I'll get all hyped up, and then he'll realize I'm too smooth-brained or too far behind to teach. And I'll feel even more hopeless than I do now.

But I don't say any of that. Instead I say, "It's a lot of work for you."

"I don't mind." He smiles. It's such a sweet, earnest smile.

Something catches in my throat—a sudden knot of emotion I wasn't prepared for.

It's pathetic. I'm not used to being shown kindness like this.

"Thanks," I mumble, half-expecting him to change his mind.

For a while, we wander around Harvard. Everything is so pretty—red brick everywhere, high-end storefronts casting a warm, buttery glow over the sidewalk. The campus itself is so different from MIT, with old-timey architecture reminiscent of a classic fairy tale. Even though the two schools are only a mile apart, they may as well be trapped in different centuries.

Khoi shows me the famous John Harvard statue in the Yard. Apparently the students pee on the same golden feet that tourists rub for good luck. We manage to sneak into Widener Library even though it's not open to the public. The whole place smells like old books and old money. The interior is carved from white marble, with soaring ceilings and reading rooms full of mahogany furniture. It's the most beautiful library I've ever seen.

Once the sun is starting to set and it's about time for dinner, we decide to go back to our own campus. Even that thought feels like a small astonishment. *Our campus*, as if it's mine, too, at least for now.

As we're passing Bow Street, I notice that across Massachusetts Ave there are two girls walking. One South Asian and one white, both in sports bras and yoga pants. The white girl has hair the color of pink cotton candy. The South Asian girl looks familiar . . .

I point. "Hey, it's—"

Khoi yanks me behind a bush. "Get down!"

I oblige, more out of confusion than anything else. We're smushed up against each other, because this bush is *not* big enough to shroud two people from view. He smells like sandalwood soap. His too-quick heartbeat is on my skin. My entire body feels jittery.

A curious turkey approaches us. It's my first time seeing one IRL. Beady eyes, razor-sharp talons. Those cute hand turkeys I used to draw in elementary school were a total lie. This thing looks like it eats other birds' dreams for breakfast.

"Don't touch the turkey," Khoi whispers. "They can attack if provoked."

I want to ask why Harvard has turkeys, but there's a more urgent question on my mind.

"Why are we hiding from your girlfriend?" I whisper. "I thought you needed to talk to her. Isn't that why you came to our room?"

"*Yeah*, but I needed to talk to her at MIT, not at Harvard. Does that make sense?"

"No, not at all!"

Why is he acting so sus? Maybe this isn't about Aisha. Maybe this is about the person next to her. "The girl she's with, is that your ex or something?"

"Why is that your first thought? How many ex-girlfriends do you think I have?"

"I don't know, ten? Twenty?" Khoi could be a secret fuckboy.

The sandalwood soap is a pretty damning piece of evidence.

"*Twenty?*" He seems genuinely offended. "Am I the world's first underaged *Bachelor* star? Should I get ready for the next rose ceremony? Choose who I want to take to the fantasy suite?"

"You seem to know an awful lot about *The Bachelor*."

"My aunt is a die-hard fan!"

"Khoi, admitting you have an addiction is the first step to recovery."

"I'm—it's not—I don't—I hate-watch it—*ugh!*" He shakes his head. "Okay, they're gone. Let's go back to campus."

We hop on the 1 bus, and Khoi makes the mistake of answering yes when some woman asks if we have a moment to talk about our lord and savior Jesus Christ, and then he's too polite to interrupt so we miss our stop. We end up in Boston. He offers to call an Uber, but I'm morally opposed to using rideshare services for walkable distances, so we trudge back across the bridge spanning the Charles River. By the time we get to Simmons, dinner has ended, so he buys us burritos from a nearby food truck.

And he never explains why we had to hide from Aisha. And he never denies that the other girl was his ex.

Chapter Sixteen

But whatever. Maybe he doesn't need to explain. Over the next several days, he keeps his word and helps me after class. We spend nearly every single spare moment together. We meet in his room because he has a monitor setup and a gaming chair, and Obi usually posts up in the student center anyway.

I learn a lot about Khoi. I learn that he is the most brilliant programmer I've ever met. I learn that he can subsist on a diet of strong coffee and blueberry muffins. I learn that he's got God-tier patience when explaining stuff that's not clicking for me.

My struggle isn't really that I don't know a certain syntax or library. It's that I've never approached coding as an art form, with underlying principles that spin into harmony. I've always Frankensteined together scraps from the internet to fix whatever problem was in front of me. It's like the difference between engineering a car and duct-taping a motor to a trash bin that might get you across town before falling apart.

But talking to Khoi helps. It isn't because he can explain

Dijkstra's algorithm and load balancing. There are plenty of YouTube tutorials for that. It's that he operates on a different frequency. He holds some deeper intuition about how everything connects. But slowly, my brain also begins to see the same patterns.

Thursday is Juneteenth, so we have the day off. Khoi isn't at breakfast and half of the Alpha Fellows are on a trip to Cape Cod, so the dining hall is nearly empty. After scarfing down a bowl of Lucky Charms, I go to his room to see if he's there.

I freeze when I hear my roommate's voice, bright as new pennies. I'm surprised she's even here. Last night she zombie lurched in right before curfew, mumbled a few words to me, and then collapsed in bed. This morning when I woke up, she was already gone.

"I don't think this is about your personal integrity, Khoi," Aisha is saying. "I think this is about Char."

Uh-oh. When people mention you behind your back, it's never for a good reason.

"She's my friend! I'm tutoring her!"

"And how's that going?"

"It's great. She's brilliant. I think she's going to do super well on the first checkpoint."

I want to staple his lips together. Can't he see Aisha is jealous of how much time we've been spending together? He should tell her that I'm a charity case and he's carrying my ass. Maybe throw in a comment about how mid I look.

"And you claim this isn't about Char? You should see how your eyes light up when you talk about her. Denial isn't just a river in Egypt, kiddo."

My heart skips a beat. What is she implying?

"Don't call me kiddo, I'm older than you! I turned seventeen a few weeks ago!"

"Exaaaaactly. This is such typical Gemini behavior."

"I'm a Taurus cusp—"

My phone chimes with a text from Lola. She's been pinging me about her latest fling, Lifeguard Rachel, not to be confused with Prom Rachel. I scramble to silence the notification, but it's too late. Khoi and Aisha have abruptly stopped speaking.

The door swings open. Aisha. She has dark circles under her eyes, and there are wisps of hair falling out of her ponytail. "Oh. Char." She doesn't try to smile.

"Sorry, am I interrupting?"

"I was just leaving." She sweeps past me. Her vanilla-and-cinnamon perfume lingers in the air like a disapproving ghost.

Inside the room, Khoi is perched on his gaming chair, knees against his chest. He's frowning.

"What was all that about?"

He shrugs. "Ask Aisha."

I shift from foot to foot. "Is she bothered by the amount of time we spend together?"

"I don't know. Maybe?"

Why is he being this way? "Dude, shouldn't you be more

concerned over how she's feeling? Or, like, where she goes all the time?"

"Char, you don't know what's going on, so leave it alone," he snaps.

I fight back a swell of irritation. "Chill out."

His eyes are definitely *not* lighting up. They are in battery-saving mode. I don't know what Aisha is on. If he actually liked me *like that*, he'd be nicer.

"Sorry." He swivels to face me. "Isn't there a trip to Cape Cod today?"

"I grew up on the beach. Didn't seem that special." And silly to lose a full day of studying. "Why aren't you there?"

He grimaces. "Don't know how to swim."

"Whoa. Why not?" Even I know how to swim. With a pang, I remember that Michael is the one who taught me.

"When I was younger, the doctor said it'd be dangerous for me. My meds work pretty well now, so I could learn, but I haven't gotten around to it." When he sees my confusion, he explains, "Kids who get seizures are at greater risk of drowning."

"Oh." Now I feel like an ass for asking.

"It's whatever." He tugs at the collar of his shirt. "If you're not going on the trip, do you want to study together?"

Maybe I should stop meeting with him. Sure, it's not like we're doing anything other than classwork. But I don't want to make Aisha feel bad, and if there's one type of code I wish I had a tutorial for, it's girl code.

But I also need to ace the first checkpoint. And honestly, if Aisha does feel weird about all this, she should talk to me instead of whatever vanishing act she's pulling.

"Yeah, that would be amazing," I say.

The next week is a blur of cramming. I spend every spare moment memorizing algorithms, reviewing papers, and completing problem sets. At night when I close my eyes, I see syntax on the backs of my eyelids. I dream in code.

Most of the Alpha Fellows seem more chill. When the weekend arrives, some of the kids leave for summer homes in Nantucket and Martha's Vineyard. There's another group that decides to do an impromptu day trip to New York City. The camp organizes some activities—karaoke, a movie screening of a Steve Jobs biopic, a scavenger hunt around the MIT campus. Khoi goes to most of those. I skip everything to study.

On Thursday, the day before the first checkpoint, Khoi has a doctor's appointment, so I spend the afternoon studying with Jenni-with-an-i. Since there are an odd number of girls, she gets a single, so we camp out in her room.

She has stacks and stacks of flash cards, color-coded by subject. We take turns quizzing each other.

"Quickest worst-case possible runtime for a sorting algorithm?" I ask.

She squeezes her eyes shut. "I wanna say linear?"

"No, it's n log n."

"Oh, fudge." She refuses to ever curse. She's like a cookie-baking grandma trapped in a seventeen-year-old Sabrina Carpenter doppelgänger.

"Okay, follow-up. What *is* the quickest sorting algorithm?"

"Is it radix?"

Before I can respond, a male voice shouts, "What the hell?" It's coming from next door. Stella's room. I don't remember who her roommate is. Maybe that girl with the crypto cult.

Stella's voice is high-pitched and frantic. "Lucas, calm down. Don't make it a big deal."

"Don't tell me what is or isn't a big deal!"

"It's not about—"

There's the sound of a door flying open and then toddler-like stomps. We poke our heads into the hallway. Lucas is storming away. Stella is in her doorway with her arms crossed.

"Are you okay?" Jenni-with-an-i asks her.

Stella's face is screwed up and red. "Yeah. Fine. Whatever." She retreats into her own room and slams the door.

"Good talk," I mutter.

We go back inside Jenni-with-an-i's room.

"I shouldn't gossip, but," Jenni-with-an-i says, which is the universal phrase for *I'm about to gossip*. "While we were in New York on Sunday, Stella told me she didn't want to team up with Lucas. I guess he took the news poorly."

"She didn't want to work with her own boyfriend?"

"Something about wanting to do things herself. I don't

know the details. We got distracted by a Times Square street performer dressed like a giant baby. Rather disturbing. Babies shouldn't have nipple hair."

An image involuntarily pops into my head and I grimace. But this conversation also reminds me that, *oops*, I don't yet have a team. I focused more on cramming once classes began. "Do you want to team up together?" Jenni-with-an-i is sharp, organized, and friendly. She'd be a good person to work with.

"I've already agreed to team with Obi and Diego," she says. "They have an idea for climate tech. I could ask if you could be our fourth member?"

I remember Diego's spiel from the first day. I don't need another lecture about how I only got in because of my chromosomes, but he does seem smart, and maybe that matters more. And I can't afford to be choosy. "That's nice of you to offer. I'll let you know."

Suddenly it seems obvious. The only person I really want to work with is Khoi. He's been such a good friend, and he's insanely talented. It feels icky to think this way, but he's probably my best shot at winning.

He's going to team up with his girlfriend, that goes without saying. But Aisha is gone all the time. She can do what she wants, but I've done plenty of group projects where one of the members goes AWOL. I don't want to split the prize money with somebody whose greatest contribution is adding her name to the PowerPoint title slide.

No, that's unfair to assume. Khoi skips class too, and he's clearly brilliant. Maybe Aisha already knows everything and that's why she's never here. She'll just waltz into the first checkpoint and breeze through the exam.

So when I see her tonight, I'll ask if I can join them. I'll happily third-wheel if it means I don't have to go back to Chinook Shore.

Chapter Seventeen

Aisha doesn't come back until fifteen minutes before curfew.

She takes two steps into our room and face-plants into her bed. Her topknot is frizzy and loose, as if she went for a five-mile jog in the Boston heat.

"Hi?" I say.

"Dead. Tired," she mumbles into her pillow.

I feel a little bad talking to her about this when she's exhausted, but I don't want to wait until after the exam. There's not that much time before the second checkpoint. "Uh, I wanted to ask you something."

"Yes, you do talk in your sleep," she says. "Mostly about operating systems."

"Oh." I didn't know that. I wonder if sleep-me is better at computer science than awake-me. If so, I might as well take a nap tomorrow during the test. "That's . . . not what I wanted to ask about."

She flips onto her back and eyes me. "What's up?"

"I was . . ." God, why am I suddenly so itchy? I'm trying to ask something reasonable. *The worst she can say is no, and that's the same result as not asking at all.* That's the wisdom people like to parrot.

But it's not the same result. If I don't ask, I can live in the delusion that maybe things could've been different had I simply tried harder. And delusion is important for my self-esteem, thank you very much.

"I was wondering if I could join you and Khoi for the hackathon?"

"Oh!" She jerks upright, and the sudden movement forces her topknot to surrender its last bit of structural integrity. With her hair losing its fight to gravity, she looks even more disheveled and bewildered.

She's about to say no. I can feel it.

"Stupid idea, forget it," I say quickly.

"No, no. I'm flattered. But . . ." She bites her lip. "Char, I don't think I should work with anyone. I'm not even going to team with Khoi."

"Huh?"

"You've probably noticed that I'm gone a lot?"

"Maybe a little," I fib, not wanting to call her out.

She steeples her hands. "Don't tell anyone else this, okay?"

"Sure." Lola used to ask me that. I was always flattered. It implied she thought I had other friends to gossip with.

"I'm doing a dance program at Harvard. That's where I've been going. Khoi knows."

I blink, digesting this new info. "Okay . . . so why bother being here at all?" She can't be using our dorm as a crash pad. The mattresses are lumpy and there's no air-conditioning. Plus, her family lives nearby.

"I'm at Alpha Fellows because my parents don't approve of dance. They think it's a waste of time. They want me to study computer science like my older brother." She makes a face that reminds me of the squiggly mouth emoji. "Stupidly perfect Aditya. Mr. Valedictorian. Mr. Princeton. Mr. Google intern."

"I'm sorry." I can't imagine what it's like to have parents who care that much.

"But yeah, so I'd be utterly useless on a team. I'm going to do the bare minimum to get through this program so my parents are happy. You should still ask Khoi to team up, though. I know he really likes you."

He really likes you. I try to keep my heart rate steady. She means as friends, obviously.

"Are you sure? He's your boyfriend."

"That's . . ." Aisha seems to think hard about it. Then she shrugs. "That's fine. It's not like I'm around anyway."

We brush our teeth in the bathroom. Aisha has this elaborate nighttime skincare routine comprising of gels and creams and serums. She offers me some of her snail slime, and I politely decline. Some things simply don't belong on your face, no matter what TikTok says. Then HellomynameisBrenda yells for lights-out, so we go to bed.

As I lie in the dark, I wonder why I'm still anxious.

I should be relieved. Aisha didn't say no, and I finally solved the mystery of her frequent disappearances. That explains why we saw her in Harvard Square the other day.

But it doesn't explain why Khoi wanted to hide. This situation is not passing the vibe check.

What if that girl isn't Khoi's ex? What if she's his current fling, and Khoi is cheating on Aisha? He was gone for a "doctor's appointment" today, but what if that's code for "sneaking off with my other girlfriend?"

No, I'm being ridiculous. Paranoid. Just because my sperm donor was, ah, monogamy-impaired, doesn't mean every guy acts that way. Khoi has always been so genuine.

And I shouldn't be thinking about any of this. The first checkpoint is tomorrow. That's all that matters.

I start mentally listing out all the data structure implementations and drift off somewhere around min-max heap.

At breakfast, everybody is uncommonly quiet. Jenni-with-an-i is at a table alone with her flash cards spread out over the entire surface. I was planning to talk to Khoi about working together, but he's busy holding court with a steady stream of kids who keep coming up to ask questions about the material. Diego is furiously typing on his laptop. Haru is sleeping with his hoodie drawn and cheek pressed against the table. Obi has a copy of CLRS, the famous programming textbook, propped up against Haru's head.

Even Aisha tries to care. "Char, do you know what language the coding portion is in? Is it Java? I only know Java."

"Pretty sure it's Python."

"Shoot." She frowns into her bowl of cereal. "Do you think I can learn Python in the next twenty minutes?"

I look down at my scrambled eggs and realize that my appetite is currently 404 Not Found.

At nine a.m., we all file into the examination room in Stata. Aisha, Khoi, and I find seats near the back.

The test is three-and-a-half hours long, no breaks. Pencil and paper only; we have to write our code out by hand. If we need to use the restroom, we'll be accompanied by a proctor.

There's a wave of grumbling as a gum-chewing college student walks around with a bin to collect our phones and smartwatches. He even forces Obi to take off his Oura Ring.

"Dude, I *need* my biometrics! How else am I supposed to monitor my body temperature?"

"You'll live," the proctor says.

When I fill in my name at the front of the testing booklet, my hand trembles. Then somebody touches my wrist gently.

"Don't worry. You've got this," says Khoi. He smiles.

My heart does this flip. Probably from nerves. "Thanks."

"You had an amazing tutor, after all," he adds, because of course he has to ruin it.

I can't even come up with a clever clapback.

"You may start now," HellomynameisBrenda says, and throughout the cavernous room, there's the sound of paper rustling like wings against air.

About an hour in, there's a commotion. Someone gets caught using homemade smart glasses to look up the answers, and he's frog-marched out of the room by two college kids. Another hour later, Aisha stands to leave. I doubt she actually finished, but maybe she has to go back to Harvard.

At the three-hour mark, more people start handing in their exams. I've skipped a few questions, so once I reach the end, I return to the ones I set aside earlier.

In a database transaction, what does ACID stand for?

The *A* is atomicity, the *C* is consistency, the *D* is durability, but what is *I*? Is it independence? That doesn't sound right. Is it supposed to end with a *y* like the others?

"Pencils down," HellomynameisBrenda says. I scrawl *independence-y* before she snatches my paper away.

At lunch, everybody is buzzing about the test. *What'd you get for the recurrence on the master theorem? How about the amortized run time? For the multiple-choice section, I was getting a string of all Bs, that was freaky. Wait, saaaaame! They're such trolls.* I don't participate in the conversation. My brain is too mushy.

In the afternoon, while the camp counselors are grading, everyone fans out on Killian Court, the green lawn in front of the iconic dome that MIT uses on their marketing materials. A few guys toss a Frisbee. Stella and Lucas make out in the grass, his hand inching closer and closer to her butt. Guess they must've resolved their fight. Obi teaches us a card game that he learned from his cousin in finance. After several practice rounds where I do only marginally better than a potato, we're all supposed to toss twenty bucks into the pot. I don't have that kind of money to lose, so I excuse myself.

"Aw, but it's only twenty bucks! A Hamilton," Obi says.

"Isn't Andrew Jackson on the twenty?" Jenni-with-an-i points to one of the crumpled bills.

"Char, I could cover it for you," Khoi says.

I shake my head. The offer is nice, but he shouldn't pay for something frivolous like this. "I want to relax, anyway."

I sit in a shady spot beneath a tree. It's a beautiful day, everything made clean with sunlight. Somebody could take a snapshot of Killian Court right now and slap the photo on a college brochure. I'd be just out of frame. Maybe the toes of my sneakers would make it into the background.

Everyone else acts so comfortable. They know that they were handpicked to be here, that they are deserving of all this because they are brilliant and ambitious and young. I wonder when I'll stop feeling like I woke up in the wrong life.

Sometime later, Khoi slumps down beside me.

"I lost all my money," he says.

"Sorry for your loss."

"Obi is a shark." He leans against the tree trunk and shuts his eyes.

I should ask Khoi to team up. Like, right now. I don't have the excuse of the first checkpoint anymore. The second checkpoint is in a week.

Why is this so mortifying? Jesus. It's like even by asking, I think I'm good enough to collab with him. The famous Khoi Astor.

But if I don't ask, it won't happen.

Winning is too damn important. I need to get over myself.

"Khoi," I start. "Do you . . ."

He's looking at me expectantly. Something about his gaze makes my voice catch in my throat.

Maybe he'll laugh at me for thinking he'd ever want to be on my team. He knows exactly how much of a disaster I am at computer science; he's witnessed it firsthand these past two weeks.

No, Khoi wouldn't laugh. He's too nice for that. I know, I know. He's never given me any real reason to think he'd be an ass about it. I don't know where my fear comes from.

"Do you want to team up with me?" It comes out as one singular gust of a question.

I'm about to do the thing I did in the conversation with Aisha—tell him it's stupid, forget it, dismiss myself before he gets a chance to—but he grins.

"I was going to ask you!"

Relief floods me. Wow. I can't believe that worked. And I

can't believe I'm actually going to be teaming with him.

I'm sort of going feral inside, but I try to play it off like whatever. "Great."

"Do you have any ideas yet? Because I had a few. There was this one *TechCrunch* article about this brain scanner that lets you beam your thoughts to dogs . . ."

As the midafternoon sun arcs through the sky, we brainstorm. Artificial intelligence that does your homework. A virtual reality simulator for first responders, like paramedics. An animated water-intake tracker.

I could see any of these ideas popping off. But none of them feel like my vibe. I'm not thirsty, at least not literally. I don't own a VR headset and know squat about medical crises. And while it would be nice to have an AI cook my assignments, my grades aren't in the desperation zone yet.

We're riffing on the concept of Google Docs but for music composition or math collaboration or something when Dallas-or-Austin rushes past. He yells, "Brenda said that the exam scores are out!"

Chapter Eighteen

By the time Khoi and I reach Stata, there's already a sizable crowd gathered on the first floor.

Our rankings are posted on a piece of paper taped to the wall. It's weird. For a tech program, Alpha Fellows is still stuck in the twentieth century. I wouldn't be surprised if they ask us to submit our final projects on floppy disks.

It's impossible to get through the crush, so we wait near the back. I'm tempted to elbow my way to the front, but Khoi seems unbothered. "Let's just wait. It's not like the results are going to change within the next few minutes."

Easy for him to say. He definitely slayed it. Meanwhile, my heart is in my ears. What if I failed? What if I did so poorly it makes Khoi rethink working with me? No, what if my scores were so trash they boot me from the program?

"They have a flair for the dramatic," somebody nearby grumbles. "What's wrong with sending out a text blast?"

Someone else shrieks loud enough that it echoes through the lobby. I can't tell if it's a happy shriek or a horrified shriek. A girl staggers away, shoulders heaving with sobs. My stomach roils.

Obi comes up to us and throws an arm around Khoi's shoulder. "Astor, you bastard."

Khoi seems bewildered. "Huh?"

"You didn't see, man? You got number one!"

"You're serious?"

"As serious as the brightest star in the night sky." Obi's mouth twitches. "Get it? Sirius?"

I'm too keyed up to even muster a pity laugh at the pun. Somehow the news about Khoi getting first makes me feel worse, not better, even though I should be doing mental cartwheels. This is amazing for our chances at winning.

But if I didn't do okayish, it'll be obvious I'm dragging the team down.

Khoi glances at me. "What about Char?"

"Oh, uh . . . didn't check. But I'm sure you did well too," Obi adds quickly.

The crowd has thinned, so I take the opportunity to push through to the front. I start reading names from the bottom-up. With relief, I see that I'm not dead last. The first name I recognize is Aisha Chadha, ranked #92, which makes sense given that she bailed halfway through the exam. Haru Watanabe landed at #71—impressive for someone whose bloodstream is mostly THC.

And then it's me. Charise (Char) Tang, #24.

I exhale.

Number twenty-four. That's top quartile, just barely. Sure, it isn't earth-shattering. Nothing to write home about (hypothetically—the idea of penning a letter to Michael or Olive about this is freaking hilarious). But it's respectable. Decent. It means I could still come through with the win as long as I commit to the grind.

Out of curiosity, I peep the rest of the rankings. The only girl who did better than me is Jenni Wheeler, #21. The top twenty names is a total sausage fest. There's Obi Udechukwu, #10. Diego Rodriguez, the competitive programming TikToker, is #4.

And Khoi Anh (Astor), of course, at #1. Huh. I wonder if Anh is a middle name or a last name. He hasn't mentioned it before. I already knew he was Vietnamese, of course.

There's an asterisk next to his name noting that he also got a perfect score. Of course.

As fawning kids swarm him, I hang back in the shadows.

There's no rational reason to be anything other than hyped for him. I shouldn't be shook. I should feel lucky that he even wants to work with me.

I don't know why it feels like a metal claw has reached into my chest and squeezed tight.

I need to do something. Something to prove that I'm contributing to the team too. But what? Khoi has the money, and clearly the brains. I guess I can be the funny one. The personality hire.

I remember Stella on the yacht babbling about how she got

a recommendation letter from one of those rich guys. Maybe I could find a mentor too.

A name floats up. The obvious name. The big one.

Usually, I'd hesitate. It's stupid. He's not going to respond. I shouldn't even bother.

But I did well on the first checkpoint. I'm working with Khoi. And I'm tired of letting the world tell me I don't deserve anything good for myself. I'm tired of believing it.

I lean against the wall and unlock my phone.

Ten minutes later, I send an email to Edvin Nilsen.

When Khoi and I sit down for dinner, I immediately sense that the vibes are off. Kids are whispering, glancing over. I look down to check if there's something on my shirt. No, it's just a Snorlax graphic.

Khoi doesn't seem to notice anything. "Okay, so I started this Notion page for our project. I'll add you."

I nod. I don't mention emailing Edvin Nilsen. Now that the adrenaline has faded, I feel ridiculous for doing that. Why would this tech billionaire help me with my summer camp project? Sure, it's a summer camp he started. But he's more of a figurehead than actually involved. He hasn't visited even once.

When I go up to refill my water glass, somebody taps me on the shoulder. It's Haru. "Oregon," he mumbles.

"Okay, can we come up with a different nickname for me?"

He shrugs, because Haru's entire existence is one big shrug.

"Something with Khoi. They were talking to me about it. Showed me some article."

"Who is they?" Is? Are? Grammar is weird.

"Dunno. Kid with the dumb hat. Wears it to cover his bald spot."

I thank Haru and head straight to Lucas's table.

He's sitting with a few guys whose names I don't know for sure—I think one of them is Aiden or Jayden or Okayden. Stella isn't around.

They're talking loud and brash. Somebody should've taught them the concept of "inside voices." I'm ten feet away when I hear them say the name *Khoi*.

"What's going on?" I ask.

Lucas exchanges a smirk with another boy. "Haven't you heard? Your boyfriend's dad is a grifter. Guess the apple doesn't fall far from the tree."

"He's not my boyfriend. And what the hell are you talking about?"

With too much glee, someone hands me their phone, which is open to an old article from *The New York Times*.

QUANG ANH SENTENCED TO EIGHT YEARS IN PRISON

Quang Anh was sentenced on Friday to eight years in prison. The disgraced founder of Pegasus Cryptocurrency who was convicted of stealing millions of dollars from customers, Anh was found guilty of fraud and money laundering last month.

Mr. Anh remained stoic as the sentence was read. His wife, Linda, burst into tears as his eleven-year-old son, Khoi, stared at the floor.

I drop the phone onto the table. "What's the point of showing me this?"

Sure, I've wondered why Khoi lives with his aunt and uncle. But I never asked. I mean, I get what it's like to have a complicated family that you can't explain.

"When the test results got posted, I saw that his legal name is Khoi Anh, so I decided to do some googling. It seems kind of sus that he's trying to hide his identity."

"By using a different last name? If he wants to distance himself from his past, fine. Why are you dredging all of this up now?"

"Char? Everything good?" Khoi is at my shoulder. Ugh, did Haru talk to him too?

"Yeah, fine." I want to protect him. I don't want him to see any of this. Maybe it's not too late to—

"So, Astor, how'd you cheat on the exam?" Lucas drawls. "Or should I say *Anh*?"

Khoi's gaze falls on the unlocked phone screen, which still has the article open. His face clouds over. Silently, he pivots on his heel and walks away.

"That video game he made, *Imposter Syndrome*," somebody

says. "You think he used his daddy's money for that?"

Lucas leans back, hands behind his head. "These types always have offshore bank accounts. They probably have millions' worth of Bitcoin stowed away somewhere in the Cayman Islands."

My blood boils. "You're pathetic," I spit out. "What, you couldn't beat him on the test so you decide to bully him to make yourself feel better? Guess what! He's still number one."

They're all silent until Lucas says, "Get off your moral high horse. You sucked him off so he'd team up with you?"

"Excuse me?" Not that it's any of their business, but my expertise in that department is purely theoretical, with no real-world experience.

"You don't think the rest of us noticed you going into his dorm room every day after class?"

"Don't be disgusting. Khoi has a *girlfriend*. We're just friends. He was helping me out."

"Must be nice to be a girl and be able to get that kind of *help*."

Wow. He's no different from Michael. I can fly thousands of miles and never escape the misogynistic viciousness that comes from a lifetime of entitlement and resentment.

So I respond to Lucas the same way I responded to my stepfather. The only way I know how to cope. I leave.

Chapter Nineteen

I am a CIA operative, and my mission is to locate Khoi. This mission wraps up quickly, because turns out he is in the most obvious place possible: his dorm room.

Without knocking, I push the door open. He's hunched at his desk, fingers flying over his mechanical keyboard. He's coding.

Maybe I should leave. Like, he seems to be having a pretty good time with his computer. Heck, his computer would probably be better at getting through this conversation than me.

But he's my teammate. And I'd rather talk this out than have it loom over us like some software update that keeps getting postponed.

"Are you okay?" I try.

"I'm fine." He keeps his eyes pinned to his laptop screen.

"Stop coding. Look at me."

He gives me the most obligatory two-second glance. "What is there to say? You read the article."

"We don't have to talk about that," I say, and I mean it. I don't really need to know about Khoi's dad. It doesn't say anything about Khoi himself. I have a shitty biological father too. "If you want to discuss it, I'll listen. But otherwise I'm just here to be your friend."

He doesn't say anything.

I grab Obi's desk chair and sit next to Khoi. "What are you building?" He's writing in Python.

"Just something silly. It's an open-source Pokémon game. Not officially approved by Nintendo."

For a few more minutes, I watch him make a subclass for Fire-type Pokémon. I suspect he uses coding to bury his sadness. I'm kind of becoming a Khoi expert.

"Are you going to leave?" he asks.

I shrug. "I'm sticking around to see how you implement the Psychic types."

"You're not going to leave." He laughs. It's the most bitter sound I've ever heard him make. "Okay, since you know about my sordid and shameful past, you have to confess something about yourself. It's only fair."

My immediate instinct is to tell him about the time I called my second-grade teacher Mom, but maybe it's better to be more vulnerable. After a moment, I say, "It was my stepdad."

"What?"

"You asked me before where the bruises on my arm came from. It was my stepdad, Michael. I was sneaking out to catch my flight, and Michael caught me. He didn't want to let me go."

"Why didn't he want to let you go?"

"Because he loved me too much, obviously." I smirk, but Khoi doesn't laugh.

"You don't need to do that," he says.

"Do what?"

"Make a joke out of something horrible. You do that a lot."

I blink, surprised by the observation. Nobody else has ever said that. "Hey, we all have our coping mechanisms. You have programming. I have my bad jokes."

"I don't use programming as a coping mechanism." But his eyes are wet. I scoot closer and grab his hand. This sends a tingle through me, which I ignore. Probably static electricity.

"Hey, talk to me. I promise I'm a better conversational partner than GitHub Copilot."

"Copilot doesn't even generate good code," he mutters.

"Khoi."

"Okay, okay. Gosh. Where to begin? My parents had to take me to the hospital a lot because I was so sickly. They wanted a second kid but my medical bills were too high for that. Eventually our family got rich and things got better. Then my dad went to prison and everything was awful. My mom moved abroad to get away from the people my dad screwed over. I moved in with my maternal aunt and uncle. Also, I started using my mom's last name. There. That's my entire life story." He glares at me almost defiantly, as if he's waiting me to leap out of my chair and bolt for the door.

But obviously I don't do that.

"I don't speak to my biological father either," I say. "He cheated on my mother and now he lives in China with his new family."

"I'm sorry."

I don't need him to say that. I didn't tell him for sympathy points. "Like, I get having a shitty dad."

He laughs sort of shakily.

"Sometimes I wish he had died instead," I say.

The words surprise even me. I've never said them out loud. Maybe Khoi will think I'm deranged.

But when I look at him, he's nodding sadly. "Yeah, because then your grief would be something other people can understand."

He gets it.

Something inside of me sings bright and strong. Like there was something broken within me all this time and now the fracture lines are flooding with gold. Like it's finally okay to acknowledge the brokenness. What's that Japanese art of repairing pottery shards called? *Kintsugi.*

He continues. "I can't talk about this with anyone. Because I don't want people to see me as the son of the crypto fraudster. You saw how Lucas and the others reacted."

"Lucas is a walking ick factory."

"Indeed," he agrees. "This is why I don't hang with the smart-kid circuit. Like the kids who are at every science fair and quiz bowl. Aisha is cool, but the others . . ." He shakes his head. "They're this toxic mix of entitled and insecure. And their biggest problem is, like, if they'll get into Harvard."

"God forbid they have to settle for Yale."

"Or worse, Dartmouth." He cracks a smile. "You know, this might be the first time I actually tried talking to someone. Usually I just code away my sorrows."

I give his hand another squeeze. "You can always come to me." I mean it. I want to be here for him.

His eyes flicker with something dark and indescribable. "I really like you, Char." And his voice triggers a thrill I can feel everywhere.

He tilts his face down toward me. And suddenly he's close. Too close. I catch another whiff of his sandalwood soap. His eyelashes are so long . . .

There's this electric millisecond where I'm tempted to lean in, close the distance between us, meet his lips with my own.

But then my logic catches up to my lust. He has a girlfriend. I can't do this to my roommate. This is all wrong.

I scoot away and spring to my feet. "What are you doing?" The question sounds more panicked than angry.

He stands too. "Char—"

"You're not single, Khoi. This isn't right." I turn to walk out.

"Char, wait." He catches my elbow, but I shake him off.

"Leave me alone. I need to go." It's late. Aisha is probably back by now. I have to tell her what happened.

I'm so sick of people's bullshit. I didn't think he'd be the type to cheat on his girlfriend.

I'm furious at myself, too, for letting things escalate. I can't believe I let myself get so lost in the sauce.

There's a prick behind my eyes, but I will myself not to cry. He's not worth that.

God. Maybe I should swear off boys forever. I'm going to live my best life as a crazy cat lady. At least cats won't betray you.

When the door slams shut behind me, he doesn't follow.

When I get back to my own room, Aisha is already in her pajamas, scrolling Instagram in bed.

"Khoi tried to kiss me," I blurt out as soon as I see her.

There's a beat. I wait for her to throw something at my head.

She puts her phone down and sits up. Her face is weirdly neutral. "Oh, so he finally got his shit together."

What's she on about? "I'm really sorry. I ran here immediately to tell you."

Aisha considers me. "I guess he didn't mention?"

"Mention what?"

She sighs. "Okay, promise to not tell anyone else this."

"Sure?" How many secrets does this girl have? She's like a total plot twist of a person.

"Char, Khoi and I aren't dating."

I blink.

"It started as this lie last fall because I'm seeing a girl I met through dance. We're actually both doing the Harvard program. She lives in Roxbury, and I didn't want my homophobic parents to know. Khoi is my friend, so he agreed to fake a relationship. My parents track my location, so it gave me an excuse for why I was traveling into the city all the time."

I need to download all this. My heart rate steadies as I chew through the info dump. God, I'm so relieved to find out Khoi isn't really a cheating f-boy. Now I feel bad for freaking out on him.

My mind is pinwheeling with questions, but the first thing I can think to say is, "You guys really couldn't come up with a better story than fake dating?" This isn't a K-drama.

Aisha shrugs. "Probably could have. But it was funny at the time? And now we're committed to the bit."

It's low-key annoying. Like there was this big joke everybody was in on. Everybody but me. "Okay, so you lied to your parents, but why'd you have to lie to *me*?"

"The first time we met, my parents were also in the room. And after that, I figured the truth didn't matter and it seemed safer to keep it a secret. And I'm not ready to come out to everyone."

"Of course," I say quickly. I wasn't trying to act like she owed me that.

"Obviously Khoi wanted to spill to you, because he caught feelings." She waggles her eyebrows suggestively.

I'm not discussing Khoi and his *feelings* right now. I still have more questions about Aisha's secret agent life. "But you said your parents track your location? So can't they see when you go to Harvard?"

"I give my phone to Khoi, and he carries it around while I'm gone." She taps her chin. "Come to think of it, maybe I could've just done something like that from the beginning. Oh well."

"Is this *really* easier than telling your parents the truth?" The mental gymnastics needed to keep up this lie . . . She's really doing the most.

"Trust me, it is." She doesn't say more, and I don't probe further. Family drama can be a lot. We've all got our own shit to work through.

There's a knock on our door.

It's Khoi. "Char? Sorry, I know that you said you wanted space, but I don't want you to go to sleep mad . . . Please, will you listen to me?"

I let him in. His eyes are round and frantic. It makes me want to smother him in a fluffy blanket and reassure him everything will be okay.

"Aisha told me the entire story," I say. "I know you two were fake dating."

"Oh." He slides into a relieved grin. "Great!"

Ugh. He thinks that because I now know the tea, we can be all hashtag relationship goals. But it's not that simple. I have literally no idea what I want. But I have this sinking sense that it isn't smart to get more entangled with Khoi.

Sometimes boys are adorable and sweet and kissable. That doesn't mean I should catch feelings.

I go, "So I'll see you tomorrow?"

"But—"

"It's almost curfew anyway." It's five minutes to eleven.

"Promise we'll talk tomorrow, though?"

"Dude, you're my hackathon teammate. Of course we're going to talk."

"No, but about non-hackathon stuff," he says. "I don't want to act like we're coworkers and, like, only talk about sharing public SSH keys."

This guy. He's lucky he's cute. "*Yes*, Khoi, we'll talk about other stuff too. Now *good night*."

He finally leaves.

Chapter Twenty

I don't want to think about Khoi, so Aisha suggests we get wasted, and that sounds like a great idea.

She has a bottle of soju and a flask of bourbon that she smuggled in. We're supposed to have our lights out, so we drink in the dark, sitting cross-legged on our beds facing each other.

She shows me TikToks from her girlfriend, Trinity, the girl with the pastel-pink hair I saw earlier. They met at a workshop last summer. "I was trying everything to get closer! Asking her to show me a new move, and she'd be all, *I'm not that good, you should ask someone else.* I thought she was rejecting me. But no. She was also down bad. We were just being useless lesbians together."

Aisha guffaws when I tell her that I guessed Trinity was Khoi's ex. "Have you *seen* that boy? No rizz whatsoever. I don't think he's ever had a girlfriend." So I guess he was acting so weird at Harvard Square because he didn't want me to learn Aisha's secrets before she was ready to share them.

When she asks if there was anybody back home in Oregon, I shake my head instead of bringing up Drew. I'm still embarrassed that I let the Mulan thing go on for so long. Alpha Fellows is my chance to delete all that. Hit refresh on my entire life.

"Who needs boys back home? Khoi *likes* you." She starts singing. "Char and Khoi, sitting in a red-black tree, K-I-S-S—"

I whip a pillow at her. "Red-black tree? You *are* a nerd, even if you won't admit to it."

"No! I *will* beat the nerd allegations. I'm cool and fun! I dance! I have sex! I've kissed more girls than eighty percent of the guys here at this dumb nerd camp!"

"That's statistically likely," I allow.

"Sooo . . ." She scoots closer to the edge of her bed. "Are you gonna date Khoi now?"

"I don't know," I say. "I didn't come here for a boyfriend. I came here to win." The words feel strange in my mouth. *I came here to win.* I'd usually be mortified to admit something like that, to admit I even think I can win.

But maybe I *can* win. Maybe that's just the bourbon talking, but I did decent on the first checkpoint. I have a cracked teammate. Crazier things have happened.

"Why are we doing this?" Aisha asks suddenly.

"Doing what?"

"*This*." She points at the bottle she's clutching.

"What do you mean? This is roomie bonding time. *You* suggested this."

She jabs a finger at me. "You're running away from something."

I take another swig of my flask as I figure out how to respond. It seems like the conversation has suddenly shifted into a serious vibe that I'm not ready for. Maybe I should distract her. Ask to see another TikTok of Trinity twerking.

Suddenly, there are footsteps, and HellomynameisBrenda's voice wafts in. She's maybe ten feet away. "Hey, it's lights-out."

Saved by the Brenda.

"Shit," Aisha whispers. "Hide the booze." She shoves the half-empty soju bottle behind her desk. I slip the flask underneath my pillow.

A door creaks opens. "Sorry!" Jenni-with-an-i's dreamy-light voice. "Was reading. I just got this fascinating textbook on plant reproduction morphology. Did you know most flowering plants have both male and female reproductive organs?"

I can't help but giggle. Aisha shushes me.

"Um, I did not know that," HellomynameisBrenda says, sounding thoroughly uncomfortable.

"And guess what the name of my textbook is? *Plant Parenthood!* Get it? Like Planned Parenthood?"

I let out another gust of a giggle, louder this time. Aisha hisses, "Shhhh!"

For a beat, there's only silence.

"Hold on, Jenni," HellomynameisBrenda says. Then there are footsteps again, and a knock on our door. "Everything okay in here?"

If she opens the door and sees us, smells our breath, she's going to know we've been drinking. And sure, some of the kids here totally get away with all sorts of stuff. Haru is high half the time and nobody says a peep because Watanabe Technologies is a major donor to Alpha Fellows. But me . . . I'll be packing my bags for the next flight back to Oregon.

I swallow, as if that'll erase the alcohol from my voice. "Yeah, all good!" I hope that sounds sober enough.

"Alrighty then," HellomynameisBrenda says, sounding somewhat unconvinced. Then there are footsteps fading and the *ding* of an elevator. Guess she didn't want to continue the plant sex conversation with Jenni-with-an-i.

Aisha says that she's tired, so ten minutes later I'm lying in bed staring at the ceiling while my roommate snores softly.

You're running away from something.

She's not wrong. I'm definitely running away from Chinook Shore. This entire summer has been an escape from that hellhole.

My mind wanders to Khoi.

I don't know how to handle a boy who has a crush on me. It's never happened before. No, that's not true. In third grade, there was this boy who sat behind me and yanked on my pigtails. According to my teacher, that meant that he *like*-liked me. As if that were an excuse for his behavior. Ew.

But at least the hair-pulling was straightforward compared to this.

Up until an hour ago, it didn't matter how I felt about Khoi. And now . . . I don't know anymore.

What if Khoi thinks I asked to team up because I had a crush on him? But that's not why. I asked because he's my best shot at winning this thing.

Oh, no. What if he said yes because he had a crush on *me*?

The thought makes my stomach twist. It feels manipulative, like I'm leading him on. Except obviously I didn't know he liked me like that. I mean, c'mon. The dude was supposed to have a girlfriend!

But for a fleeting moment there, I was definitely tempted to kiss him . . .

No, I can't be kissing Khoi. Not if I'm serious about winning. It'll be too distracting. Instead of hacking, we'll be hooking up. Instead of making an app, we'll be making out. Instead of coding, we'll be cuddling . . .

(For several minutes, I amuse myself by thinking of more wordplay like this. Most are absolute flops, but there are a few with potential. Like, *GitHub and get it on* could be the next *Netflix and chill*.)

Anyway. I'll tell him tomorrow that we should just be friends. That's obviously the safest, most responsible option. So now I've made my decision and everything is chill and I can forget all about the almost-kiss.

For three more hours, I can't fall asleep.

Chapter Twenty-One

In the morning, Khoi wants to dodge the dining hall because he's not ready to deal with the whispers or knowing glances. Instead he takes me to Flour, one of his favorite cafés that happens to be two blocks from MIT. He insists on paying because I could've gotten free breakfast at Simmons. I try not to think of it as a date. It's merely another opportunity for free food.

The shop is brimming with sunshine and the bright chatter of customers. I order a latte and a cauliflower sandwich. Once we're situated with food, he looks at me expectantly, and I know I can no longer curve this conversation.

"Khoi. I'm really flattered." This isn't a lie. I am shook that he's interested in me *like that*. He has everything going for him. People actually know who he is. He's good-looking and accomplished and I don't know what he sees in me.

Well, if there's anything I've learned from Drew, it's that sometimes boys like you just because you're there. It doesn't necessarily mean you're pretty or smart or even nice.

And if it weren't for Alpha Fellows, maybe that would be so valid. I don't need Khoi to be the love of my life. And if I'm being completely honest, I haven't kissed a boy since Drew and I miss the fireworks of someone else's skin on mine. I'd be down to mess around with Khoi for a summer.

But there's the competition looming and I'm not going to squander my chances by hooking up with my teammate.

"I like you, Char," he says. "And we had something last night."

I wish he would stop looking at me like that, all wide-eyed with sincere adoration. Like a puppy. It's going to make this conversation so much more difficult. I don't get some sick pleasure from kicking puppies.

"Look, I think you're cute too, but—"

"I don't just think you're cute. I mean, when we first met, yeah, sure, you caught my interest because you're cute. But it's deeper than that now."

Outside on the sidewalk, a couple is fighting, both of them gesticulating wildly. Their wedding bands glint white gold in the morning sun. Their faces are etched with annoyance and exasperation.

Once, they must've loved each other very much. I wonder if they woke up one day and *poof*, the love was gone, or if it was a gradual thing, love leaking out over years like their marriage was a rusty pipe nobody bothered to fix.

But I'm imagining things. I don't know anything about these

two strangers. There's no need to make up a story for them.

I turn my attention back to Khoi.

"We have a fantastic friendship," I admit. And as I say it, I realize how true it is. Before coming here, I didn't have any real friends besides Lola, and I never expected to get close to anyone the way I've gotten to know Khoi.

I recall last night's conversation. I never knew what it could be like to feel so seen. Or to be able to give someone else that same gift. "You've been amazing. I'm grateful for your help. But . . ."

"Char, there doesn't need to be a *but*. You're making this more complicated than it has to be."

I barrel on. "*But*, we should keep things platonic."

"This isn't because of my dad, right?" The question is quiet and sad.

I resist the urge to seize him by the shoulders and shake sense into him. "Khoi! Of course not."

"I don't know how to shut off my feelings," he says miserably. "And it would be one thing if you just didn't like me back. I can get over a rejection like that. But I don't understand why you're doing this."

"Maybe I *don't* like you back," I snap. The words come out harsh. But this schtick is irking me. He's not owed a romantic relationship.

Khoi's gaze is unwavering. "Fine. Look me in the eyes and say that you don't feel anything for me. And I'll forget about all of this."

I open my mouth, but I can't do it. I can't deny how my heart flutters when I see him, or how I want to be near him all the time, or how often my mind wanders to him. I tried to ignore these things before, when I thought he was off-limits, but now they're neon-lights obvious.

Here's the thing, though. Infatuation isn't enough. I need to be logical.

"We're hackathon teammates. There are six weeks left in the summer. We need to focus on that. Not on this." And even if we did have a fling, what would happen after the camp is over? I shove the thought away. Doesn't matter.

"But we can do both." He smiles. "Like that one meme with the little girl. Por qué no los dos?"

He's not getting it. For him, Alpha Fellows is a fun opportunity, but whether he wins or not, his life will be the same. He'll still be Khoi Astor, creator of *Imposter Syndrome*, and even if he takes home the grand prize, his biggest achievement so far will be something else.

But for me, it could change my entire trajectory.

"The day I left for this camp, my stepdad, Michael, told me to never come home," I say. "I don't know if he meant it. Maybe it was something he screamed in the heat of the moment. But even if he lets me move back in at the end of Alpha Fellows, I don't want to live there anymore." I don't bother to explain why. It should be obvious.

"In my hometown, Chinook Shore, most people get stuck

forever. They live and die there. The median household income is thirty thousand dollars. My best friend is joining the military so she can snag her mom a green card and better health insurance." I don't know if he's understanding any of this. We're from such different worlds. "Khoi, I need to get out of there. I need to get into a decent college that gives financial aid."

Another nightmarish thought: What if Michael straight-up refuses to fill out the FAFSA? Could I even still get financial assistance?

"You will," he insists. "You're smart. You have solid grades, right?"

"I do, but it's not enough." Being here is a constant reminder of that. "I'm not some science fair winner or math prodigy. I don't have any fancy accomplishments. I need to win, okay? I need that way more than I need a boyfriend."

"Char, I could help you financially," he mumbles. "I got a lot from the *Imposter Syndrome* acquisition . . ."

"Khoi. No." We've known each other for all of two weeks. I can't be taking his money. That's absurd. "You've already helped enough."

He takes a deep breath. "Okay. I get it. And I'm sorry your circumstances are so tough. I can't pretend to know what that's like."

Maybe afterward, I want to say. Maybe if we actually win this thing and we both get into MIT or something. Then maybe we could try dating for real. If he's still into me.

But I don't say that. I don't want to get his hopes up. I don't want to get my own hopes up.

Our sandwiches are sitting there untouched. I guess neither of us had much of an appetite.

Khoi gets up to use the restroom, and I check my phone. It's Lola's eighteenth birthday today. I want to call her as soon as she wakes up. It's ten a.m. here, which means it's only seven a.m. there. I should wait another hour or two.

There are a few email notifications. Mostly marketing crap, one Nigerian prince asking for my banking info, and a response from Edvin.

hey char good to hear from you. i'm actually in town today, can you meet me at the nexus office @ noon? my personal assistant janelle (cc'd) will coordinate details.

I triple-check the message to make sure I'm not hallucinating. Oh my God. Edvin Nilsen wants to meet. With me. With me!

"Maybe we can pack up our sandwiches?" Khoi says. He's back. "Let's find an empty classroom somewhere on campus and brainstorm."

Oh. Right.

Maybe I should let him know what's happening. We could pull up as a team. Actually, it'd be kind of weird *not* to invite him.

But the minute he saunters into the Nexus office, Charise Tang will become totally irrelevant. Edvin will start simping for the wunderkind who built a viral game, just like everyone else.

And to be one hundred percent clear, I'm not mad at Khoi for that. It's not his fault. But I want this just for myself.

I slide my phone into the pocket of my denim shorts. "Sure." There's this throb of guilt, which I ignore.

Chapter Twenty-Two

We find a classroom with a chalkboard, and Khoi immediately gravitates to the rainbow assortment of chalk. As he amuses himself by doodling a surprisingly accurate portrait of Hellomynameis-Brenda, I check my email. There's a message from Janelle Lim, Edvin Nilsen's assistant, saying that a car will pick me up from campus at 11:30 a.m.

For the next hour, we bounce concepts back and forth. A sustainability social game that incentivizes users to compete with friends on "going green." An app that uses computer vision to identify plants—Jenni-with-an-i would like that. But honestly? These ideas feel pretty beige.

"How did you come up with *Imposter Syndrome*?" I ask.

Khoi blushes. God, I wish he looked less adorable doing that. "It's sort of pathetic."

"Try me." I'm well-versed in pathetic.

"You know that game *Mafia*? It's also called *Werewolf* sometimes."

I nod. Classic social deduction game. The underlying mechanism is the same as the one in *Imposter Syndrome*: There are a few secret bad guys who go around killing everyone else. The good guys have to figure out who the bad guys are before they succeed in wiping out the rest of the players.

"I really liked it as a kid. But then in sixth grade, after my dad's trial, my classmates and I played it. And every single time, they'd point the finger at me first, even though I was never the killer. So I'd immediately get voted out, and then I'd sit out the rest of the game." He sighs. "It took me three rounds to realize they were doing it on purpose."

"That's mean. I'm sorry." I want to hug him but we're supposed to be keeping things platonic, so I settle for patting his elbow.

"Yeah, I transferred schools and changed my last name after that." He shrugs. "But I always wished I could play the game again. So I made a mobile version where nobody's real-world identity mattered."

Khoi probably spent hundreds of hours building *Imposter Syndrome* while also attending high school. He only could've done that if he was actually obsessed with the game. Perhaps it filled a yawning emptiness he didn't even know he held.

Any winning idea will have to bloom from something deeply rooted within us. Someplace where we hide our pain, somewhere that is yearning to be seen.

My phone flickers with a new email from Janelle. The car is five minutes away.

I stand. "I have to go. I'll be back in a few hours. You should do lunch without me."

"Wait, where are you going?"

I don't want to lie but I don't want to tell him about Edvin Nilsen either, at least not until after the meeting. I don't want him to come along. "Uh. Just talking to someone."

"Okaaay . . ."

I know he's waiting for more, but it's not like I owe him my whereabouts at all times. We aren't even dating. We're just teammates. So I pick up my backpack, give him an awkward head bob, and walk outside.

The car is already idling next to the curb. When I slide in, the seats are buttery leather. There's a blast of air-conditioning.

"Hi," I say to the driver, and then I notice there is no driver. It's a self-driving car. Mesmerized, I watch us drift away from the curb and zoom down the road. The wheel turns as if it's being operated by a ghost.

I've heard of these before, but I've never been in one. I've never even known somebody who's been in one. Honestly, I half figured they were mythical creatures, like unicorns or tech bros who shower regularly.

It's eerily quiet in here. Since I don't drive, I've never been in a car alone. Oof. Is this truly the future of America? Everyone cloistered in their own separate metal boxes, speeding along the freeway, at the mercy of a faceless algorithm?

To escape the silence, I decide to call Lola to wish her a

happy birthday. It's already eight thirty in Oregon.

She picks up my FaceTime on the first ring. "Char!"

She's still in bed and her sleeping mask is propped up on her forehead. I swear, her face is an instant serotonin boost. I forgot how much I missed Lola. We used to spend, like, every second together. These last few weeks might be the longest stretch we've gone without seeing one another since we first met.

"Happy birthdaaaay! You're an adult now! Did you decide on a tat?" For months she's been talking about how she's going to get inked to celebrate her eighteenth.

She pushes her lower lip out, contemplating. "Do you think a butterfly on my shoulder is too basic bitch?"

"It is a tad basic," I admit. "But basic doesn't equal bad."

"My mother's name, Mariposa, is *butterfly* in Spanish, so it does seem meaningful. But also I like the aesthetic?"

We spend a few more minutes spitballing about tattoos. I tease her about getting a tramp stamp of the name *Rachel*, since apparently she likes Rachels so much.

But then Lola's expression shifts. "Char, I gotta tell you that I'm shipping out next week for training. It won't be easy to contact me."

July snuck up on us. I won't even be in town to send her off. Of course I always knew that. It just suddenly feels a lot more real. I blink rapidly. "Oh. How are you feeling?"

"Darlin', to tell you the truth . . ." She heaves a sigh. "I'm terrified? I can't even say why. It's not like they're tossing me into a combat zone. It's training."

I wish I could say something to comfort her, but nothing comes to mind. Maybe I could talk about how scary it was to leave Chinook Shore to come here, to Massachusetts, but it doesn't seem like the same thing at all. It's not like I have to do push-ups in the rain while someone screams about how much of a loser I am. Although some of the guys here have huge drill sergeant energy. Their talent for making their own anger management issues into everyone else's problem is truly wasted on the software industry.

She continues, "Mari's been crying when she thinks I'm not looking. I'm worried about what's going to happen to her once I'm gone."

With a stab of guilt, I realize I haven't thought much about how Mom is faring back home. Before, I was too upset with her, and then things got so busy at camp. It was easier to stress about everything happening here.

What's her life like right now? She's at the Lucky Panda. Summer is high season for tourism, so probably her tips are great. Nobody's handing out twenties faster than a bridal party that's two mimosas deep. But is Michael treating her fine? Even if he's being a monkey's ass, what can she do about it? It's not like she's swimming in friends. Her English isn't the best, so she struggles to build relationships. Back in Portland she knew other Chinese international students at her university, but in Chinook Shore we're considered "exotic."

Cynically I wonder if that's why Michael moved us to a far-flung beach town. To isolate us from any support system we might've had. No, that's not fair. His dad kicked the bucket and he inherited the house. I know that.

Lola and I chat until the car rolls to a stop in front of a sparkling skyscraper.

"I have to go." Dammit. I wish I could've talked to her longer.

"Kick ass, darlin'," she drawls.

I peer out the window. We're in Boston's Seaport neighborhood. Everything is glossy and sleek, glass and steel. How would it feel to work and live here? To exist in such a beautiful, wealthy place?

"You have arrived at your destination," the car chirps.

Chapter Twenty-Three

I enter a gleaming lobby with sweeping ceilings. There's a receptionist who asks to see ID—I flash my Alpha Fellows lanyard—and then cross-references a list of guests. "Edvin Nilsen?" she asks. I nod. "First elevator on the left."

I pass through a glass turnstile that silently slides open and shut. The elevator doesn't have buttons, which I've never seen before. It's kind of freaky, like I'm no longer in control of my own destination.

I get deposited at floor nine, where a rosy-cheeked East Asian woman greets me. "You must be Charise? I'm Janelle. We emailed." I shake her hand. Even her manicure feels expensive.

Janelle offers coffee, but I decline. I'm too anxious for caffeine.

She leads me through the Nexus office. It's Saturday, so it's mostly empty, although there are several frazzled-looking employees typing away at desks. There are colorful beanbags scattered everywhere, a foosball table in the corner. Whiteboards covered in pseudocode. The view overlooking Boston Harbor is incredible, and I wish I could linger at the window for longer.

We enter a conference room with floor-to-ceiling glass walls, and there's Edvin Nilsen. Not even ten feet in front of me. He's dressed in a T-shirt and jeans, and he looks less handsome than his *Forbes* cover. His age is starting to catch up to him: he has a receding hairline, and his jowls are pronounced. But there's still something magnetic about his aura.

He looks up from his phone. "Oh, hi there. Char?"

Janelle settles into the corner to jot down notes.

"Thank you so much for taking the time to meet," I manage.

"Of course. When I was your age, I cold-emailed Bill Gates. This was back when email was still new. And to my surprise, he actually replied! His guidance was so helpful in getting me started. That's why I started Alpha Fellows. If I can do that for other young people, that's something no amount of money can buy."

"I really appreciate this." I'm still in disbelief.

He interlaces his fingers. "So what can I do for you?"

Right. His time is precious. I should get to it. "I'm in Alpha Fellows this summer, and we're—" I catch myself. "*I'm* having difficulty ideating. It's my first hackathon. It would be great to get tips."

"Fair warning, I'm not on the judging panel, so if you're looking for a cheat code, talking to me isn't going to get you anywhere," he says. "But I've been running this camp for a long time. Seen lots of winners. I'm happy to give advice."

I basically info dump our best ideas.

"All of these are garbage," he says.

"Oh." I blink, taken aback by his blunt response. No, this is good. Refreshing. He's not sugarcoating it. This is what we need. "Why?"

"Do you know why teenagers rarely build anything fantastic?"

"Because . . . they can't code?" I venture.

"That's part of it, and that's something our camp tries to address with the first checkpoint. But there are plenty of kids who can code. The barrier to entry is low. Lots of free online resources." He shakes his head. "But most kids with the time and educational background to learn how to code don't have any real problems to *solve* with those skills. They can't think of anything interesting. At Alpha Fellows, we see a lot of homework planners. Study buddies. Apps where you can compliment your friends anonymously. *Boring.*"

"Um, okay." I'd appreciate a compliment every now and then, but I guess the idea doesn't sound too promising. The internet was basically invented to anonymously insult others.

He jabs a finger at me. "I remember your application. Oregon, right?"

God, I hope he doesn't start using that nickname too. "Yeah . . ."

"Your application was . . . eh. Nothing special. No offense. Perfect grades and test scores, sure, but everybody has that. That script you wrote to catch the test bank thief took some cleverness, but it didn't have any impact outside of your no-name school. The admissions committee was torn. People didn't see the point in accepting you when we were already rejecting USAMO qualifiers and ISEF finalists."

I don't ask what those words even mean. Probably other competitions I've never heard of. "Uh."

"But I wanted you," he says, like he's a savior swooping in to deliver clean drinking water to an impoverished village. "You reminded me of myself. From bumfuck nowhere. Surrounded by losers."

My spine stiffens. I don't like the way he's talking about my background, even though he's not entirely wrong.

"When I was a teenager, I was homeless for a while," he says. "But I figured out how to survive. Got into college. Dropped out to catch the dot-com bubble. Made money." From Edvin's Wikipedia page, I already knew this origin story, but it hits different hearing him say it out loud.

"Most of the students we admit, they're babies. They don't have any grit. They don't need any. I wanted you because you seemed resilient. Strong."

I drink in the compliment. It's embarrassing how good it feels that Edvin Nilsen thinks well of me. "Thanks."

"So do me a favor. Prove that I was right to take a bet on you instead of Kevin Chen or whoever from Fremont who's been winning math contests since they were in diapers." He crosses his arms. "What's something unique about you? Something you could solve?"

I think. What's special about Charise Tang? I'm a girl in a camp full of guys. "Maybe I could work on something related to reproductive health? Like a menstrual cycle tracker?"

"It's not a bad idea, but there are already plenty of those out there," he says.

From her corner, Janelle adds, "Also, the government can use that data to prosecute women for illegal abortions."

"Oh." That's messed up. I hate that.

"Keep thinking," he says.

I recall what Lola told me in the car. *I'm worried about what's going to happen to her once I'm gone.* Her mother doesn't have a large support system. Neither does mine.

Back in Portland, my mom used WeChat to find new friends, join local groups. Everyone typed in Chinese characters. But once we moved, she couldn't do that anymore because there were no Chinese people around.

"Maybe an app for helping immigrants connect with each other?" I try. It sounds so trite. "It's so difficult to move to a new country, especially if you don't know people like you."

For the first time since I walked in, Edvin seems intrigued. "Say more."

So I tell him about how, before I was born, my mother lived in some dingy one-bed apartment with another roommate. She slept in the living room. It took her months to realize she was paying double rent, and that was only because one of her school friends knew the tenant who Mom had replaced.

Edvin shakes his head. "Scamming a pregnant woman? Disgusting."

That's an obvious example of scum-of-the-earth behavior, but I'm thinking of all the little moments too. Like once, when my mom and I spoke Mandarin, a stranger asked why we even came here if we weren't going to speak English. Or when she started going by Quinn instead of her birth name. When she stopped calling Michael out for wearing shoes inside the house. When she stopped cooking the dishes of her childhood. All the tiny sadnesses.

Being an immigrant in a new country means falling asleep under foreign stars that will never align themselves into the constellations you once knew.

Later that afternoon, when I tell Khoi about the meeting with Edvin Nilsen, he's annoyed.

"Why didn't you invite me? If the roles were reversed, I would've brought you along."

"It's not the same." Khoi already *has* the clout. People already respect him. He doesn't need to build this connection the way I do.

"How is it not the same?"

I don't know how to explain it. "Sorry? I didn't know you were dying to see Edvin Nilsen in the flesh. He's less handsome up-close."

"I'm not *dying to see him*! It's about the *principle*. We're teammates. We shouldn't hide things like this from each other."

He shakes his head. "Be careful. He didn't get rich by being benevolent. Guys like Edvin always want something."

"What are you suggesting? That he's only interested in me because he wants something gross?" That's so insulting. Besides, he's married. Third wife, Australian actress who's been in a string of Netflix rom-coms, I think. Or maybe he got divorced last year? Maybe I'm getting him confused with Elon Musk.

Anyway, he clearly wasn't interested in me in some pervy, old guy way. His assistant Janelle was in the room the entire time.

"No, that's not what I'm saying." He presses the heels of his hands to his eyes. "Forget it. Did you get anything useful out of the meeting, at least?"

Great, we're moving on. "We ideated. I was thinking an app for immigrants to connect with each other, exchange info for putting down roots in America. Edvin likes it a lot."

"I don't know, Char," he says. "I don't want to implement Edvin's ideas."

Of course we're back to this topic. Why's Khoi being such a hater? "It wasn't *his* idea. It was mine." But Edvin was one who came through with the questions that inspired the concept, and his encouragement gave me the confidence to actually pursue it further. Otherwise I would've assumed it was too niche or too social justice-y.

"Do you even know what Nexus does?"

His question is condescending, but I try to answer in good faith anyway. "Something about data analytics?" I've looked it up, but they're very secretive. Yet the vibes at their office were so playful and open. They can't be, like, sacrificing kittens.

"They have defense contracts," Khoi says. "I've heard . . ." But he trails off.

That doesn't seem bad. "If you're so against Edvin, why are you even at a camp that he started?"

"It feels different when he's not as involved. He's barely here. And I wanted to meet other kids like me," he says. "Kids who like to code."

"Edvin Nilsen can't be that evil if he's running a program like this for free, right? He probably poured tons of money into this."

"There are lots of other corporate sponsors for Alpha Fellows. Like, Haru's dad with Watanabe Technologies." He chews on his pen. "But forget all that. Your idea is good. My dad's family came as refugees when he was a kid, and they struggled to find community. My mom was an adoptee, and she also felt out of place in her lily-white family."

That makes Khoi a second-generation immigrant. Like me. "What was it like for you, growing up here?"

"In elementary school, I was the only Asian kid in my grade," he says. "Other people would always try to guess 'where I came from,' like it was a game they could win. And then they'd always get it *wrong*. Nobody ever thinks Vietnam."

"Or when they pull the outer corners of their eyes," I say.

"Right! Why do they do that? Nobody actually looks like that."

The first time I knew I was different was maybe first grade. One of the girls in my class decided that Charise was too hard to pronounce, so she start calling me Ching Chong instead. Soon, everyone had started doing it. To six-year-old me, this was incredibly bizarre—*Ching Chong* sounded nothing like Charise, and besides, I went by Char. In a meeting with both my mother and me, my teacher had to explain that the kids were being racist.

"Ignore them," Mom said after the meeting. "Americans, they're soft. When I was in school, kids used their fists. Bullying with *words*? That's so cowardly."

Did Mom think my bullies should start throwing hands? That was kind of disturbing.

I decided to shut up and swallow my anger. And never talk to anyone about this ever again. Until right now. It feels like I've been navigating around a sinkhole in my living room for so long that I forgot why I was even taking the detour.

Chapter Twenty-Four

For the rest of Saturday, we make the high-level decisions for our project. The proposal is due on the Fourth of July, which is next Friday. We have to deliver a pitch, wireframes, and design documents.

We decide to name our app Hello World. I like the layered meaning—it's a reference to the first program every developer write but also evokes the excitement of moving to a new country.

Next we decide on the functionality. I'm thinking something similar to Nextdoor or Reddit, with forum discussion as the main conceit, but with a strong translation feature, since the language barrier gatekeeps immigrants who would otherwise use those websites.

We argue playfully over the tech stack—Khoi is a fan of Flutter since it's cross-platform, but I'm more familiar with Swift. He wants to use MongoDB to host our databases, but I prefer PostgreSQL. I let him win most of the arguments because he knows way more than me, but he can pry SQL from my cold, dead hands. Those relational databases are giving the only relationships that actually make sense.

Sunday is for product research. Khoi and I brainstorm questions to ask, print out a sign and an information sheet, then claim a table in the MIT main lobby for better visibility. Curious passersby begin to wander up to us, but nobody agrees to a research interview. One tourist asks us where the John Harvard statue is.

After ten minutes go by without yeses, I'm starting to fret. "Maybe we should offer an incentive for talking to us. Besides the inherent joy in getting to interact with our wonderful selves, obviously."

"Obviously." Khoi drums his fingers against the table. "How about . . . a compliment?"

"Huh?"

"At the end of the conversation, we give each interviewee a heartfelt compliment. Like this." He takes my hands into his and stares into my eyes. "Char, you have irises the color of Earl Grey tea."

God save me from this strange boy and his idiosyncrasies. I pull my hands away and break our shared gaze. "Khoi, don't flirt. *Just friends*, remember?"

"People love compliments! Haru is making an app for anonymously complimenting your friends." Oh, Edvin's going to love that.

I puff my cheeks out. "Also, my eyes are *not* the color of Earl Grey. They're the first strong steep of pu'er."

"A storm in a teacup," he mutters, but I pretend not to hear him.

A moment later, one man licking a Popsicle stops by. *"Are you an immigrant?"* he reads. "I'm here to get my PhD and then I'm going back to Pakistan. Do I still count?"

Honestly I'm unsure, but I nod anyway. It makes sense that we're going to get grad students, since we're on campus. "Sit down! We'd love to chat with you." I pat the chair beside me.

He plops down. "You have until I finish this Popsicle."

Turns out he really likes talking about himself. Once his Popsicle is gone, he sticks around until I've finished all the questions.

For the next few hours, more interviewees trickle in steadily. There are all sorts of people passing through MIT. A college student from New Zealand with the coolest accent. A Syrian refugee who's waiting for a Tinder date. A Filipino man who fell in love with a New York lawyer. A few people who are second-generation immigrant kids, like me.

There's only one tense moment. At around eleven a.m., while I'm interviewing a teenager whose parents were born in Istanbul, a woman comes up to our table, reads our sign, and wrinkles her nose.

"This app isn't right," she says. "You're excluding people like me."

The teenager cuts in. "So what? It's not built for you. But the rest of this country is."

"You know, technically, everyone is an immigrant," she says.

"Were Native people immigrants? How about slaves? And are we really going to call colonial settlers *immigrants*?" The questions spray out rapid-fire.

Khoi and I exchange startled glances. I feel like we should step in before this escalates into a full-blown shouting match, but I don't know what to do.

To my relief, the woman only nods. "I suppose I haven't thought of that before." And then she trots off.

When we break for lunch, I'm overwhelmed. Some people said they didn't feel out of place at all in America, while others said they could never quite fit in. People cited myriad reasons for coming here: more job opportunities, a better life for their children, civil unrest or war in their birth countries, or just a fresh start. They struggled with divorce, coming out, grief.

And I . . . I have no idea how to distill all these experiences down into a single app.

As we devour pizza—pineapple for him, sausage-and-pepperoni for me because I don't hate my taste buds—I say, "Most of my town is white. I've never met so many immigrants with all these different stories."

"Same. My family's from a very white suburb." He chews thoughtfully. "Honestly, I don't know if I count as an immigrant."

"But you're Vietnamese?"

He lifts a shoulder. "A lot of the people we spoke to talked about feeling torn between the country of their birth and the country they now reside in. But I've never felt like I had to choose. My mom was adopted. I've been to Vietnam plenty of times, but it never felt like home."

"I don't remember anything about China," I say. I've visited Beijing once, for a funeral when I was four years old. Maybe it's bad, but I don't even remember whose funeral it was.

When someone once told me to "go back to my own country," the comment didn't piss me off. It confused me. I was born and raised in America. What other country could I ever possibly call home?

Monday morning, Khoi shows me how to use Figma, a software for creating design mockups. We want the app to be intuitive, simple, responsive. I choose a sky-blue palette since that's Mom's favorite color.

We each assign ourselves to designing two pages that our app will have—login, user profile, discussion forum, private messaging—and work side by side.

Khoi begins playing something orchestral and cinematic from his laptop speakers. The cellos slide into crescendo. There's a swell of woodwinds punctured by timpani.

"Really?" I give him a look.

He pauses the symphony. "What's wrong with Beethoven?"

"Nothing's *wrong* with Beethoven. I'm sure he's a cool guy—"

"He's not. If he were alive today, he'd totally get canceled for being an asshole."

"I'll take your word for it. Anyway, outside of movie scores and concert halls, his music is low-key pretentious. Don't you have anything more . . . recent?"

"How recent are we talking? Like Liszt? Tchaikovsky? We're already deep into the romantic era, Char. There's not much more recent we can go."

"Recent like . . . Cardi B?"

He tilts his head in confusion. "Cardiovascular disease?"

"No, *B*, not *D* . . . never mind." I turn my attention back to my computer screen. Khoi unpauses the symphony.

A few minutes later, he says, "Let's play a game."

"Maybe later." If this is another one of his tactics to winning over my heart, it's not going to work. I am totally immune to his flirting.

"Like a game while we code. It'll make the time go by faster."

I don't look up from my laptop. "How's that work?"

"We ask each other questions and respond with the first thing that comes to mind. The idea is that you exert almost no mental effort into responding."

"So all my responses are thoughtless?"

"So all your responses are *honest*."

Sure, whatever. "Fine. Go ahead. Ask something."

"You first."

I narrow my eyes.

"What? You can learn a lot about a person by what questions they ask."

Okay. I've got something. "Would you rather fight one hundred duck-sized horses or one horse-sized duck?" It's a classic. During our sleepovers, Lola and I kick off Would You Rather with this one. She thinks she could destroy the horse-sized duck. I'm a duck-sized horse truther. It's our friendship's longest-running argument.

"I'm a pacifist *and* I believe in animal rights," Khoi says. "I don't want to fight either of these things."

"Sorry, dude. You're in an empty field and both options are charging toward you right now. You only have your fists to defend you. Pick your poison."

"I would step aside and let them duke it out with each other," he says.

I try to arch an eyebrow at him, but I was not blessed with the lifting-a-singular-eyebrow gene. "Just answer the question."

"Fine! Um . . ." He thinks for a second. "How large are these horses? Are we talking miniature pony? Thoroughbred?"

"Bruh, I don't know. Normal horse–sized?"

"I'll go with the second option," he says. "I'd feel less bad fighting a monster duck than a bunch of adorable tiny horses."

"That's precisely why I'd choose the first. Adorable tiny horses are easier to take on than one monster duck."

He sucks in his teeth. "Wow, that's cold, Tang. Remind me never to get on your bad side."

I flash him a smug smile, then go back to Figma.

"My turn. Who's your favorite poet?"

"Dunno . . . maybe Pablo Neruda?" I don't know a single Pablo Neruda poem, so I'm not sure why I name-dropped him. It just popped into my head. Isn't he the guy that Lola's ex Hot Sarah wanted her to read during sex? "You?"

"Ocean Vuong," he says. "He's Vietnamese too. Look him up."

He spells the name out, and I google it. I click on the first link. The poem has a lot of unnecessary line breaks. Why do poets do that? It's like they write four words and then get bored, so *might as well press the enter key!* At least in Python, white space means something.

"I don't get it," I say.

"You're not supposed to *get* poetry. You're supposed to feel it."

According to my AP Lang teacher, you're supposed to dissect it for metaphors and imagery, but I'm not so sure I appreciate that surgical approach to literature. "I wouldn't have thought you of all people liked poetry."

It's weird. I guess I had this impression of Khoi in my head as a huge nerd who only cared about computer science. I mean, he's still a huge nerd, but one who cares about anything and everything. I like that. I like that a lot.

"Why not? Poetry abstracts the world, just like code. It distills everything down to its purest form." He gets this dreamy, wide-eyed expression. "Science can't account for everything. Let me give you an example. You're from the Oregon coast, right?"

I nod.

"Sure, the tides are caused by the moon's gravitational pull. The blueness is due to water's absorption of sunlight. But you know that scientifically unaccountable sense of enchantment and beauty that comes when you look at the ocean?"

Once upon a time I must've felt something like that. When we first moved to Chinook Shore after Michael inherited the house, I was so excited to live right next to the beach. I always begged my mom to let me go into the water, even though it was ice-cold. I loved its enormity. I loved how, no matter how far it receded from shore, the sea always returned like a promise.

But nowadays, the Pacific Ocean is a constant reminder of everywhere I am not.

"Okay. Yeah."

"That's poetry."

This boy. I fake gag so he won't notice how charmed I am by his hopeless poetic wonder.

"Your turn."

"Yep." I try to think of a good question. "If you started a cult, what kind of cult would it be?"

"Man. I would be such a terrible cult leader." He shakes his head. "I'd be the cult leader for, like, people with no rizz. For the introverted and the socially awkward. We'd bring cats to parties and then recruit the people who come play with said cat instead of talking to others."

"You could pose as waiters and recruit those who say 'you too' when you tell them to enjoy their meal," I suggest.

"People who get profiled by *Wired* magazine but their interviewer keeps referring to their app as 'Imposter Symptom' instead of 'Imposter Syndrome,' but they don't want to be rude by correcting her."

"Khoi, that sounds like a situation specific to only you."

"Fair. What kind of cult would *you* start?"

Hm. I take a second to think. "The cult for people who shamelessly love bad pop music. I'm talking the classics. Justin Bieber. Kesha back when she still had a dollar sign in her name. I know it's like junk food for your brain and I don't care." When it comes to music, I'm like a little kid at the candy store: going for anything sugary sweet, colorful, and easy to reach for.

Khoi shudders. "Char. I want to respect your choices. I really do. But this is going too far."

"Why do people hate on pop music so much? Is it because they think it's cool to be edgy and different?"

"No, it's because most pop music is atrocious. Music is mankind's most universal art form. It exists in every known culture. There are instruments that are thousands of years old. All of that history and lineage, and somehow the most popular song in the world right now is about how much some guy wants to sleep with a woman he met at a nightclub?"

"Well, sex is mankind's second-most universal art form," I say. "Okay. Your turn to ask."

He leans forward, resting his chin on the top of my laptop screen. "How are you doing?"

I blink, confused. Is this part of the game? "I'm fine. You?"

"Nonono. People always do that, right? They brush off the question with some generic one-word pleasantry. What's even the point? But actually, this is my question. How are you doing?"

I cast about for a response. How *am* I doing? I'm . . .

I'm *happy* in a way I haven't felt for a long while. I don't know when that happened. Obviously the competition is stressful and half the kids here are either insanely toxic or straight-up insane, which is unfortunate, given that they're the future leaders of Silicon Valley.

But I don't have to be careful. I don't have to hide money beneath my bed or watch what I say. And honestly? That's a vast improvement from my previous situation.

"I'm happy," I say, and when he smiles, something inside of me melts.

Chapter Twenty-Five

The next week flies by. I spill my heart out in our pitch. *To some people, Silicon Valley and artificial intelligence are the gold rush*, I write. *To others—to my mother—the United States itself is that mine replete with luxurious things. In Mandarin, America is* mei guo, *or beautiful kingdom, but in our family's worst moments, I've wondered if there was any beauty at all in this country. Sometimes I don't know why we even stayed.* It feels weird to be vulnerable in something that's going to be read by faceless strangers, but I figure that if whoever is judging thinks the same way Edvin Nilsen does, they'll probably want to know about my background.

When Khoi reads what I wrote, he hugs me but says nothing. He doesn't need to.

Tuesday, the program organizes a game of capture the flag on MIT's campus, and Khoi convinces me to go. "C'mon, Char, you can't skip *everything* fun. And this next checkpoint isn't like the last one. It isn't an exam you can cram for."

I relent. For some reason my team decides to stick Haru

on flag-guarding duty, and he dozes off. Austin-or-Dallas gets lost somewhere in the tunnels below building 16, and his twin, who's on the other team, pretends to be him to infiltrate our defenses. Khoi, Obi, and I cook up a triple-pronged tactic that is much more complicated than it needs to be, and we all get captured anyway. An embarrassing defeat for my team, but it's the most I've laughed in a long time.

We take another break from work on Thursday evening when Aisha invites us to her midsummer showcase over at Harvard. The dances are mesmerizing. Bodies weave in and out perfectly in sync as music flows from frenetic to tranquil. There's even a traditional Chinese fan dance, which I've never seen in real life. I wish my mother was here too.

Then a funky drum splits the air, and Aisha rushes onstage with several other dancers, their hips swaying to the beat. She kicks, her leg arcing through the air like a calligrapher's brushstroke. Levitates, as if she's no longer bound by the same gravitational forces that anchor the rest of us. She radiates pure joy. This is so obviously what she's meant to spend her life doing. I applaud until my palms hurt.

At five p.m. on Friday we upload our proposal to the Alpha Fellows portal. To celebrate, Khoi and I go to Toscanini's, an ice-cream shop near campus, and we split a scoop of their most iconic flavor, B3: brown sugar, brown butter, and brownies.

After dinner, there are Independence Day fireworks along the river. Some of the Alpha Fellows want to watch the show on sailboats. They're really determined to get permission. After enough begging, they finally wear the camp counselors down.

"That's the secret to life," Obi says as we walk over to the MIT sailing pavilion. He sounds a little too smug. "Be super-duper annoying until you get what you want."

This other girl shoots him the nastiest look and takes a big, dramatic step back like he's got the plague.

"Wait, wait, hold up," Obi says in a panicky voice. "I didn't mean it like that!"

I fall back to walk next to Khoi. "Growing up, I never got to see fireworks," he says.

"What? Why?"

"The sound reminds my dad of a pirate attack." It sounds so silly—like something out of a Disney movie—that I almost laugh, but one glance at Khoi's face tells me he's dead serious. I don't know too much about the history of the Vietnam War, but I know that Vietnamese refugees fled the country on boats.

The world can be horrible in ways I can't even imagine.

"PTSD is an asshole," I say. "My stepdad has it. He served in Iraq." I've never told anyone about Michael's condition before.

He reaches down to give my hand a squeeze, and his grasp is warm and soft and perfect. I have to remind myself to let go.

On the dock, we strap ourselves into puffy orange life jackets. The sailboat bobs in the dark water. I end up in a group with Jenni-with-an-i, Haru, Aisha, and Khoi. Jenni-with-an-i, who got certified to sail last year, asks the rest of us to slide in before she unties the boat and jumps in.

As we cut through the waves, she explains the basics of sailing. There's a mainsheet, which, counterintuitively, isn't actually a sheet—it's a rope that controls the orientation of the sail. There's also the till, a glossy wooden lever that is used to steer.

For once, Haru seems enthralled. He keeps asking Jenni-with-an-i questions about the boat mechanics. Aisha and I exchange knowing smiles. Somehow I don't think Haru is truly that interested in tacking versus jibing.

We find a windless spot to float. It's a pleasantly cool night, that perfect summer twilight vibe I'd spend the entire school year waiting for. The moon is plump and yellow and it looks the same as it does back home.

While we wait for the fireworks to start, we idly swap gossip—one of the girls at Alpha Fellows is Elon Musk's secret daughter, three camp counselors are in a throuple—while passing around Aisha's flask.

After I have a sip, I offer it to Khoi, but he whispers, "Can't have alcohol with my meds."

There's a whistling, and then a deafening crack as the first firework shatters into gold-and-crimson shards.

"Char!" Khoi shouts. "Look! It's in the shape of a heart!"

I mean. It's kind of impossible not to smile.

We fall silent as the sky splinters into bright, luminous colors: midnight blue, vibrant green, deep purple. I've seen fireworks displays before, of course, but somehow this one feels uniquely magical. I don't know if it's being out on the water, or next to my friends, or just the alcohol zipping through my veins.

I cut my gaze to Khoi. The fireworks are reflected in his eyes, and he looks so giddy, like a little kid seeing them for the first time. It's adorable. Then I notice Aisha watching me watch Khoi. Blushing, I turn my face back toward the sky.

Once the last firework fizzles into nothing, Jenni-with-an-i is about to steer us back to shore when another boat speeds past.

"Race you to the Esplanade!" Diego shouts. Next to him, Obi pumps his fists in the air.

"Bet," Aisha yells. She's drunk. "Captain Jenni, after them!"

Jenni-with-an-i frowns at the water. "I don't know, the winds are starting to pick up . . ."

"Babe, fuck the winds! *Fuck* them!"

"Not anatomically possible," Haru mumbles.

"It'll be fun," I say, not wanting the night to end just yet.

With a sigh, Jenni-with-an-i tacks, and soon we're whizzing after the other boat.

She's right; the wind *is* stronger than before. Hair whips into my eyes and mouth. On the bright side, at least it's my *own* hair.

"Woooo!" Aisha hoots. "Somebody do *Titanic* with me." She stands up and holds her arms out. "I'm the king of the world!"

Then there's an aggressive gust and she totters.

Khoi rushes over to her. "Are you okay?"

With Khoi on the left, the boat tilts from the uneven weight distribution. Jenni-with-an-i stumbles. Haru drops the rope and throws his arm out to keep her from falling.

"Fudge, the sail is luffing!" Jenni-with-an-i cries. "Somebody secure the sheet!"

The boat lurches again. The hull is almost entirely perpendicular to the river. I scramble for the rope, but I'm not quite sober and it's slicker than I thought. It slips out of my grasp.

The metal arm of the sail swings back wildly and knocks Khoi clean into the Charles.

It takes me a moment to remember he can't swim.

Before I realize what I'm doing, I've plunged into the icy water, the cold slicing through my clothes. I frantically grope for Khoi in the darkness. My fingers finally find fabric—his shirt. I lock my arms around his midsection and kick upward with all my might. The water breaks over our heads, and we both gasp for air.

"Char, what are you doing?" he sputters. "We're wearing *life jackets.*"

I stop thrashing. He's right. We're both buoyant. We're fine.

"Oh," I say, feeling immensely dumb. "Right."

They've tilted the boat upright again.

"Y'all alive?" Jenni-with-an-i calls.

"Babes, you're lucky this is a coding camp and not a swimming camp!" Aisha shouts.

Our friends drag us back onto the boat and we decide to

head to shore. Even though it's, like, eighty-five degrees out, I'm shivering. My body is one giant goose bump. As we sail, Haru brags to Jenni-with-an-i about his motorcycle, which was apparently a bribe from his dad during his parents' divorce. He says "torque" like it's the most erotic word in the English dictionary.

"We could go for a ride," he says to her. "The suspension is phenomenal. Buttery smooth. You gotta feel it for yourself."

Jenni-with-an-i squirms. "Ummm, aren't motorcyclists twenty times more likely to die in a car crash?"

"I'll ride with you, dude," Khoi offers in his completely oblivious Khoi way. Aisha makes a choked-up noise that sounds like a stifled snicker.

"Maybe if we have time," Haru says in a tone that means he's never bringing this up again.

Meanwhile, all I can think about are fluffy cotton towels and a mug of hot chocolate. Not the powdered packet crap. The rich, smooth stuff that makes your insides feel like liquid gold.

I decide that the minute we reach dry land, I'm bolting for the nearest shower.

But I don't get the chance. Once we dock and Jenni-with-an-i starts derigging the boat, Khoi touches me on the shoulder. "Can I talk to you?"

We sit on the far end of the dock, away from everyone else, still dripping wet. Khoi's shirt clings to his torso, and I make a point of looking away.

The water is so serene, like dark glass. Deceptively serene. Who knows what's lurking beneath the surface?

"Do you know the common advice for saving a drowning person?" he asks.

"Check that they're actually drowning first?"

"The advice is to not jump into the water yourself. Because somebody who is drowning will drag you down with them." He shakes his head. "Char, why would you even try? I weigh more than you."

"You never know. Maybe I've got superpowers," I say. Now that he says it like that, it does feel ridiculous that I tried to save him. "It's not that serious."

"No, it *is* serious. You could've gotten hurt."

Why is he so hung up on this? "As you pointed out, we were both wearing life jackets."

"I don't want you to try to save me."

"Khoi, you're always so eager to help everyone else. Now that I tried to help you, you're being weird." I mean, he's usually a little weird, but he's being even weirder than normal.

"Because it's different when *I'm* not the burden!" He screws up his face, like he's said more than he intended to.

Something inside me twists.

"You're not a burden," I say quietly. "Who told you that you were a burden?"

He's silent for a long time. I wait.

When he finally speaks, he says, "Growing up, my parents were always stressed about my medical bills. We were upper-middle-class but my health issues were expensive. And when my dad got arrested, it felt like I was the reason he had done . . . what he did."

"Khoi, I'm sure that's not true."

He does this noncommittal nod-slash-shrug that indicates he thinks I'm wrong, but he's too polite to say that out loud.

"When my dad left, I thought he did that because I was defective in some way," I say. "It took years to realize that, even if that were true, it doesn't excuse my father's actions. He was a grown-up who couldn't face his responsibilities. That's on him. Not me."

"Char, I'm so sorry."

"I'm sorry too."

Khoi lays his head on my shoulder and I let him, even though it feels like a not-entirely-platonic gesture.

"My dad did bad things because he chose to," he says to the river. "I was a child; he was the adult. Sure. I know that intellectually. But even if I repeat those facts over and over, I never feel less guilty."

"That's a mood," I say. "Knowing that I shouldn't feel inadequate only goes so far."

"Too bad we can't debug our brains, right?"

"Khoi, I think that's what alcohol is for."

He laughs, a gorgeous bellyful of mirth, and something flutters inside me. For the stupidest second, my brain decides I'll do anything to make him laugh again.

Anyway, it makes sense now, why he's always tried so hard to help me. To help others, too—his fake relationship with Aisha, his conversations with other students whenever they ask for advice. As if he's trying to prove to himself that he's good and useful. That he's enough.

But he's already enough for me.

Chapter Twenty-Six

When I squelch back to our dorm, Aisha immediately pounces. "What's going on with you and Khoi?"

"Nothing?" I don't know what she's getting at.

She crosses her arms. "Char. Babe. I love ya, but if you were drowning, I'd call the Coast Guard or something and let them rescue your ass. I wouldn't try to play the hero."

"He's my teammate. If he died it would completely ruin our chances at winning."

"Riiight. So you jumped into the water because you were so concerned about your hackathon project."

"Yep," I say. "You get it."

She does an overly dramatic, heaving sigh. So much theater-kid energy, and she's not even a theater kid. "Did I ever tell you about my first girlfriend?"

"Trinity?"

"No, no, this was a girl I was besties with in middle school. Her name is Emma. We were crazy inseparable. We were on the dance team. I'm a huge simp for dancers."

"Your middle school had a dance team?" My middle school didn't have any extracurriculars. You showed up at eight thirty, tried to avoid getting thrown into a locker, then left at three.

"Yours didn't?" She shrugs. "Anyway, I caught feelings in seventh grade while we were backstage getting ready. She was applying my lipstick, and this lightning bolt zapped through me when she cupped my chin with her palm. And I knew this wasn't how I was supposed to feel about a friend."

"Sooooo you fessed up?"

"No! I spent the next year in complete denial. I even went to the school dance with some boy from homeroom. Alvin James, bless his heart. I didn't want to be queer. It felt like I was making my own life more difficult. At night I would pray to the deities that I'd wake up hetero. Which didn't work, by the way. Hinduism. What's the point of having so many gods if they're all asleep at the wheel?"

"Aisha, I'm sorry."

"Also, I thought she was straight. I didn't want to get hate-crimed."

I nod. Lola's told me similar things before, about being scared to hit on a straight girl. After she came out, somebody scrawled DIKE on her locker. She put on this act like she was outraged only by the terrible spelling, but I know that it chipped away at her heart too.

Aisha continues. "Like, Emma's celebrity crush was that boy from *Stranger Things*."

"Finn Wolfhard?"

"Nah. The cute one."

"But Finn Wolfhard is the cute—"

"Let me finish! On the last day of eighth grade, I finally confessed. She was moving to London, and I was heading to boarding school, so I thought even if she rejected me and told everyone we knew, my life wouldn't be over. But it turned out she'd felt the same way the entire time."

I crack a smile. "That's sweet." Sickeningly adorable, really. Then something occurs to me. If Aisha is with Trinity, she's not dating Emma anymore. "What happened?"

"Oh. We broke up three months later when she flew across the pond, although we stayed in touch. She has this fake British accent now."

I'm pretty sure Aisha is doing story time because she's suggesting something about Khoi and me but her tale isn't super compelling. All this struggle and angst just to date someone for like, one summer when she was fourteen. The math isn't mathing. Not sure what the point of love is if it ends before the next iPhone even drops.

She notices my skepticism. "It was worth it. Because of Emma, I found out that I like girls. And having that experience gave me the confidence to pursue other relationships in high school. Plus, our memories are really awesome? First date. First kiss. First kiss with tongue. First—"

"Okay, I get it," I interrupt.

"But I do wish I'd confessed *way* earlier. We could've been girlfriends for so much longer. I wasted so much time and energy hiding."

"You waited until you felt comfortable. That makes sense." I can't imagine how intense it is to come out, especially at that age.

"Yeah, yeah. Sure. I still regret not speaking up sooner."

It's almost curfew and I'm still sticky from the river, so I excuse myself to shower.

As I lather shampoo into my hair, I can't stop thinking about what Aisha said. It must've taken serious guts to do something about her crush. Major moves for a fourteen-year-old.

And I know what she was trying to tell me. Aisha is about as subtle as an elephant.

White foamy suds slide down my bare skin and slip into the drain at my feet.

Why *am* I so sure that catching feelings for Khoi is going to screw up the hackathon? Not once did Drew ever mess with my GPA. But I basically did Chinook Shore classes on autopilot. Alpha Fellows hits different. This program demands all my brain cells and then some.

But the way Khoi got me to take breaks from the grind this week? Probably good for my neurons. It's not like we could've leveled up our second checkpoint submission by throwing another hour at it. I mean, it's a pretty fire proposal. *And* I got to play capture the flag.

So who knows. Maybe I'm using this hackathon thing as an excuse to avoid my own emotions.

Saturday afternoon, we're at a liquid nitrogen ice-cream social when HellomynameisBrenda announces that the second checkpoint results are posted. There are abandoned cardboard cups, pink pools of melted ice cream, and a stampede to Stata.

In the lobby, there's a crowd again, but Khoi is taller, so he pops onto his tippy-toes and cranes his neck. Then he does a triumphant whoop. "Char! We're ranked first!"

"No way??"

"Way!" He shoves me forward playfully. "Go see for yourself."

I weave through the crush. Maybe it's my imagination, but people seem more willing to step aside and let me pass. And there it is. Our names at the top of the sheet. Khoi Anh (Astor) and Charise (Char) Tang. The team of parenthetical names.

A squeak of delight escapes my lips.

"It isn't fair," someone mutters behind me. "Astor is a professional developer. Of course he knew how to sell it."

"Wish I was a pretty girl," someone else grumbles. "Then he'd want to work with me."

"She's not even pretty," the first voice says. "In the Bay Area there's a girl who looks like her working at every boba shop." Which is such a specific insult, I have to respect the effort.

If they want to munch on sour grapes, they can have the

whole vineyard. We're still first, which is going to definitely help propel us to the top during final judging, since results from all three checkpoints get combined.

I twirl to find Khoi. He's standing in a pool of afternoon sunlight, which etches him beautiful and gold. My chest swells.

I dash over. When our eyes meet, he smiles and opens his arms. I run into the hug, and he lifts me off the ground and spins me around.

And then his face is right there, wide-open and wanting. So even though we're in front of everyone, I kiss him.

His lips are shy at first, but then he reciprocates hungrily, like he's been dreaming about this for a long while. Warmth floods my entire body, and I reach up to rake my fingers over the nape of his neck, through his hair.

Someone whistles. Suddenly embarrassed, I break away from the kiss and turn toward the source of the noise.

Our roommates are standing shoulder-to-shoulder. Obi looks confused. Aisha is grinning from ear to ear. She's probably the one who whistled.

"Shut up," I tell her. My cheeks are hot.

She throws her palms up. "I didn't say anything!"

"Yeah, but you were totally thinking it."

Obi frowns. "Aisha, you cool with this?"

"Don't worry about me," she says quickly. "I, uh, dumped Khoi."

Khoi tilts his head, like, *Why am I the dumpee in this fake scenario?*

"Wait, so Char, are you two girlfriend-boyfriend?" Obi asks. "Or is there some new Zoomer trend where we're kissing our platonic friends?"

I have a flight to PDX in August, but who knows if I'm going back? I can't commit to anything when the future is such a question mark. "No labels yet," I say.

"As long as you don't sexile me," Obi says. "You are *not* keeping me away from my A100."

Khoi blushes. "Understood."

"I'm serious. I don't care if you're naked. I *will* karate-chop the door down." He pantomimes with a stiff palm.

"I have a condom from health class," Aisha adds mischievously. "Want it?"

Khoi doubles over in a furious coughing fit.

Chapter Twenty-Seven

The next two weeks of July are an absolute whirlwind. Once, at the aquarium, I saw this swarm of fluorescent fish. My parents—this was back when they were still together—were busy amusing themselves by pointing out which creatures were good to eat, but it was the bright swirling school that caught my eye. It astonished me, how they swam as one shape. But now that's Khoi and me as we write lines upon interlacing lines of code.

The hours pass by quickly. Khoi—Khoi's *good*. He's quick and experienced. He anticipates problems, thinks three steps ahead. Working next to him makes me all amped up, like I've downed too many espresso shots.

And when we get bored or tired, we make out. It's nothing like making out with Drew. With Drew, I was always hyperaware of our surroundings. My brain had plenty of RAM for non-Drew-related thoughts, even when we were kissing. But with Khoi, it's like everything else falls away except for this pink-and-gold bubble we've made for ourselves. I think I could spend my entire life inside of the bubble.

Tuesday afternoon, Khoi and I are on my bed. His mouth is hot and tender. He kisses each mole on my chin, my neck, my collarbone, and each kiss feels like the first. Our limbs are entangled, but I pull him even closer.

He tugs at the hem of my top. "Can you take this off?" The urgency in his voice stokes the fire within me.

"No," I say.

His eyes widen. "Sorry, was that—"

"*You* take it off for me." I give him a wicked smile, and he blushes.

We take turns removing each other's shirts. And he's beautiful, which is a word I never thought I'd use to describe a boy. His skin is so smooth. It reminds me of a marble sculpture at an art museum.

I'm leaning down to kiss him when the doorknob rattles. There's this scraping sound like somebody is working the key into the lock.

Khoi calls, "Aisha, give us a minute!"

The door opens anyway. I dive for the blankets, because there's no time to put my shirt back on.

It's not Aisha. It's her parents, clutching Tupperware containers full of food.

Oh my God oh my God oh my God. How did they even get in here? How do they have a key? Maybe they're allowed to trespass, or maybe Aisha gave them a copy? I zoned out when Hellomynameis-Brenda gave parent-related info, since that stuff was irrelevant to me.

The adults stare at us. "Khoi?" Mr. Chadha asks. "What are you doing?"

We're half naked. Barring some laundry emergency, it's fairly obvious what we're doing. I burrow deeper into the blankets. Khoi reaches for his shirt.

"How can you do this to our daughter?" Her mother demands. "And you!" She glares at me. "You—*floozy*—"

"Stop. Stop. Don't insult Char. Aisha and I . . . uh . . ." Khoi improvises as he yanks his shirt over his head. "We broke up."

Her father shakes his head. "Sorry to hear, but perhaps it's for the best. You both should focus on college apps."

Mrs. Chadha is still staring at me like I might try to steal her husband too. "And where is Aisha? Find My Friends says she's here."

"She's probably . . . somewhere?" Khoi offers.

"Indeed. Thank you for that helpful contribution." She checks her phone. "It says her location is right here. Simmons Hall. This very room."

"You know, the GPS on Apple devices can be super inaccurate," I say. "I read a *Wired* article about that."

"I'm going to call her." Mr. Chadha speed dials. A second later, Khoi's backpack vibrates.

Without asking for permission, Aisha's mom kneels down and unzips it. She digs out Aisha's rose-gold iPhone. "Why is her phone here?"

"Maybe she . . . forgot?" God, Khoi is so bad at coming

up with these answers. We'd be better off with ChatGPT. Or a Magic 8 Ball.

"She forgot her phone in *your* backpack?"

"Do you mind if we take a look around?" Mr. Chadha asks me.

It doesn't feel like there's much of a choice. I nod. I'm just praying this interaction ends without anyone seeing my boobs.

They sort through Aisha's dresser, shake out her bedsheets, sift through the scattered papers on her desk. It's like they're FBI agents. I wouldn't be shocked if someone busts out a fingerprinting kit.

"Priya," Mr. Chadha says. "Look at this."

When I see what he's holding, my heart sinks. It's a program for the Harvard dance showcase from June.

"Her name is here. See?" He jabs his finger at the page. "This is for some high school dance camp."

Mrs. Chadha's face is stormy. She mutters something in Punjabi.

"Wait," Khoi says. "That's, um. That's not . . ." But his voice dwindles, because there is no lie that might explain this away.

"The situation is clear," Aisha's dad says. "Our daughter's been lying to us about where she's going. Did you help her with this deception?"

Khoi opens his mouth and then closes it again wordlessly.

"Google Maps says this building is a twelve-minute drive from here," Mrs. Chadha says, looking up from her phone.

"I'm disappointed in you, Khoi," Mr. Chadha says as they leave. "I thought you were a good kid."

He is a good kid, I want to say, but don't.

The door slams shut.

As soon as they're gone, Khoi jams his feet into his shoes. "Char, let's go!" Without waiting for me, he starts running.

As soon as my shirt is back on my torso where it belongs, thank you very much, I chase Khoi down the hall. "Where are you going?" I holler.

"We have to get to Harvard before Aisha's parents. We have to warn her!"

My brain connects the dots. Oh, hell. It's one thing if the Chadhas discover that their daughter is at dance camp. It's another if they discover that she's queer before she's ready to come out. And we can't even call or text her, since she doesn't have her phone. We're basically prehistoric again.

He suddenly halts in front of a room and pounds on the door.

Haru answers with a yawn. "What?"

Khoi's all, "We need to borrow your motorcycle." No greeting. No explanation. Not even a *pretty please*.

"No thanks." Haru moves to shut the door.

"Please!" Khoi wedges his foot in the doorway. "This isn't for me. It's for Aisha."

"So? I barely know that girl."

"Okay. How about this. Let us borrow your motorcycle and I'll debug your code for you." Khoi smiles big, as if this is some incredible once-in-a-lifetime opportunity.

Jesus. If I'm ever in some hostage situation, he better not be the one negotiating for my release.

"Yo, you think I care that much about this dumb competition?"

My teammate seems stumped, so I jump in. "You like Jenni, right?"

Haru reddens. "How do you know that, Oregon?"

I ignore the question. "If you were kind enough to let us borrow your bike, maybe I'd be tempted to mention how amazing you are . . ."

Three minutes later Khoi and I are on Vassar Street next to Haru's motorcycle.

"How did you know that he likes Jenni?" Khoi asks as he swings his leg over the seat.

I slide in and wrap my arms around his waist. "I'll explain later. How do *you* know how to ride a motorcycle?"

"My most recent visit to Vietnam, my cousin taught me. Everyone there rides. Even the kiddos." The keys jangle. Of course Haru has a pot leaf keychain.

"When's the last time you were in Vietnam?"

Khoi frowns. "Maybe age ten?"

Ten-year-old Khoi on the roads. That's so cursed.

Chapter Twenty-Eight

As we screech down Massachusetts Avenue, wind whipping our faces, I shout in Khoi's ear, "Do you really think we can get there before the Chadhas?"

"It's difficult to find parking around Harvard Square. And maybe they won't be able to locate the exact building? It's not that easy if you're unfamiliar with the campus." Sounds like he's huffing hopium, but I say nothing.

He's unbelievable with the motorcycle. Unbelievably atrocious. He makes sharp turns and sudden swerves that send my heart into overdrive. Weaves past other cars, which should be a violation of traffic law. It's like he hasn't improved at all since he was ten years old. And we're not even wearing helmets, so that's just brain damage waiting to happen.

A horrible thought occurs to me. "Khoi, do you have a license for this?"

"Nope," he chirps cheerfully.

I cling to him tight and squeeze my eyes shut. On the bright side, if I'm going to die, at least I'll die doing what I love: holding on to a cute boy.

Ten terrifying minutes and several near-death experiences later, we're in front of the brick building where Aisha rehearses. As we dash up the stairs, I glance over my shoulder to see an older South Asian man and woman across the grass, marching in our direction.

"Khoi, hurry. The Chadhas are right there."

He follows my gaze. "We better make this count, then." His mouth is a grim slash.

We run.

The dance studio is on the second floor. When we burst in, the dancers are on a water break. There are clusters of girls standing around. Aisha is chatting with someone with pink hair. Trinity.

My roommate's face is flushed and happy until she sees us. "Khoi? Char? What—?"

"Your parents," I pant. By the way, running? Still the worst thing ever invented, thanks for asking. "They—they're here."

"Here where?"

"*Here* here. They caught Char and me," Khoi says. "They found out about the dance program. They're going to be here any minute."

Horror floods Aisha's expression.

Trinity immediately understands. "Probably best if I make myself scarce, right?"

"Y-yeah."

Trinity pecks her on the cheek and melts away into a separate conversation.

Aisha's face slams shut. "Okay. I don't want them coming in here." She steels her shoulders and slips out into the hallway. We follow.

At the other end of the corridor, her parents are walking toward us. Their anger is this black, poisonous fog. They see Aisha, and Aisha sees them. It feels like I'm about to witness an execution.

"You guys should go," Aisha mumbles out of the corner of her mouth. "I don't want you to get caught in the crossfire."

Khoi folds his arms. "We can't ditch you."

"It'll be worse if you stick around." She jabs a thumb over her shoulder. "Take the back stairwell."

"But . . ."

I touch his arm. "Khoi, we should leave." If Aisha wants us gone, then we should respect that.

We turn away. When we're picking our way down the stairs, Mr. Chadha starts shouting in Punjabi. As his voice echoes, we exchange worried looks.

"Should we stick around to make sure she's okay?" Khoi asks.

"I don't know if she wants us to hear this," I say. Whenever Michael was being terrible, I never wanted an audience. There is something uniquely humiliating about being powerless against an adult authority figure.

"We can't do *nothing*."

I grit my teeth, irked. Khoi freakin' Astor. In his world, everything can be fixed. Everything is possible, like it's Narnia or something. Why can't he understand that there are certain heartbreaks that can't be mended with a hug?

No, I'm not being fair. It isn't like he's lived such a cutesy, wholesome life either. I know that. It's just easy to forget sometimes.

We're both silent as we exit the building. It's a muggy, overcast day, like the clouds are on the verge of bursting. Like the sky is about to cry.

"Suggestion," I say. "Let's walk the motorcycle instead of riding it."

We trudge back to the dorms and return the keys to Haru. Khoi seems sad, and he excuses himself to crash before dinner. So I try to work on Hello World, but my thoughts keep floating back to Aisha. Her parents had major control freak energy. No wonder she was trying to hide her dance stuff from them.

What's it like to have parents who are total opps? I hate how conflict-allergic my mother is, but I can't imagine her getting pressed with me for doing something I love. I can't imagine her trying to make me into someone I'm not. Even when I ran away for Alpha Fellows, she never gave me shit. She just wanted to know I was okay. I never realized that other parents might've been absolutely unhinged about it.

Aisha limps into the dorm room around dinnertime, followed by her father. My roommate's eyes are red and puffy, ringed with smudged makeup.

"Where's your luggage?" Mr. Chadha asks.

"Under my bed."

Aisha drags out her suitcase and silently starts packing—stacking books, pulling clothes out of the dresser, tossing loose papers into the wastebasket. Watching her sweep her life into a suitcase makes me feel awful. It's like she's deleting her entire presence from this room.

"Do you need help?" I offer, because I don't know what else to do. "I'm pretty good at rolling socks."

"We're fine, thanks," Mr. Chadha says curtly.

Once Aisha's things are packed, Mr. Chadha moves to leave, but she says, "I still have stuff in the bathroom."

"Go get it, then."

She leaves, and then it's me and her father standing in awkward silence.

I shouldn't say anything. This situation is above my pay grade.

But Khoi would speak up. Khoi would want to try. And even though his naive optimism can be so extra, it also makes me feel like I should do more.

It's now or never. I can't sit this one out. I can't just let her leave like this.

"Have you ever seen Aisha dance?" I blurt.

He turns to me. "What?"

"She's incredible onstage. It's like the music reshapes itself around her." He doesn't respond, so I keep yammering. "She works so hard for something she truly loves. It's super inspiring. Please don't make her leave."

Mr. Chadha considers me. "Are your parents immigrants too?"

"Yes . . ." Where's he going with this? I don't want to get into my family lore.

"Perhaps you'll understand. It isn't that I don't want Aisha to dance. But our family doesn't have the resources to support her in such an unstable career. And when is the last time you saw an Indian American dancer?"

Error 503: Brain temporarily unavailable.

"It doesn't happen for people like her." His eyes size me up. "People like you too, maybe. This country wasn't built for us. There are many games we cannot even participate in. The best we can hope for is to win at the ones they *will* let us play."

I want to argue back, but he's sort of spitting facts. Even in tech, there are plenty of Asian women who are software engineers, but how many of them get to be actual CEOs or company presidents? Diversity only happens when the gatekeepers—overwhelmingly white and male—decide to care. It's almost impossible to climb to the top rung of America without a ladder built by a white person.

Aisha returns holding a shower caddy.

"Ready?" her father asks. Without waiting for a response, he steps outside into the hallway.

She wraps me in a bear hug. "Thanks for being the best roomie, Char."

And then she's gone, leaving nothing but a lingering whiff of vanilla-and-cinnamon perfume.

Chapter Twenty-Nine

Later that night, Aisha texts that she's grounded until senior year and won't have access to her phone anymore, crying-face emoji. Without her and her stuff, the dorm room is too empty. It's the first time in years I've had a space to myself.

It's weird. I've been manifesting my own room for years, pretty much ever since I discovered how smutty those Sarah J. Maas books can get. But now I'm too sad to even care.

So I call Mom.

Honestly, the Chadhas were kind of a vibe check. At least Mom's never actively prevented me from pursuing my dreams. I mean, I don't know if I ever had any specific dreams to pursue besides getting through the hellscape that is high school, so maybe that's not saying much. But still.

She picks up on the first ring.

"Char?" Her voice is all hushed, wind against grass. Like she's at the library, which I don't think she's visited in years.

"Why are you whispering?"

"Michael is sleeping."

I check the time. It's ten p.m. here, so it's seven over there. The sun hasn't even set in Oregon. "He's already asleep?"

"He's not doing so well lately."

"Is he sick?" Maybe he has food poisoning. That would be cool.

"He's fine," she says. "He lost some money. He's stressed."

"Is he treating you right?"

"Char, don't act so suspicious."

"Mom, if Michael is—" I try to reach for the right words in Mandarin. "If he's not being a good guy, I want to know about that."

"Your stepfather has been good to us, *baobei*. Even if you can't see that right now."

She cannot be serious. I grit my teeth. "What. Am. I. Not. Seeing?" I'm not tripping, right? Because I *am* seeing the alcoholism, the gambling, the toxic, controlling energy, the straight-up unhinged rage. It's not like I'm hallucinating those things.

"He gave us a roof over our heads, he put food on the table. He pays our bills. He helped me get a green card and then citizenship. Once you get older, you'll see those things don't come easily."

There must be other ways of securing all that, I want to say. But my mind is giving nothing. My mother dropped out of her doctorate program, and besides, the degree was in art. I don't know what employment opportunities are out there, but the job market probably hates her. Maybe if I could work too . . .

"He's been here consistently," Mom continues. "Unlike your father."

Of course. The bar is so deep underground, it's paying rent to Satan.

"Quinn? Who you talking to?" Michael's voice sounds faraway. "I heard Chinese."

Raising her voice, she calls in English, "Nobody, honey! Telemarketer." I can't decide if it's more insulting to be described as nobody or a telemarketer.

My stepdad says, "Which one is it? A telemarketer or nobody?"

She whispers, "I have to go."

"But—"

"He won't be happy if he finds out it's you. I'll call you back later."

Before I can get another word in, she hangs up.

I stare at my phone, feeling like I've been punched in the gut. God. I can't believe she's so terrified of him, she won't even speak to her only daughter. I know I should put aside my own anger and focus on Mom's well-being—it sounds like things are deteriorating back in Chinook Shore—but I'm too upset to care.

Why won't she ditch his ass? At the very least, it's not like her citizenship is going to get revoked if she divorces him. I think.

I guess he makes decent money with his veteran's pension

and that job where he scams tourists on overpriced timeshares. And because he inherited the house, we only pay property taxes and utility bills. I know not everyone is lucky enough to even have that. A few of my classmates have had their homes foreclosed on.

And he used to be nice. He bought my mom these beautiful sable brushes so she could paint. He talked about how her stuff would hang in the Louvre someday. He took us camping in Oregon's high desert, way out east. He showed us the constellations and taught me how to make a campfire.

Like, yeah, he always had bad days. PTSD is a bitch. But his bad days were balanced out by plenty of good days, so it was okay.

But life happened. Olive's mother, who he coparented with, dipped to go live her best life with an Italian tour guide. Michael's dad passed and we moved to Chinook Shore. His chronic pain got worse, which led to more drinking. He started playing cards with some bar regulars. One night he and his friends hit up the casino on a nearby reservation, and then he started going there by himself. Summarized like this, it sounds like a bad episode of *Euphoria*, but you have to remember this happened over a stretch of years. It was this awful train wreck in slow motion, so slow that I didn't even get what was happening until it had already demolished half the town.

And if Mom isn't going to leap off a train that's barreling straight for the cliff, it's on me to save us both. And this hackathon could give us the money and the connections to find a new life. Otherwise . . . well, I don't even want to think about otherwise.

So, no pressure or whatever, but I have to win this whole thing.

On the last Sunday of July, Khoi isn't at breakfast, which is weird.

"Maybe he's at church," Obi suggests.

I frown. "Last I checked, his only Bible was Stack Overflow."

"Who knows. Maybe he found a bug so unholy, he's seeking divine intervention."

So that's on me for expecting Obi to be helpful. Anyway, maybe Khoi slept in, which isn't like him. He's usually such a chipper morning person, it's like he swallowed a rooster.

So after finishing my Canadian bacon—which is just ham with a foreign passport—I go up to his room.

His door is ajar. He's still in his pajamas, frantically digging through his dresser drawers.

I lean against the doorframe. "You good?" I hope this isn't some random side quest of his. I want to get back to working on Hello World.

"Char, I can't find my meds." His hair sticks up in all directions, and his eyes are wild and confused. He reminds me of one of those cautionary "After" photos on posters that warn you not to snort crystal meth. "The bottles are always on my desk. I saw them this morning before my shower. I think someone stole them."

Which is a lot of paranoia for Khoi. "Why would someone take your medication?" I don't know anything about seizure meds but they don't seem like a hot commodity on the dark web. I would know. Haru spends a lot of time talking about where he gets his weed.

"Lots of people would kill to get their hands on Adderall. At my school, kids use it to study. There's an entire black market. Goes for ten bucks a pop."

Oh. "I didn't know you took that," I say. "Do you have ADHD?"

"Not as far as I know. Keppra—which is for my seizures—makes me really tired. So my doc prescribes Adderall for focus and energy."

I nod. I'm not trying to be nosy about his medical situation. But it's kind of weird that we're so close and yet he never told me this.

I don't know. It's not like we're girlfriend-boyfriend. Maybe we're just hooking up. Maybe that's how he thinks of us.

"I'll help you look," I offer, stepping inside. The sooner we handle this, the sooner we can get back to the grind.

Twenty minutes and a way messier room later, we conclude that Khoi has too many mysteriously orphaned socks ("They're being eaten by the washing machines, I swear!"), there is a previously unknown microbial ecosystem flourishing in the boys' trash can, and the medication is not here.

"Who else knows about your Adderall?" I ask.

"Obi?" Khoi wrinkles his nose. "I couldn't hide it from him."

"I don't think he would steal your meds, though."

"We don't keep our door locked. It really could've been anyone."

So he was giving "please rob me" energy. I decide against doing a whole TED Talk about not getting your stuff stolen. Instead, we find Obi to ask if he knows anything.

Khoi's roommate is slumped over in his usual spot on the first floor of the Stratton Student Center, and when I tap him on the shoulder, he wakes with a jolt.

"Hmmmph?" He looks at us blearily. "Oh, it's you two. My favorite and second-favorite Alpha Fellow. What's up?"

"Wait, which one of us is first-favorite?" Khoi asks.

I cut in because I'm not sure I want to know. "Obi, can you help us with something?"

After we explain the situation, he shakes his head. "I've been here since seven a.m."

"Do you have any guesses as to who might've taken it?"

He shrugs. "No clue."

"Okay . . . Did you tell anyone else about Khoi's meds? You're the only person at camp who knew about them."

"Oh!" He brightens up. "At dinner Lucas and some of his

minions were talking about how they wanted Adderall so they could pull more all-nighters. And I cracked a joke about how they could buy it off you."

"*Obi.*" Khoi buries his face in his hands.

"Don't worry, bro. I don't think they actually thought you were a drug dealer."

"That's not the *point!* I didn't want them to know I take Adderall!"

"Sorry, I didn't know it was meant to be incognito!"

"You didn't know *what medications he takes* was supposed to stay private?" I ask.

Khoi groans. "These guys already hate me. They call me a grifter. Now they think I'm cheating my way to the top by abusing drugs. If I'm going to be known as a drug addict, I want to at least be doing a *cool* drug, like ecstasy!"

"Ecstasy isn't even cool anymore," Obi says. "These days, it's all about ketamine."

I touch Khoi's back. "Forget them. If they stole your meds, we have to do something."

"You're right." He squares his shoulders. "I'll go to Brenda. No, Courtney."

I was thinking more like confronting the thieves directly. "You sure that's a good idea?"

He frowns. "Why wouldn't it be?"

"Do you really think the adults will do anything to help?"

"Of course. Isn't it their job to solve a problem like this?"

I'm pretty sure their main job is to keep Edvin Nilsen happy, but maybe he's right. Maybe a lifetime of being failed by grown-ups has made me way too cynical. Besides, it can't hurt to try.

"Do you want me to come with you?" I ask.

He shakes his head. "No, you should work on Hello World. We still have to add web socketing for the chat feature."

Then he marches off to find HellomynameisCourtney.

"Wait, so are you guys mad at me?" Obi asks.

The next day at breakfast, HellomynameisCourtney walks into the dining hall and claps to get everyone's attention.

People fall silent. She's all business. "One of the students has misplaced his Adderall medication. If it has come into your possession, please come forward."

There's a beat, and then everybody turns back to their conversations.

Khoi is stricken. "Wait, this is so not helpful! Nobody is going to fess up like that."

It's like he just found out that Santa isn't real. I bite back the urge to say *I told you so.* "Yeah, adults are useless," I say. "More breaking news at eleven."

"I really thought that going to the administration would help," he says.

I stab at my scrambled eggs. I'm not sure what's worse—the Adderall theft or Khoi's naiveté. He's a baby cow, and it's adorable, but you know what happens to baby cows? They get sent to the slaughterhouse. "What can they do about it? It's not like they can search every single student's room to find the culprit."

"But they don't *have* to search every room. It's probably in Lucas's room."

"Nobody else at this program is enough of an ass to steal medication," Obi adds. "That shit is low, even for Lucas."

"Right, but there's no real proof that it was him. And now that Brenda's made the announcement, I bet he's going to get psyched out and throw the pills away," I say. "Khoi, can you get a refill at the pharmacy?"

"Adderall is a controlled substance. I can't get a refill until August." He groans. "Maybe I can chug Monster. Or stop taking my seizure meds so they won't make me tired?"

I shake my head. "No. Absolutely do not do that." Skipping seizure medication sounds super risky.

"Monster is D-tier," Obi says. "Ever heard of Red Bull?"

I locate Lucas across the dining hall. He's still chatting with his friends, seemingly unfazed. He can't get up now, right after that announcement, without looking sus. But as soon as he gets a spare second, he's scramming to flush those pills down the toilet.

"We need to break into his room," I say.

Chapter Thirty

There's one major problem with my plan—the door to Lucas's room is locked.

I jiggle the doorknob again, as if maybe it'll magically click open. No shot.

"Do either of you know how to pick a lock?" I ask.

Both boys stare blankly at me.

Ah, yes. The most brilliant technical minds of our generation, foiled by a simple single-cylinder deadbolt.

We're searching up lockpicking tutorials on YouTube when there's the familiar *ding* of the elevator, signaling it's about to open on this floor.

"Hide, hide," Khoi hisses.

We scamper to the boys' room across the hall. Of course *now* they've bothered to lock their door. Khoi fumbles for the key, and we've barely crammed our bodies into the room when footsteps echo down the corridor.

We keep the door cracked open and press our faces against

the narrow gap. It's an East Asian girl in a lavender babydoll dress. Stella from Texas.

I'm expecting her to pass by the boys' section and head toward the girls', but instead she pauses in front of Lucas's door. Then she looks around surreptitiously, as if she's checking that nobody else is nearby. It's very James Bond.

She fishes a silver key out of her dress pocket and slides it into the lock, then twists.

Once Stella's disappeared into Lucas's room, Obi whispers, "How does she have a key to his room?"

I shrug. "She's his girlfriend?"

"Is that normal? Khoi, you better not have given Char a copy of *our* key!"

Hey! "You're worried *now*? You guys don't lock your door anyway. That's literally why we're in this mess!"

Khoi shushes both of us.

The door opens again, and when Stella reappears she's holding a transparent orange bottle with a white cap. A pill bottle.

Obi's jaw drops.

Her eyes scan the other doors, as if she's searching for a specific name. Then she's strolling in our direction.

We all immediately clock what's happening and scramble away from the doorway. Obi dives beneath his bed. Khoi and I flatten ourselves against the wall. My heart is in my throat, even though we're not doing anything wrong. Khoi and Obi are allowed to exist in their own room, and I'm their guest. But somehow it feels like we're the ones sneaking around.

Stella pauses in front of the door. She places something on the floor and then walks away.

More footsteps, and the *ding* of the elevator again.

Another minute crawls by before anyone dares to move. I quietly tiptoe to the front of the room. Khoi gives me an approving thumbs-up, and I push the door open.

At my feet, there's the bottle of Adderall, full of chalky blue tablets as if nothing happened.

It's past midnight. We're on my bed, pair programming. That's not some euphemism for a sexual act. I'm writing code while Khoi's looking over my shoulder.

He randomly mumbles, "It's unfair that Lucas just got away with everything."

Sure, the situation is absolutely freaking infuriating, but I don't see the point of dwelling on it. There's nothing we can do. Besides, Stella returned the Adderall.

I drum my fingers on my laptop keyboard. "Be better about locking your door."

"Feels like you're victim blaming."

Why does he want to harp on this? The hackathon is so much more important than this petty bullshit. I try not to sigh. "I'm not *victim blaming*. Obviously it's on Lucas to not be the human version of 4chan, but since he *is* the human version of

4chan, you have to install some firewalls. Metaphorically speaking. Besides, we should focus." I nudge his knee with my own. "We can still kick his ass in this competition. That's the best revenge."

After a beat, he nods. "You're right." He kisses my forehead and warmth spirals through me.

For the next two days, life seems totally normal again. We build out SMS authentication with a Twilio integration so users can use their phone numbers to log into Hello World. And Khoi buys more Google Cloud storage to support photo and video uploads. I don't protest, even though it feels like an unfair edge over other teams. It's not against the competition rules.

While he's setting that up, I fiddle with our translation features so immigrants can communicate in their mother tongue. I figured it would be an easy addition with the Google Translate API, but that was silly to assume. It's so much more than what I signed up for.

Lots of languages, including Chinese, don't use ASCII characters, so we can't slap on our current font. And other languages, like Arabic, are right-to-left instead of left-to-right, requiring even more changes to the user interface. I stay up until four a.m. implementing everything.

On Wednesday, Khoi goes home to celebrate his uncle's fiftieth birthday. Obi is avoiding his teammates—apparently Diego and Jenni-with-an-i are fighting all the time, in the least surprising plot twist ever—so he and I work in the student center. Obi has a strong rule about being within a twenty-foot perimeter of Tea-Do.

Around ten a.m., both of our laptops chime with an email notification. The subject line is *check this out!!* and the sender is some throwaway account. The cc'd recipients are a good fraction of the Alpha Fellows.

Confused, I click on the attached video.

It's Stella. Or not exactly Stella, but some uncanny valley, plastic robot imitation of her. Her naked body is contorted like she's a circus performer, and she thrusts her hips mechanically against some faceless guy. Her mouth emits a high-pitched, unnatural noise.

For two seconds, I'm more confused than anything else. Then things click.

A deepfake. Somebody must've slapped her face onto a porn actress's body.

A sharp wave of nausea overwhelms me.

"Don't click on the email you just got," I tell Obi.

"Why?" He glances over my shoulder and glimpses the screen. "What is that?"

I slam my laptop shut. "Nothing worth looking at."

He tilts his head, clearly unsatisfied. If I don't spill, he's going to open the email anyway.

"It's deepfake porn of a girl at camp," I say.

"Yikes, that's disgusting," he says. "People need to touch

grass." He navigates to his inbox and deletes the email without opening it.

"Why would anyone do that?"

"Thirsty? Bored? Insecure about their own pathetic, lonely NPC lives spent trapped in their mom's basement?" Obi shrugs. "Why does any internet troll do anything?"

He turns his attention back to his own screen.

I force myself to forget about the email. There isn't anything I can do for Stella, and I have to debug. Now that we have a multimedia integration, the Hello World data pipeline needs to be retooled to handle larger files and mixed formats. It's a spaghetti nightmare. I miss Khoi. His skills are God-tier compared to mine.

An hour later my laptop battery is dwindling. And because I'm a genius, of course I left my charger in my dorm room. So I head back to Simmons to grab it.

When I stroll through the girls' section, quiet sobs drift from Stella's room.

Yeah, I feel awful for her. I only viewed the video for like, zero-point-two seconds, but that was long enough to traumatize me, and I'm not even the one who got deepfaked. But this isn't my problem. I have a hackathon to win.

Still, it feels too heartless to walk away. Khoi would never do that. Khoi would be hacking into the MIT servers to track down this asshole, even for a girl he barely knows.

And she *did* return the Adderall. So maybe I owe her one.

I knock on her door. "Are you okay?"

"Go away," Stella moans.

"What happened is really horrible," I say. "I'm so sorry."

There's a pause, and then the door opens. Her face is tear streaked and puffy. Her usually glossy hair hangs in limp strands.

"How are you doing?" I ask.

A laugh-sob escapes her throat. "How do you think?"

We sit on the floor of her room as she quietly weeps. I don't know what the move is here. I can't even come through with Kleenex. If we were friends, I'd hug her, but we don't really know each other like that. We haven't spoken since that night on the yacht.

"You could go to the police," I say. "There are laws against this stuff. And you're a minor."

She shakes her head. "I don't want my parents to find out. Besides, I already know who did it."

"Who?" I assumed it was some horny loser at camp. Which could be, like, half the people here.

"Lucas van den Berg." She sniffles.

"Lucas . . . your boyfriend Lucas?"

"I broke up with him on Monday. After he stole your boyfriend's Adderall."

"Khoi's not my . . ." I decide to let it go. She's clearly not trying to hear about my situationship status. "Hey, it was nice of you to return it. That took courage."

"Fat lotta good that did me," she mumbles. "I should've

known Lucas would be nasty about the breakup. I heard that after he got dumped by this other girl, he spammed her with scary anonymous texts for *months*. She had to get a new phone number. But I wanted to give him the benefit of the doubt, since she couldn't *prove* it was him . . ."

"Lucas is a bastard," I say.

Stella covers her face. "I'm scared he's going to send more stuff. Or send it to people at Andover, or my parents." She does this shaky gulp for air. "He always gets away with everything. He has that slouchy bored-skater-kid aesthetic, but he's rich. There's a building at Yale with his family's name on it."

"Well, it's only Yale," I say. "Not even Harvard."

She doesn't smile at the joke.

I switch tactics. "Stella, if you expose Lucas, Alpha Fellows will *have* to kick him out, even if he's rich. You aren't powerless here."

"Do you actually think so?"

I'm not confident, but I nod anyway.

She sniffles some more. "How are we going to do that?"

We? Looks like I'm part of this now. Let's be real, as soon as I knocked on Stella's door, I was going to be part of this. And even though there are a million other things on my to-do list, I'm kind of living for the chance to take Lucas down.

I say, "We need to prove that the email came from him."

Chapter Thirty-One

For the next hour, we brainstorm ways to nail Lucas's ass.

No way tracking his IP address helps. Like, congrats, bestie, he's on the MIT network. So is everyone else at camp.

"I could pretend to get back together with him?" Stella suggests. "Act apologetic and get him to confess to making the deepfakes. Secretly record the whole conversation."

"Do you think Lucas is gullible enough to fall for that?" It's a genuine question. She knows him way better than I do. If she truly thinks he could be tricked by this, then so be it.

She considers, then sighs. "No."

What if we track down whatever deepfake service he used and force them to fork over the user data? Thing is, there's no watermark on the image, so it would take serious detective work to determine exactly which pervy hellhole it came from.

A quick Google search reveals that there are a million apps out there that allow creeps to produce this stuff. I hate the world.

Maybe technology was a mistake. Things were better when we all lived in caves.

"Could we steal his phone?" I ask. "Do you know his password?"

Stella shakes her head. "I'm certain he's changed it by now. And he's superglued to that thing. Sleeps with it beneath his pillow. We'd have to pull a heist."

For a few seconds, I fantasize about how awesome it'd be to do an *Ocean's Eleven* on Lucas. But I'm not trying to get expelled here.

"What if we run a man-in-the-middle attack?" I suggest. "Trick him into connecting to an insecure network and intercept his data packets?"

She wrinkles her nose. "That's a pretty sophisticated cyberattack. Can you pull that off?"

"Probably not," I admit. I know the theory behind this stuff, but I've never done it for real.

Coincidentally, that's also how I would describe sex.

God, I'm on the struggle bus here. I wish Khoi wasn't busy cramming his face with birthday cake. He'd know exactly what to do.

No. I don't need him to play tech support twenty-four-seven. I can handle this on my own.

This situation reminds me of last year, when someone emailed the school with chemistry test answers and I made a script to catch him. Sent him an attachment with the message

Hey! I also got the answers for bio. As soon as he downloaded the attachment, it triggered a script that used browser fingerprinting to collect as much data as possible. That's how I discovered that the thief was Tommy Gavel and that he had a furry porn addiction. Honestly, I regret doing such a deep dive. Some foxes you can't unsee.

But that only worked because Tommy was basically asking to get hacked. He clicked on a sketchy attachment. He didn't disable his cookies. He wasn't even using incognito mode. It was giving major "my password is the word *password*" energy. Made me feel kind of bad about the whole thing.

Lucas *cannot* be that smooth-brained.

But. What if he is? Why am I so convinced that these kids at Alpha Fellows are so much savvier than everyone back home?

"I have an idea, but it might not work," I say.

Since no mainstream email server would let us send a script like this, I use an SMTP connection with Python. It takes a hot minute to set everything up, but I did this last year in Chinook Shore.

Then we have to compose the body text of the email. And now I'm staring at the blinking cursor in my terminal like it might magically come up with the perfect words.

"If we're going to get him to click on an attachment, the message has to be spicy," Stella says.

I nod. "Maybe like, 'Here's the proof to the Riemann hypothesis'?" I learned about that from Khoi.

"What's that?"

"An unsolved problem in mathematics." Like the holy grail of math problems. Whoever solves it will get instant legend status.

"What? You think Lucas cares about that? Does *anyone* care about that?" She shakes her head. "No, no. It has to be . . ." She snaps her fingers. "Give me the laptop."

I oblige. She types something and then tilts the screen toward me.

Bro Stella is so hot!! She sent me these n00dz last yr bro wanna see bro

"Maybe remove one of the *bro*s," I say. "Also, you really had to add in a line about how you're so hot?"

"Just keeping it realistic."

I fake-gag and she giggles. Something loosens between us. Even though this entire situation is horrible, I can't help but smile.

"Can we send the email now?" Stella asks, and the feel-good moment is over. She slides the laptop back to me.

I add a few more lines of code to hide the script in the attachment, then hit execute. For a few seconds, my cursor does that annoying thing where it freezes like it's having a meltdown.

From the tracking pixel I slid in, I can see that he opens the email almost immediately. *C'mon, dude, be the dumbass I know you can be. Take the bait . . .*

He clicks the attachment. I let out a whoop.

Stella grabs my hand all hyped, then lets go once she remembers we're not tight like that.

My script chews through his browser data and sends along whatever it finds. Lots of it is useless—I don't need to know what version of Google Chrome he's on, and I *definitely* don't need to know what's in his "baddies" bookmarks folder —but he *is* logged into both the email he used for those deepfakes and his normal email account from Exeter, his private school. Caught in 4K.

Ten minutes later, we've secured all the receipts to prove that Lucas is the creep. I bundle everything into a CSV file and send it to Stella so she can decide how to end this fool's whole career.

"I'm going to talk to Courtney," she says.

I nod. "You can probably go to the cops too. But obviously that's a whole ordeal." Personally I want to report his ass to law enforcement, but it's not my place to tell her how to handle this.

"Thanks, Char. For everything."

Well . . . time to bounce, then. I stand.

"Wait, before you go," she says. "Why did you start ignoring me?"

"Hmm?"

"We were totally chill that first day. Good vibes. And then . . . it's like you ghosted."

"Oh. That." I blink.

I could crack a stupid joke. Dodge the question completely. But maybe she deserves to know.

"Honestly, I didn't like how you and Lucas talked about Khoi." And I felt bad that I didn't defend him.

There's an understanding in her eyes, and then regret. "I don't feel good about that either. It's like I became a different person when I was around him."

I shrug, because I'm not the one she should apologize to.

When I walk out of her room, something bubbles in my chest, like, *Huh. I'm kind of that bitch.* Kicking Lucas's ass with that computer script, calling Stella out on her mean behavior, all before dinner.

It sort of reminds me of when I let Lola cut my bangs. I didn't recognize the new Charise Tang in the mirror, but she was someone with main-character energy. Someone I wanted to get to know.

Chapter Thirty-Two

Lucas disappears—no official statement is made by the administration, but everybody knows he's been expelled. His roommate, a lanky boy from New Jersey named Chris, throws a party to celebrate and promptly gets shut down by HellomynameisBrenda.

August simmers in. Khoi and I finish implementing all the functionality for Hello World and start testing edge cases. Our app breaks a lot. As we work, he hums a tune: *Ninety-nine little bugs in the code, ninety-nine bugs in the code / patch one down, compile it around, 122 bugs in the code* . . .

A week before our project is due I receive this email from the College Board reminding me of my upcoming SAT. It's scheduled for the Saturday of final presentations. Oof. I completely forgot I signed up for that, way back in June when Aisha's mom got on my case about it. I hate it when Past Char makes decisions for Future Char. The decisions are often bad.

"Should I even bother taking the August SAT?" I ask Khoi. "I haven't studied at all. I could just take it in October."

He taps his chin. "If you're already signed up, you might as well?"

"But it's the day of final presentations."

"We can ask for a presentation slot after your exam."

"What if it jeopardizes our chances at winning?" I don't know if I can prepare for both the SAT and our presentation on the same day. Multitasking is such a struggle. Like, I can barely walk and text at the same time.

"Alpha Fellows is just one summer," he says. "College is the next four years of your life." He smiles. "Besides, I thought we were going to apply to MIT early? Your October test scores might not arrive in time for the November deadline."

"Thought you were doing Harvard early," I say.

"No, I said that to appease the Chadhas. I want to apply to MIT. Better engineering program." He shrugs. "I mean, if you want to go to Harvard, that's cool too. They're both in Cambridge. We could still be together."

"Khoi, what are you on about?"

We haven't even discussed what's happening to us once summer's over. Why is he out here acting like we're going to attend college together? As if I'm even going to get into any of these universities he's name-dropping.

He looks confused. "I guess I assumed you wanted to go here, since you're doing a summer program at MIT. My bad." Then he nods like he gets it. "Ohhhh. You're a West Coast, Best Coast believer. You're thinking Stanford?"

"No!" The exclamation comes out harsher than I mean it to. He flinches. "I don't know what I'm doing for college apps."

"But it's already August," he says. "Did you ask teachers for rec letters yet? Have you signed up for the Common App portal?"

His questions make me feel like I'm wearing an itchy sweater. "No."

"Do you need help?"

"Khoi, chill. This is my business. I'll figure it out myself."

"But it's *my* business too!"

"How is it your business?" I snap.

His eyes widen. "I want to spend our college years together," he says softly. "Don't you want the same thing, Char?"

Something inside of me unravels. He wants to *spend our college years together*. He wants to be with me for real. He looks at me and sees something more than a fling. He sees his future.

For a second I indulge the fantasy of enrolling here with Khoi. Attending lectures together, completing problem sets side by side. Sneaking onto the famous MIT dome. Making out in our dorm rooms when our roommates are away, stealing kisses in the library stacks. Existing together in seasons besides summer: crashing the Harvard-Yale football game, carving pumpkins, sipping hot chocolate along a frozen Charles River, studying on the grass of Killian Court during the first searingly gorgeous day of spring.

And for a split second, there's so much yearning I think it might flood my heart.

But I can't want any of this. If I want it, it'll hurt so much more later.

I let the daydream pop like a rainbow soap bubble.

"We can talk about this after we submit," I say. "For now, let's just focus on Hello World."

Several days later Edvin Nilsen slides into my inbox to say he's back in town. He wants to link up before the final deadline.

This time, I tell Khoi about the meeting beforehand. He does this passive-aggressive side-eye, but doesn't say anything, so whatever. It's about the small wins.

It's a weekday, and the Nexus office is bustling with activity. Everyone is on edge, frenetic, like they drank too much coffee. As I pass by the desks, I hear someone say, "Screw this defense contract." There's that phrase again. *Defense contract*. Khoi had mentioned it too.

What even is a defense contract? Like, Nexus is working for the military or whatever? I guess the military has hella data to analyze.

Edvin Nilsen greets me in the same conference room as last time. In the corner, Janelle taps away at a tablet.

He's in a muscle tee and gym shorts, as if he just finished a jog along the harbor. I guess someone like Edvin never has to stress about looking unprofessional. Meanwhile, Janelle is in a crisp navy blue pantsuit. She's giving Hillary Clinton.

"I heard about what happened with Stella Zhou and Lucas van den Berg," he says. "Seems like you were involved?"

I blink, surprised that he knows or cares. Maybe Edvin is more involved with the day-to-day of Alpha Fellows than I thought. "Yeah."

"It was kind of you to help your friend out," Edvin says. Stella isn't exactly my friend, but I don't correct him. "But there are two weeks left in the summer. You gotta focus on your own project. No distractions."

Makes sense. "So probably I shouldn't take the SAT in August?"

"What?"

"I signed up for it, but I haven't studied yet, and . . ." I stop talking because he's shaking his head adamantly.

"What's the point? That stuff is for rule followers, pencil pushers. *Bo*-ring. Why do you need to fill in a Scantron to prove that you're smart? You already know you're smart."

"I want to go to college?" A four-year college. With Khoi, even.

"College is useless. Look at Bill Gates, Mark Zuckerberg, Steve Jobs. All dropouts."

I don't even bother pointing out that they were also all dudes. If I want to be taken seriously, I need the credentials.

"What are you going to do in college, Char? Waste time in gen eds and intro courses that have nothing to do with building something real? Get on your knees for some shitfaced frat boy?" When I flinch, he laughs and claps a hand on my shoulder. "Kidding, kidding. But my point is, you're too good for the normie path."

Hearing him say that is like drinking champagne. Or what I imagine drinking champagne is like. There's a warm glow in my chest. "Thanks, Edvin."

"But you gotta focus," he repeats. "Don't let anything distract you. None of that bullshit." And his blue eyes are so intense. It's almost like he knows about Khoi and me.

That evening, Khoi and I go up to my room after dinner as usual. The minute the door slams shut, he kisses me hard and everything in me sharpens with desire. We stumble backward and fall into my bed. He smothers my body with his. But when he fumbles for the hem of my shirt, Edvin Nilsen's dry-gravel voice rings in my head. Total mood killer.

I push Khoi off me.

He caresses my face. His touch is gentle. "Char, what's wrong? Did I do something?"

"No. No, you're perfect. More than perfect." I look away. "It's not you. I don't . . . want to get distracted."

He frowns. "Am I a distraction?"

"Not *you*, but this is." If I'm down bad whenever I'm around Khoi, I'm clearly not focusing on Hello World. "Maybe . . . maybe we should stop doing this. At least for now. I want to full-send our project."

His shoulders stiffen. "Are you dumping me?"

I straighten up. "No! No. I just don't want to spend too much time fooling around. That's what Edvin said."

"Edvin Nilsen told you to stop fooling around with me?" he asks slowly.

My cheeks burn. "Well, *no*, obviously not like that, but he said I should focus on winning."

"Char, why are you meeting with him anyway?"

"He's mentoring me!"

Khoi raises an eyebrow. Ugh, I'm so jealous that he can do that. "Haven't you met him, like, twice? Some mentor."

"He's busy. And didn't he help with the project idea? It's really nice of him to give advice when he's, you know, *Edvin Nilsen* and I'm some stupid teenager. "

"Don't call yourself stupid," he says. "And Edvin gives me bad vibes."

I tip my palms up. "I don't get why you don't trust Edvin. He hasn't been sus at all." Obviously I've heard the horror stories of rich, powerful tech bros taking advantage of younger girls. Who hasn't?

But with Edvin, it hasn't been like that. Not even close. Every time we meet, his assistant Janelle is there.

Khoi studies my face. It looks like he's on the verge of saying something. But when he opens his mouth, all that comes out is, "If he's a good guy, then I'm happy for you."

Chapter Thirty-Three

The next morning, Khoi and I are in my room, fudging with performance improvements. He's showing me how to benchmark our code to assess our latency bottlenecks—basically, see which parts of our code are slowing the whole thing down—when my phone rings.

It's Olive. We haven't spoken since I left Oregon. I'm so surprised, I pick up.

"Char?" Her breath comes out all choppy. "I'm worried for your mom."

"What's wrong?" My mind takes a dumpster dive through the possible worst-case scenarios. Car accident? Stroke? Tsunami? All three at once?

"My dad," she says, and my heart sinks. "He's been drinking more lately. He lost a lot of money back in June. It's getting bad . . ." She doesn't elaborate. She doesn't need to.

"Olive. Do you have a safe place to go?"

"I'm at, um, Drew's," she says. There's an awkward pause as we both remember I used to fool around with her man.

"Your mom is trapped in the house. He won't let her out. Or, like, he *says* she can leave, but he won't let her drive, and he's always tracking her whereabouts on her phone, so basically she's trapped."

Panic rises in my chest, but I force myself to keep talking. "That's awful. Did you call the cops?"

There's a pause, and then she says, "He's still my dad."

Of course. I squeeze the phone tight. "So you left her there all alone?"

"Don't be so judgmental," she says. "You're the one who ditched us first."

I'm tempted to hang up right then and there, but I can't. I've got to come up with a plan. "Okay. I'll call the police, then."

"No, that won't help," she says. "He'll just play nice when they drop by to do a wellness check, then take it out on your mom. You know how it goes."

She's right. I do know how it goes, because that's how it has always gone in the past.

The answer is obvious. I have to be the one to save her. I can't be here, safe and happy in this cushy camp thousands of miles away, while my mother is caught beneath the thumb of a monster. I've been lying to myself all summer. But I can't run from the truth any longer.

I thank Olive for letting me know, then end the call.

Khoi is staring at me. "What's happening?"

My body feels taut, wired with energy. Quickly I explain the sitch while my brain kicks into overdrive. I'm not sure if I can scrape together enough money to buy a last-minute flight back to Portland. And let's say I can orchestrate a jailbreak. I don't know where we'll go after that. Maybe I should google women's shelters in Oregon.

"I'll buy the flights," Khoi says. "We'll bring her back here. She can sleep in Aisha's old bed until you figure out what to do next."

His expression is so sincere it makes my heart hurt.

"Khoi. This is too much. I can't accept this."

"I'll come with you," he adds.

"No, don't," I say. "I can go by myself. You should stay here, work on Hello World." The submission deadline is this Friday, two days from now.

"Char, if this is about your stepdad—the one who gave you those bruises—then I think, for your safety, I should come with you." He takes my hands into his own. "You know I don't care about the money, right?"

But it's not about the money.

I don't want him to come to Chinook Shore. I don't want him to see the fist-sized hole in our living room wall, the empty beer cans littered on our kitchen counter, the overgrown weeds strangling a lawn nobody has bothered to maintain. I don't want him to see all the ugliness, all the shame.

Khoi and I can be together in this sparkling, hopeful place where everyone expects their future to be bubblegum pink. I don't know if we can be together elsewhere.

If he sees who I really am, and the horrible place I come from, he won't want to be with me anymore. He'll run away. I wouldn't even blame him.

But his expression is stony, determined. I can't fight him on this. And I can't afford to dawdle. I have to rescue Mom. Even if it means losing Khoi.

"Fine," I say. "Let's get on the next plane to Portland."

About nine hours later, Olive is waiting at Arrivals. She's driving Drew's dad's girlfriend's car—the same one that I used to kiss Drew in. It still has that same melted-crayon smell. I buckle myself into the passenger seat and ignore the torn condom wrapper in the cup holder. Khoi slides into the back.

"Hey, I think you might have a moth infestation," he says suddenly. "There's a little hole in this seat."

"That's a cigarette burn." My stepsister glances at him through the rearview mirror. "I'm Olive. Are you Char's boyfriend?"

He blushes. "Um, uh, I, we, uh—"

"We're figuring it out," I say.

"Okaaaaay." She turns her attention to the road. That's one great thing about Olive. She knows when to stop asking questions.

As we cruise down the freeway, Khoi tries to keep the convo alive. He exhausts all the usual small-talk topics: the weather, summer plans, college apps. Olive gives nothing but clipped, one-word answers, which doesn't deter him from firing off yet more questions. I have to respect the guy for trying, but like, c'mon. Read the room. Or the car, I guess.

After Khoi asks for her favorite math theorem, she's had it. Instead of answering, she cuts her eyes to me. "Does your mom know that you're coming?"

"Uh. No . . . I was scared to text. She wouldn't pick up any of my calls." I know Michael has full access to her phone. That never struck me as weird or controlling until recently. I wonder what other glaring red flags I missed.

She purses her lips. "Then what's the plan?"

Step 1: Distract Michael.

This is Khoi's role, since my stepfather won't recognize him. He suggests setting off firecrackers to lure Michael out of the house, but both Olive and I veto that idea. "He might come after you with a shotgun," I say.

Khoi laughs and then stops upon catching our faces in the rearview mirror. "Oh, you guys aren't joking."

It's surprisingly difficult to come up with a schtick that will buy a few minutes. Michael isn't big on politics, so posing as a canvasser won't work. Khoi isn't the right age or gender to be slinging Girl Scout cookies. And after I get him to do his best impression of a Jehovah's Witness? Let's just say that he should strongly consider other careers besides cult leader.

"Dad really likes to gamble," Olive says. "If you try to

convince him to take a crazy bet with huge upside, that could work."

So Khoi decides to spread the gospel of Bitcoin.

Step 2: Fetch Mom.

Olive pulls up a block away from the house. She's still got a key to the back, so while Khoi climbs the steps to our front door, I dip around. The doorbell rings, and then there are heavy footsteps from inside. The door opens and Michael hits him with, "Whaddya want, son?"

"Hi, sir! Do you have a few minutes to hear about a fantastic money-making opportunity?" Khoi's voice is plastic and two octaves higher than normal—a dead giveaway he's freaking out. But he powers on. " I'll give you this amazing twenty-dollar bill if you listen to my entire pitch."

"Why not."

Michael steps out onto the porch, and the front door closes.

I immediately unlock the back door and rush inside, not bothering to take off my shoes. Michael can scrub away whatever muddy footprints I leave behind. I hope they stain.

My mother's curled up in the master bedroom, swathed in blankets. The lights are off and the blinds are shut. Everything is bathed in a grayish gloom. The faint glow of the TV flickers against the wall. It's playing some C-drama on low volume, so the dialogue comes out muffled and distant. The air smells faintly of stale tea.

She looks listless and sad. Her hair hangs around her face in damp, limp strands. I can't recall the last time she seemed truly happy.

But when her eyes land on me, there's a spark of life. "Char? You can't be here. Michael will be upset."

"Get up. We need to go."

She pauses the show. Onscreen, Wang Yibo freezes mid-sentence. "What are you talking about?"

"Olive is parked around the corner. We have a plane ticket so you can come stay with me at MIT. But we have to go, *right now*."

"Why would I leave? I'm fine here." But she says it like she isn't sure she believes her own words.

"No. This is *not* fine." I gesture wildly at our surroundings. "This is not a life. Mom, when's the last time you even went outside? How long has he been keeping you in here?"

"I have to pack," she says. "Everything I have is here. I'm not ready at all."

"I *know* you're not ready." Frustration simmers in me. "It doesn't *matter*. Michael is keeping you trapped. This is fu—um, messed up. How do you not see that?"

"Stop," she says. Her eyes glimmer with tears. "Please stop."

"Mom. Right now, my—my *friend* is distracting Michael, but I don't know how long he's going to be able to do that. We have to run. We have to leave before Michael returns. *It isn't safe here.*"

She still isn't moving, so I pivot. "If you're not going to leave for yourself, leave for me. I can't ever be happy, even if I'm thousands of miles away, if you aren't safe."

"You can learn to be happy, Char," she says. "I'm so proud of you. And the new life you found for yourself. You're so brave. Unlike your old mother." She says it like she's on her deathbed, and it makes me want to cry.

"I'm not leaving until you leave too. And how do you think Michael is going to react if he sees me here, in his house, after he told me never to come back?" I fold my arms and stare her down.

Here we go. It's finally time to find out if she loves me enough to conquer her own fear.

Please, I silently beg. *Please, make the right choice*. Because if Michael actually catches my ass here, I don't know what he'll do. Not even Khoi will be able to save me from my stepfather's wrath.

After what feels like a century, she stands up. Relief floods me.

Without a word, she takes my hand and we're shadows, sneaking out of the bedroom and past the kitchen. She slides on her shoes and snags her purse.

"Leave your phone," I whisper. "He can track your location with it." Thank God Michael never cared enough to add me on Find My Friends.

"But—"

"Mom, we'll buy you a new one. Your data is uploaded to the cloud anyway. *Leave it.*"

After a pause, she unzips her purse and gently places her phone on the floor.

Just as we slip out the back, I hear the front door creak open.

Step 3: Run.

Chapter Thirty-Four

We book it at a full sprint. For a few moments nobody follows us, and I think maybe Michael won't notice my mom's gone before we reach the car.

But then there's a roar of anger and the back door flies open. I toss a glance over my shoulder and yep, it's my stepfather, gaining on us fast. My heart throbs in my ears.

Khoi is chasing after him. "Sir!" he yells. "Sir, I have more to tell you about Bitcoin!"

He ignores Khoi. Of course the one time I'm praying Michael gets sidetracked by sketchy financial advice, he wises up. "Char, I'm going to kill you, you bitch!" he shouts.

Khoi, like the absolute legend that he is, yanks off his lemon-yellow Croc and chucks it at Michael's head. And dude's got shockingly decent aim—it nails him right in the neck. My stepfather whirls around, more from surprise than actual pain.

Then Olive comes tearing round the corner and screeches to a halt in front of us.

I scramble for the door and shove my mother inside, then dive in after her.

"We can't leave Khoi!" I scream.

Olive slams her foot on the gas pedal and Khoi starts running in the opposite direction, away from Michael. We fly past my confused stepfather and meet Khoi in the middle of the street. He tumbles into the back seat.

I crane my neck to check the rear windshield. There's Michael, standing in a dim orange pool spilled by the streetlight. His face reminds me of a blinking cursor at the top of a blank file.

Then Olive's fully in her *Fast & Furious* era, lunging onto the main road, and I lose sight of him.

I don't remember how to breathe until we've blown past the WELCOME TO CHINOOK SHORE sign at the town limits. Khoi does this shaky half laugh, half sigh.

"You just. You just threw a Croc at my stepfather," I say.

He shrugs. "Hey, at least now I won't have to remove it during airport security."

I dissolve into giggles, more out of relief than anything else.

Step 4: Freedom.

We drive in heavy, stunned silence. Night has fallen. The sky is full bellied with clouds. Few cars pass us by. Flickering gold lights from distant small towns dot the horizon.

At one point, Khoi tries to strike up the same painful

small-talk convo with Mom, but quickly clams up after I hit him with a look.

Olive drops us off at the airport. Khoi and Mom hop out of the car but I linger. It feels like I need to say something to my stepsister.

"Thank you," I say. "You didn't have to help us."

"No, I did." She tries to play it chill, but her eyes betray fear. She's the one who has to handle Michael afterward. We'll be jetting off to the opposite coast.

My gut clenches.

"Come with us," I blurt out. I don't really know how this would go, since Olive is still a minor. Like, could my mom even get full custody? Whatever—that's a problem for future us.

She shakes her head. "Char, he's my father. I'm all he has." Olive's mother, his ex-wife, lives in Sicily with her new husband.

"He's dangerous. If he hurt me and my mom, he can hurt you too."

"I know. Do you think I don't know?" For a moment doubt flickers in her face, but then she seems to decide something. Her mouth straightens. Hardens. "I'll be fine. I'm turning eighteen in two months. And I can crash with Drew. Or maybe I'll hit up my mom in Italy."

Something shifts between us, some newfound understanding. We spent so long ignoring each other that I never saw it until now. Michael didn't just happen to my mom and me—he also happened to Olive. And we're luckier than her, maybe. At least we can actually ditch him. Carve him out from our lives like he's a malignant tumor.

No matter what Olive does, she'll always be shackled to Michael through blood.

"Take care of yourself," I say before stepping out. "You can always call me if you need anything."

She waves at us through the car window. "So I guess . . . have a nice life?"

It's weirdly underwhelming, like the ending of some bad Netflix movie. I feel like I should say something profound or poetic. *It's been an honor serving with you* stuff, but for a sister.

The only suggestion my brain coughs up is *What Disney princess nickname did Drew give you?* But bringing up the Mulan crap would kinda ruin the mood. Besides, Olive is totally an Aurora.

I wish I knew more about her.

We spent years living on top of each other, yet we're basically strangers. It's a real shame. Why *didn't* we try to bridge the gap between us?

But as I watch my stepsister's taillights wink into the darkness, the answer hits me. The reason, of course, is Michael.

Mom barely says a word during the whole flight and taxi ride to campus. I keep sneaking glances at her, trying to figure out what's happening in her head, but her face is a blank slate. Meanwhile, Khoi is on high alert, constantly reaching for my hand like he's scared I'll go *poof*.

We finally roll up to Simmons at eight a.m. Khoi crashes in his own room. I show my mother to mine and we both pass out cold.

When I wake, it's early evening. Golden-hour light filters through the windows, painting a yellow grid on the floor. Mom is still knocked out, so I tiptoe outside to find Khoi in his room. He's awash in the bluish glow of his laptop. There's a crease between his brows that only appears when he's intensely debugging.

And I've seen Khoi code a thousand times before, but for some reason, my heart does this stupid little somersault.

"When did you wake up?" I ask.

His eyes dart to my face, then back to his screen. "Not too long ago. I got a notification saying our most recent deployment failed. Throwing some build error . . ."

I sit. Should we even talk about what went down in Chinook Shore? Maybe now that Khoi has met Michael, now that he has truly seen the Chernobyl-grade meltdown that is my family, he's ready to bounce.

I want to run far, far away from this ugliness. The thought of Khoi knowing everything makes my stomach churn. He is so pure and kind and sweet and I'm scared to drag him into this chaos.

But I have to say something. I have to let him know that I see it—this enormous gift he's given me.

"Thank you," I say. "For buying the flights to Oregon. For standing up to Michael. For helping me with my mom."

It doesn't feel like enough. I don't know how to express my gratitude. I mean, the kid basically saved my life. I don't know if I'll ever deserve this boy.

I misjudged him before. He's soft, but he's no coward. Khoi freakin' Astor.

Khoi freakin' Astor who can't ever stay in his own damn lane, but maybe that's one of the best things about him.

He sets his laptop down and turns to me. "Char. I will *always* be there for you." His eyes are so wide and sincere.

There's a familiar swell in my throat.

Nobody has ever told me that before. And I've never believed anybody ever would be there for me.

I wish Khoi was less . . . good. I wish he could say something cruel. I wish he would see everything that is broken within me and nope out. Because at least I would know how to deal with that.

I don't know how to not ruin this.

I swallow hard. "Tell me more about the error."

Chapter Thirty-Five

After dinner, I sneak some leftovers upstairs for Mom. "Sorry, there weren't that many . . ." I try to recall how to say *lactose-free* in Mandarin. "No-milk options." The plate is piled high with items from the salad bar. In English, I add, "It was mac and cheese night."

"Char, you shouldn't have to do this," she says. "I'm your mother. Why are you taking care of me?"

I don't get why she's picking *now* to suddenly feel guilty. Maybe if she'd cared this much years ago, we wouldn't be in this mess. No, I'm being unfair. I lift a shoulder noncommittally. "I have to go work."

Khoi and I camp out in his room. Obi's gone—his squad has been grinding long nights at the student center. Obi says it's because the Wi-Fi is marginally faster there, but honestly, I think they just want to be within refill range of the boba shop.

We're *this close* to hitting submit.

I want to check Hello World's responsiveness on larger screens, so I slide over to his desk to hook my laptop up to his monitor. As I reach for the HDMI cable, my knuckles knock into an orange pill bottle that feels surprisingly light.

I squint. The label says levetiracetam—Keppra, his seizure meds. There are no pills inside. "Khoi, why is your medication empty?"

"I ran out a few days ago. I was going to visit the pharmacy for a refill yesterday, but we went to Oregon instead," he says. "And then I had a very busy schedule today, with all the sleeping and whatnot. I'll get it tomorrow."

"Is that safe?" I'm no doctor, but I'm pretty sure meds need to be taken regularly.

"It's whatever."

He kisses me, and even though I know it's his way of shutting down the convo, I kiss him back. His lips are tender, then urgent. Something within me uncoils. Something that used to be tight and pinchy.

I dip my hands beneath his shirt. He gasps as my fingers trace the skin of his abdomen. I didn't know a boy could sound so—vulnerable. My body responds with a desperate stirring, almost a howl.

Edvin Nilsen said I should focus, stay sharp.

Edvin Nilsen can go kick rocks.

"Let's go to your bed," I murmur into his mouth.

He steps away and searches my face. "Char. You sure? I know you said no distractions . . ."

"I want to be with you," I say. "If you're ready."

He hesitates, and my heart lurches. Maybe I'm asking for too much. Maybe I totally misread him. Maybe, after everything, he doesn't want to be with a train wreck like me.

Then he says, "Um, I didn't think we'd get this far, so I didn't do any research or . . ."

And I'm tempted to smack him.

"Khoi. Do you think I give a fuck? I just want you." I swear, he better not whip out his phone to ask ChatGPT for top-ten best sex tips.

To distract him from any AI-related shenanigans, I close the distance between us, pressing my body against his. His eyes darken with desire. They look like molten glass. "I want you too," he says. "You're . . . everything. I'm so lucky."

No, I'm the lucky one, I want to say, but I don't get a chance before he drags me into another kiss. This time, he doesn't let go.

Afterward, we're sprawled on his twin XL, both naked. My head rests on his chest, rising and falling with his breath. My fingers trace the secrets of his skin, each tiny new miracle I've discovered in the last hour. The mole on his hip. A small scar on his inner thigh from a bike injury in Vietnam when he was eight. I want to memorize every inch of him.

He's stroking my hair, slow and deliberate, and it sends shivers down my spine. I don't recall the last time I felt this calm, this safe. I want to scoop this moment into a glass jar and live in it forever.

Out of nowhere, he drops the question: "Why won't you be my girlfriend?"

Just like that, the peace has been shattered.

I roll onto my back and gaze at the ceiling as if the answer to his question might be written up there. "Dude. This program ends in, like, three days."

"So? You're not returning to Chinook Shore, right? Char, you *can't* go back." He props himself up on one elbow and stares me down.

"Chill. I'm not going back." Mom and I need to put as many time zones between ourselves and Michael as possible. Heck, maybe we should go to the moon. One of those space-obsessed billionaires must have an extra seat on their rocket ship. "But I can't commit to a romantic relationship. That's just not a priority right now."

"I'm not a priority to you?" His voice is small.

I swallow my sudden irritation. "That's not what I meant. Obviously you're important to me, Khoi. But I don't know where my mom and I are even going to live."

"You guys can get a hotel around here," he says, like someone who thinks Hilton rewards points grow on trees.

I know he wants me to stick around Boston even though we have zero ties here. No housing, no job opportunities, no community that might help us get those things. (If only Hello World were a real app with users, and not a hackathon project.)

I could fight him on it. I could pull up whatever bank

accounts Mom and I can still access, whip out an Excel spreadsheet, really drill it into his head that *we're too broke for this zip code*.

But I don't *want* to argue. Not now. Not after he's been so kind, and definitely not before the final presentations on Saturday.

I sit up and reach for my clothes, which are wadded up in the corner of his bed. "Let's just try to win this damn thing."

Chapter Thirty-Six

Friday morning, Khoi's all moody and quiet, and I know that he's still upset over the girlfriend thing. Part of me wants to call him out for being unfair. That he doesn't understand what it's like to constantly be in survival mode.

But the smarter part of me knows when to shut up. We're hours away from the finish line. I'm not about to mess up our chances at winning by getting into it with my teammate.

Sitting in Khoi's room, we upload links to our GitHub repository and a video demo. An entire summer's worth of work concluded with a silent button click. The final project submission deadline comes and goes.

I don't know. I was sorta hoping for something more dramatic, something more eleventh-hour. Like somebody throttling the Wi-Fi network to sabotage the competition. Code getting leaked. A fistfight over server space. Some rogue drone crashing through the window.

But no. All I get is the spinning rainbow wheel of doom while we upload our submission.

Afterward, the rest of the camp heads to Chinatown to celebrate with karaoke, but Khoi bails, saying that he's tired. I join everyone else in screaming our lungs out to "Mr. Brightside" and try not to think about what's coming this weekend.

Saturday rolls around, and we've got a midmorning slot to present in front of the judging panel. When Khoi and I meet in his room to practice beforehand, he looks off. His face is hollow and pale, as if he hasn't slept a wink.

"You good?" I ask as he fiddles with his monitor screens.

"Hmm?" His reaction time is sluggish too. "Yeah."

Something occurs to me. "Did you end up refilling your medication?"

"Not yet," he mumbles.

"*Khoi.*" I check my phone for the time. There's still an hour before we have to meet the judges. "Is the pharmacy open on Saturdays? Do you want to do it now?"

"After our presentation." He shakes his head.

"We have time to get your meds."

"We should try to win," he says. "I thought that was *important* to you? I thought that's all you cared about?"

Okay, that's enough. "Grow up," I snap. "What are you expecting me to do? Right now this contest is my only chance at securing a better life for myself and my mom. And if you're too immature to get that, then maybe we *shouldn't* be together."

He's silent, and for a moment I think I've gone too far. I didn't really mean that. I don't want to break up.

God, of course I had to go and ruin things.

But then he crumples onto his desk and an unnatural spasm shudders through his body, like his muscles are at war with each other.

I rush over. "Khoi? Khoi!"

He doesn't respond. I don't even think he's conscious. His face is stiff except for this horrible gurgling sound that oozes from his mouth. Even though I've never seen a seizure before, I'm deathly sure that's what this is.

Fuck. Fuck. He never told me what to do in this situation. But I should've asked.

Should I turn him on his side to ensure he doesn't choke on his own vomit? Or is that only for drunk people? Do people even vomit during seizures? I hate myself for not knowing. God, I need an actual adult right now. My mom is down the hall, but let's be real. In a medical crisis, she's not much better than Reddit.

With trembling hands, I dial 911.

By the time the EMTs arrive, Khoi's stopped jerking, thank God, although he's still out cold. As one of them checks his vitals with easy confidence, the other asks me how long he was seizing for.

"Um, maybe a few minutes?" It felt like forever to me. I feel like an idiot for not having a better answer. Why didn't I think to time the seizure?

"If it was longer than five minutes, it's considered to be *status epilepticus*, which can be life-threatening."

The word *life-threatening* makes my stomach knot up, and I force myself to take several deep breaths. I have to keep my shit together. For Khoi.

They say he'll probably be fine as long as he gets back on his meds—withdrawal seizures are a common side effect of missing multiple doses of Keppra—but they want to whisk him to urgent care just in case. The paramedics let me ride in the ambulance and I hold his hand the entire time. At least his breathing has steadied. He looks so small and pale on the cot, like a porcelain doll, and it makes me want to never let go.

Once we arrive, they disappear with him in the back and I collapse in the waiting room. My entire body is vibrating with anxiety.

The dude next to me, who's definitely old enough to be my dad, shoots me a low-key flirty look. Yeah, no thanks. Maybe it's an overreaction, but I bounce to the other side of the room. Not today, sir.

Ugh. I feel so useless. There's nothing I can do for Khoi. I can't even call his aunt and uncle to let them know about what happened because I don't have their phone numbers. I think MIT Medical might be taking care of that.

No, wait. There is something I need to do.

The clock's ticking. We've got, like, ten minutes before we're supposed to present. I should tell the judges that we had a medical emergency and can't make it anymore. Beg for a do-over slot later. So I call HellomynameisCourtney.

"Hello?" Her voice is crisp, efficient. Like metal scraping against metal.

"This is Charise Tang, I'm in Alpha Fellows, my team is supposed to be presenting, like, right now, but we're going to miss our time slot, my teammate Khoi Astor, he suddenly had a seizure . . ." The words tumble out all piled up.

"Charise. Charise. Take a deep breath."

I oblige, but it doesn't calm me down much.

"Great. Now, is he okay?" she asks sharply.

"I don't know." I haven't even had time to doomscroll WebMD. "He hasn't been taking his medication."

A horrible thought hits me. What if the last thing he ever hears is me saying that we shouldn't be together? No, I'm spiraling. The paramedics said he'd be fine. And people don't just die from seizures. I think. But what if they do? I don't know anything about this. I should've asked him more about his condition. Why did I never ask? It's such a huge part of his life. He didn't seem to want to talk about it . . . but maybe I'm just making excuses for my awfulness.

"I'm very sorry to hear that," she says. "Health takes priority, of course."

"But the presentation?" I feel shitty for even asking, but I have to know.

"Well, you're perfectly fine, right?"

The implication is obvious, but I want Khoi there too. I don't want him to miss out on this, especially when he poured so much of his soul into Hello World.

Plus . . . I don't know if I can do it by myself. Without him.

"They might let him out soon," I say. "They're just, uh, observing him?" Like he's a goldfish in a fish tank. "What if we presented later?"

"Unfortunately our schedule is tight and we won't be able to allocate a different time slot to your team," she says. "You have to present by yourself or not at all."

"Please—"

"Charise, it's eight minutes to ten," she says. "If you don't want all your hard work this summer to go to waste, I suggest you go *right now*. If not for yourself, then for your teammate."

Then she hangs up and I free-fall into panic.

I hurtle through the hallway, trying to figure out where the hell the actual judging room is.

I've been through this set of doors before. I've passed by this bathroom like three times already. But the mythical final boss room? Nowhere to be seen.

I wave at a random nearby college student. "Hi hi! Do you know where this is?" I show her the room number from the Alpha Fellows portal.

"Oh, that's on the other side of the building," she says. "So, the way Stata is designed, there are multiple towers, and you can't cross to one from another on this floor. You should take the elevator down to the first floor and then try the west side."

It's giving *The princess is in another castle!*

She sees my disappointment and shoots me a sympathetic smile. "It's confusing, but kinda fun?"

We have very different definitions of fun. I thank her and rush toward the elevator, which is just about to close as I dive inside. Inside is a dude and his metal dog that growls at me when my calf brushes against its snout. Lovely. Now even the robots hate me. When the AI uprising happens, I'll be at the top of the kill list. Me and anyone who's ever kicked a Roomba.

As the elevator zips toward the ground floor, I check the time on my phone. Already two minutes past ten.

Three minutes later, I breathlessly trip into the room. The three judges, all men, are seated at the front. One of them—a guy rocking a mullet and Birkenstocks combo—gives me a look like I just showed up late to my own funeral.

Edvin Nilsen is chilling in the corner. He grins at me. I smile back, relieved to see at least one friendly face.

"Glad you could make it," another judge says. "Your app is Hello World, right? Courtney informed us of your teammate's medical emergency. I hope he's all right." His words come out rapid-fire, like he's mainlined a triple shot of espresso.

"Yep, that's us." I get my laptop and link it to the HDMI cable at the podium. Our slides pop up on the screen in full color, and suddenly it all feels so much more real. This is it. The home stretch.

I wish Khoi were next to me. It'd be less intimidating to face down this room of all dudes. He'd be rizzing up the judges, joking about their favorite Elon Musk tweets or fanboying over the latest gadget in *TechCrunch* or whatever.

But more importantly, he put in the work. Tweaked CSS pixel by pixel, wrestled with API calls, crawled through Stack Overflow rabbit holes. He should be standing up here, too.

But I don't have time to dwell. The judges are staring expectantly. I clear my throat. "Hi—hello. I'm Charise Tang. I'm from Chinook Shore."

The Birkenstocks dude frowns. "Where is Shinoo Shore?" He says the name like it's gibberish. It's especially annoying because Chinook is an Indigenous word.

"Chinook Shore. It's on the Oregon coast, an hour or two away from Portland."

He does this half grunt. "Never heard of it."

It's a small town, for sure. The job opportunities aren't gilded with money and prestige the way they might be in Silicon Valley or Manhattan. But that doesn't mean that the people who live there don't dream as brightly and love as ferociously as they would anywhere else.

I *know* that. But some part of me still wishes I were from a specialized STEM magnet school, or a posh New England boarding school, or an intense Bay Area public school. Some place that would automatically let people know that I am smart and tough and capable.

I swallow. "Um, right. So both Khoi and I have immigrant parents. We both know the struggle of finding solid footing in a country that doesn't understand you. So we decided to build Hello World—an app for newcomers to America to connect with one another and discover community."

I flip through some of our Figma designs, highlighting my favorite features—the language toggle button, the automatic discovery based on geotagging.

"I don't know," one judge cuts in. "It looks cluttered."

I blink. "Oh. How do you mean?"

"Well, you don't have that much white space. And there isn't a lot of attention paid to text hierarchy. You could've just used a search feature instead of automatic discovery."

I want to tell him that Chinese apps don't look the same as American ones. That search engines in other languages are often hard to navigate. That just because our app doesn't look like the ones he uses every day doesn't mean that it's inferior.

But I'm pretty sure we're not supposed to argue about feedback.

"Um, okay." I move on to the next slide, which describes our back end. Khoi was supposed to present this part.

It's this stereotype in tech that girls gravitate toward "softer" design and front-end work, while guys do the more "hardcore" stuff in the back end. But I worked on the back end just as much as he did. I hooked everything up to our databases, I wrote the search algorithms.

But maybe that judge's comment threw me off my flow, because now I'm second-guessing how good I'll be at explaining this slide. God, I wish Khoi was here right now.

No. I *know* our project. I've spent weeks mucking elbow-deep in this code. I've debugged at three a.m., I've fine-tuned models for language translation, I've read research papers on performance optimizations, I've dreamed in SQL queries. I'm just as good as the dudebros here who don't shower. No, better. Because I also shower.

And I can't mess this up for Khoi, either. He deserves a shot at the top prize.

I dig into some of the technical difficulties and questions we considered while building. A few slides flash by, but to be honest, they're not visually interesting—just snippets of code to explain our ideas.

Once I reach the end, one of the judges asks, "Great. Now here's a question for you. Why do you think you deserve to win?"

I stare at him. My mind feels so blank. Truth is, I don't know if we deserve to win. Our project is cool but all the other projects are amazing too. Well, maybe not *all* of them. I think that one guy who wants multiple girlfriends built a polyamorous version of Tinder.

Anyway, I'm not sure what makes us special. We don't incorporate any groundbreaking technology, and we aren't using blockchain or whatever the latest buzzword is. Our algorithm isn't particularly sophisticated—just filtered searches with some basic recommendation logic. Most decent mobile programmers could make something similar.

But then I think about my mom, about the times she wished she had someone to ask about American school forms or credit card applications. About Lola's mom struggling through health care paperwork in English. About all the families like ours, stumbling into vast, faceless systems that weren't built for them.

"Hello World has the potential to be a lot more. If it were launched as an actual platform for immigrants, it could help so many people."

Edvin Nilsen nods, like he totally buys into the vision. The actual judges seem confused.

"Did you raise venture capital already?" one of them asks. "Because if you did, that would be in violation of the competition rules."

I blink. "Uh, no?"

"So are you planning on making this a real app?"

"Uh . . ." Khoi and I haven't discussed that at all. That sounds like exactly the sort of conversation that would lead to talking about the Future™, which is, like, the problem in our relationship right now. "Maybe?"

I can tell from their expressions that this is the wrong answer. My heart plummets. Maybe I should've bullshitted about blockchain instead.

Did I just kill our chances at winning?

"Sounds good," another judge says after a beat. "Well, this was a pleasure. Hope your teammate feels better soon."

I might thank them. I'm not sure. My mind is all a jumble. And as I walk out of the room, my legs feel like lead.

After the presentation, my phone is all lit up with notifications. There's a flurry of texts from Khoi, fresh out of MIT Medical, spamming apologies for missing the presentation. I've never seen someone use that many loudly crying emojis in a row.

My thumbs freeze over the blank text box as I try to figure out what to say. I want to check in about his health, but once we start a back-and-forth, he's going to ask about how things went. And I don't want to admit that I blew it.

But before I can type a word, he double texts that he's going to hit the Walgreens pharmacy and then crash before the awards ceremony.

I go back to the dorm and start packing up. We have to check out tomorrow. Mom is nowhere to be found—who knows where she disappeared off to. I don't put too many brain cells toward that. I'm too busy freaking out about, like, survival stuff.

So yeah. I flubbed the presentation and we're not winning. No, maybe we still have a shot. We got first place on the second checkpoint and our test scores on the first checkpoint were decent. The final score is based on all three. But I'm not counting on that. That's like buying a lottery ticket as your retirement plan.

What are Mom and I going to do?

When I was six, we stayed at a shelter for a little while. Not sure how we ended up there. It might've been around the time her boyfriend Zhao got deported and we had to move out of his apartment.

It's been a decade, so my memories of the shelter are fuzzy. Besides the constant noise and occasional fights between grown-ass women, it was kinda fun. There were other kids around, so it was like a never-ending sleepover. We had these chaotic Wii bowling tournaments. But after, like, two weeks, Mom caught me playing with an empty syringe I found on the ground, and the next day we moved in with one of her grad school classmates.

I'm not six years old anymore, so maybe we can give a women's shelter another shot.

I spend the next few hours packing our things and researching nearby options. There are eight shelters in the Boston area and I call up each one. But they're all full. And the receptionist at Roxbury Sanctuary hears my surname and starts ranting about how "you people eat raw bats and bring disease everywhere."

I resist the urge to tell her that I like my bats sautéed, thank you very much.

Anyway, so that's a total bust. I guess we're sleeping on the sidewalk tomorrow night. Maybe I should dig through the recycling to snag the comfiest piece of cardboard.

But I can't keep fretting over this, because the award ceremony is at four. At three fifty I go to Khoi's room and shake him awake. He's bleary eyed and I feel bad for disrupting his nap.

"How are you feeling?" I ask.

He goes, "Hnnnnrgh."

"Do you need anything from me?"

"Grrrrrmf."

Despite my many years living with Michael, I'm not fluent in Neanderthal. I give up on the conversation. But I get Khoi dressed and out the door, so that's a win.

When we sneak into Kresge auditorium, Hellomynameis-Courtney is already onstage, so we sit down quietly in the back.

"This year we had nearly forty wonderful entries," she's saying. She goes on about how each submission was marvelous and so impressive for something hacked together in one summer. How we're the next generation of leaders, which is honestly terrifying, considering some of the kids I met this summer.

"But enough about that. Here's what you've all been waiting for. I'm so excited to present this year's winners."

She goes through the special sponsored awards. There're some pretty big names here—Apple gives out a Best Hardware prize, and Oculus has something for virtual reality. The twins win scholarships from Niantic, the company that makes Pokémon Go. For her app that generates outfit ideas using diffusion models, Stella snags a cash prize from OpenAI. Even Haru gets recognized for his anonymous compliments app.

Then it's time for the overall winner, and there's this insane electricity in the air—that heart-pounding, forgetting-to-breathe anticipation. And even though I logically know the odds are against us, I can't help but hope.

Because if we win, it would solve all my problems.

HellomynameisCourtney removes a card from an envelope and reads, "The grand winner of this year's Alpha Fellows hackathon is the team comprising of Obi Udechukwu, Diego Rodriguez, and Jenni Wheeler for an innovative portable solar power generator."

Of course.

I mean, it's not surprising. And I know I should be happy for my friends. They deserve the win. But . . . fuck. What am I going to do now?

My heart hurts.

Next to me, Khoi slumps down in his seat.

Obi rushes to the stage, pumping his fists in the air like an Olympic runner doing a victory lap, and wraps HellomynameisCourtney in a bear hug, which makes everyone laugh. Diego and Jenni-with-an-i follow with slightly embarrassed expressions. Cameras flash.

I force myself to applaud even though I feel sick.

After the team returns to their seats lugging their huge, one-hundred-thousand-dollar cardboard check, the room quiets down again.

"I say this every time, but it remains true year after year—I'm so blown away by your creativity and dedication," HellomynameisCourtney says. "It's been an honor to host a hundred of the nation's brightest young minds this summer. In a world where technology is so often used for frivolous or downright dangerous affairs, I urge you to apply your talents to building a better future for all. I hope to see every single one of you again."

Chapter Thirty-Seven

After the ceremony, Khoi stands up and mumbles he's going to step outside for fresh air. He still seems frail.

I stand too. "Do you want me to go with you?"

"No, I think . . . I think I want to be alone," he says. His voice is hollow with disappointment. I wonder if he blames himself for our loss. I should reassure him, but he's gone before I can find the right words.

And I know it's bad, but a tiny part of me also thinks he could've been more responsible about taking his meds.

People swarm the winning team. Obi serves face for every camera like it's a *Vogue* cover shoot, while Jenni-with-an-i looks mildly terrified. I should go up and congratulate them too, but my limbs feel frozen. I'm standing near the wall alone, trying to think past my panic, when Edvin Nilsen materializes out of nowhere like some ninja.

"Sorry you didn't win," he says. He doesn't sound very sorry.

Even though I'm in no mood for conversation, I say, "Thanks

for your advice this summer." It was generous of him to come through with so much help, even if we took an L in the end.

"You might like to know that I was very impressed with Hello World," he says. "You've achieved something incredible at any age, let alone as a teenager."

I shrug. Sure, praise is cute, but praise isn't going to rent an apartment or pay the bills.

"What are your plans after this? Are you going to return to Chinook Beach?"

I don't bother correcting him. "I'm not sure." Alpha Fellows hooked me up with a flight back to Portland, but keeping a thousand-mile radius from Michael is probably the move.

"You won't be able to cultivate your talent to its full potential if you stay in Oregon," he says.

I nod, barely listening. Honestly, I'm not that pressed about reaching my *full potential*. If my mom and I starve on the streets, there won't be any potential to reach.

He continues, "I've spoken to my board. After some careful deliberation, we have a proposal for you."

"What proposal?"

"Nexus is starting an incubator program. We want to invite Hello World to be part of our first cohort. You'd spend the next six months working out of our office to make it into something more than a prototype. Our team will mentor you, connect you with people who can help you succeed."

What's he on about? "Edvin, I haven't graduated high school

yet." Khoi has told me about accelerators such as Y Combinator. They're like a professional version of Alpha Fellows. Rich tech bros throw money at not-yet-rich tech bros, praying that someone's going to pop off and become Snapchat 2.0 or whatever. But those programs are for, like, Harvard dropouts. Not kids like me.

"So?" He lifts a shoulder. "Leave. And we'd give you housing and a living stipend, of course. How does that sound?"

It sounds incredible. It sounds like the solution to all my problems. It sounds too good to be legit.

I blink. "You're serious?"

He nods. "Char, you're too smart to waste away in Oregon." He has this intense look that makes me feel like I could take on the whole world as long as he's got my back.

And if there's anything I've learned this summer, it's that having someone who's got your back is a total game changer.

Maybe the universe isn't always out to screw me.

Maybe this is real.

Something light and sparkly ripples through my whole being. Hope.

I want to agree immediately, but . . .

"I need to talk to Khoi," I say. It's his app too.

"Sure, talk to him," Edvin says. "But give me your decision within the next hour. We have a press conference tomorrow announcing this program and I want to show you off as Patient Zero. Let's get this done fast."

• • •

I find Khoi outside near the river. He's gazing at the Charles, which shimmers in the late-summer light. The breeze ruffles his dark hair. He reminds me of a painting, something with careful brushstrokes.

When he sees me, he presses a kiss to my forehead. "I'm sorry we didn't win, Char."

"It wasn't your fault." Okay, it was, a little. But I also goofed on the presentation. So I guess it's on both of us.

Anyway, it doesn't matter if we're doing the Nexus incubator program.

"I should've been better about taking Keppra. I know you really needed the win. I'll do whatever it takes to make sure you and your mother are fine."

There are shadowy rings beneath his eyes. He's clearly exhausted. He just had a seizure. Maybe I shouldn't bring this up right now . . .

But Edvin said he wanted our response ASAP.

"Listen, Edvin Nilsen came up to me," I say. "He wants us to join his incubator program. It starts in September. We'd work out of the Nexus office, keep building Hello World."

I'm expecting him to crack a relieved smile. But nope. He frowns. "What about school?"

"We could drop out. That's what Edvin suggested."

He crosses his arms. "First he got you to ditch the SAT, now he wants you to leave high school? Char, what are you going to do if he decides he no longer wants to help you? You can't put yourself in a position where your future depends on his goodwill."

"Why do you hate Edvin so much?" The question sounds whiny, even to myself.

"I don't hate *him*. I don't even know him. But his company, Nexus, has these contracts with Homeland Security. You know what they do to immigrants? Do you truly think they'd be a good partner for Hello World?"

Annoyance spikes in me. "Khoi, does it matter? I don't have any options left."

"You don't need Edvin Nilsen. I've got you. Come crash with my aunt and uncle. Our house has plenty of room. It'll be fun. You can start senior year with me. We can get detention together. Make out in detention."

I know he's trying to be lighthearted, but his joke only makes me feel worse. He's not taking this seriously. He doesn't get it. After tomorrow, my mom and I might actually be out on the streets.

How would he get it? He's always had money and family to fall back on. Even when his dad went to jail, he had a home with his aunt and uncle.

"Do you not see the irony in asking me to not rely on Edvin and asking me to rely on you instead?" Mom spent her entire life believing in the empty promises of her romantic partners and look where that got her.

He blurts, "Well, unlike him, I actually love you!"

Then a heavy pause as we stare at each other in shock.

Love. My brain glitches out. The silly, frilly-pink part of me, the part that believes in Disney endings, wants to squeal into a pillow. *He loves me!* He loves me. He's seen the clusterfuck that is my life and he still loves me.

But the other part of me is smart.

His eyes are round and sincere. I know he believes completely in what he is saying. I wish I could believe him too.

I fight to keep my voice steady. "You said you'd do whatever it takes to help me. So let's sign with Edvin."

Hurt sweeps over his face. "I just said that I love you and you're acting like this is a business negotiation."

"This is so much more important than our relationship, okay?"

"Do you love me too?" he asks.

I can't have this conversation right now. I just can't. All I manage is, "Khoi."

"Char, I love you," he repeats.

"Khoi, don't . . ." But I stop talking. I don't know what I'm trying to say.

And then there's this awful, unbearable silence between us, with only bird chirps from somewhere above and faint chatter from faraway tourists.

After an eternity, he nods, like this is enough of an answer. Something in his eyes switches off.

His voice comes out low. "The app is all yours. We never drafted any contract about how ownership was split—you can keep everything, I don't care. Do what you want."

"That's not what I was asking for. I don't want sole ownership." I want to join the incubator, but I want to do it with Khoi by my side.

"But that's what I'm giving you." He inhales hard. "Take everything. We're done."

He doesn't mean that. He can't mean that. I reach for his hand but he steps away from me.

"Good luck, Char," he says. "I really hope you get everything you want. I truly mean it."

He whips on his heel. I stand helplessly and watch him walk away. The distance between us grows and grows until he disappears into a building.

An abyss yawns within me, and if I'm not careful, I might slip and fall forever.

Chapter Thirty-Eight

Everything aches. Even breathing hurts. I don't want to move. All I want to do is curl up on the grass until I fossilize. Maybe MIT scientists could study me. *Here, we have the world's first specimen of* homo heartbreakus . . .

But I don't have time to mope. I have to track down Edvin Nilsen and agree to join his program.

I walk back to Kresge, where the Alpha Fellows and their families are fanned out on the lawn. Stella pops a small wave at me, which I return. Jenni-with-an-i is posing with the cartoonishly giant check while her parents snap photos. Haru is lingering nearby with this embarrassingly lovesick expression. The twins are playing some game that involves kicking the crap out of each other's shins. Everyone seems drunk on sunshine.

Edvin is chatting with Obi and a Black woman who might be Obi's mother, but when he sees me, he excuses himself. "Char! Have you given the offer more thought?"

My heart speeds up. This is it. If I agree, there's no going back.

Goodbye, Khoi.

"Yes, I'll join," I say. "Thank you for giving me a chance." He's truly saving my life. "Quick question. Um, I don't have Boston housing after tomorrow. Do you know if Nexus could help with that?"

He blinks, confused. "You don't want to return to Oregon first? We weren't planning to onboard you for another few weeks. We need to finalize the entire cohort, and then you'd all start in September."

I'm not about to explain my family drama. "Maybe you could give me an advance payment on the stipend, and I can use it until the program starts?"

"Char. Don't sweat it. If you need a place to stay tomorrow, we can put you up in a hotel for several days."

There. Problem fixed in two seconds. I nod like this is no biggie, like his help isn't the only thing standing between us and the five-star hotel known as a park bench.

Having money must be like playing life on easy mode.

Edvin wants to meet in the Marriott tomorrow to do paperwork before the press conference. Since I'm not yet eighteen, my mother will have to sign too. We discuss a few more details, and then he excuses himself to shake more hands.

I scan the lawn. Everyone is with their parents, their families. Shouldn't the Astors be here? Surely Khoi's aunt and uncle would pull up. They live so close. But Khoi is nowhere. He's simply gone.

· · ·

When I get to the dorm, Mom is back. She says that she spent the day walking into restaurants and asking for a job. She's starting as a dishwasher at P.F. Chang's on Monday.

"At the library, I made a Facebook account and reached out to friends from grad school, but none of them have responded yet. I can't blame them. It's been years since we've spoken. I'm sorry that I can't do better, *baobei*."

She doesn't need to stress about our short-term logistics. "It's okay. I figured it out." I tell her about Edvin Nilsen and the Nexus incubator program.

"What about Khoi?" she asks. "Is he doing the program too?"

I shrug. "Nah. We broke up."

"Are you okay?" She tries to hug me, but I duck away.

"It's whatever. It was just a summer fling, and now the summer's over." I don't want to get into this with Mom, so I change the topic. "But hey, don't worry about housing. Edvin said he's going to put us up in a hotel."

I'm expecting her to be happy, but her eyes glitter with tears. "I feel like a failure. What sort of example did I set for my daughter? I'm forty years old. I don't have a job to support you. I don't even have a home for you to go back to."

If I weren't so wrecked, I would probably comfort her. Shrug, say it's fine, I've got everything under control. But I'm already barely keeping it together. So all I do is nod.

Besides, maybe she's right. She should've done better. I don't want to be too mean about it, but like, she hasn't been much of a mom recently.

Anyway, I should know not to rely on anybody else. I was straight-up delusional letting myself trust Khoi like that.

I spend most of the night staring at the ceiling, going through our last conversation like it's an infinite loop. Why doesn't he get why I had to go with Edvin? Is he really so stuck in his bubble of privilege that he can't see how this deal might be life-changing for me? And why did he have to pick *that* moment to say he loved me? God.

And it was so freaking unfair how he expected me to say it back! Like, sorry, bro, I have bigger problems here. It's like he thinks this is a fluffy romantic K-drama and I'm out here trying to survive *Squid Game*.

I can't even muster the energy for anger anymore. There's only this emptiness, like somebody has excavated my insides with a fork.

I never fall asleep. Morning arrives silently, buttery sunshine spilling through the crack between the windowsill and the pull-down blind.

My meeting with Edvin is at nine in the conference of the Kendall Square Marriott. The hotel is wedged between a bunch of biotech startups and AI research labs. Mom and I post up in the lobby. She gives me a wide berth so I can look more independent, more adult.

As I wait, my eyes fall on the television mounted on the wall. The digital clock at the bottom of the screen says it's 8:54 a.m. On TV, there's a news anchor speaking into the camera—*boring*—and I'm about to look away when the news ticker catches my attention.

DEFENSE COMPANY NEXUS ENABLING ICE IMMIGRATION RAIDS.

As a video of an arrest plays, a female voiceover says, "Recent government documents have revealed Nexus's role in aiding Immigration and Customs Enforcement agents by providing software that identified the whereabouts of undocumented people. To date, ICE has arrested over a thousand people with Nexus's help."

Onscreen, there's someone with a blurred-out face being led away in handcuffs. And even though I intellectually know the blur is *good*, that they deserve their anonymity, that they don't need their face blasted all over the news, it still hurts. Like this person isn't even a person anymore.

It feels like somebody just stabbed me in the solar plexus.

Suddenly everything that Khoi said about Edvin Nilsen makes sense. The defense contracts. *Do you truly think they'd be a good partner for Hello World?*

There's the *ding* of an elevator, and Edvin's assistant, Janelle Lim, strolls toward me with a clipboard.

"Char? Come upstairs. Mr. Nilsen is ready to see you now." Then she sees my face. "What's wrong?"

I can't muster the words, but she glances at the television screen and does this *oh, dear* kind of sigh. "Oh. That."

Her nonchalant attitude makes me blurt, "How can you work for a company that does this?"

"The media blows things out of proportion," she says. "They thrive off sensationalism."

So she's not outright denying it. "So you guys *are* helping with . . ." I wave at the television screen. "Whatever the hell this is." When she says nothing, I add, "My mom is an immigrant." And Janelle is Asian too.

"They aren't like us, Char." Janelle fiddles with her glasses. "They came here illegally. Our parents came here the *right* way."

"I don't think we're all that different," I say, thinking about the people I interviewed while doing product research for Hello World. The lady from Venezuela who sobbed because she couldn't go back to see her sick mother. Or the guy who crossed the border by himself at age fourteen.

The people in my own life. Lola's mom is undocumented. My mother only got her citizenship through marriage.

If I sign with Edvin, am I betraying all of them?

I want to hurl.

She shrugs, her face impassive. "You shouldn't make any rash decisions here. Working with Mr. Nilsen could be very good for your career."

She's not wrong. I need the cash and the clout. I need the safety net that comes with being all buddy-buddy with a billionaire like Edvin Nilsen.

I wonder why aligning myself with a white guy so often ends up with me hiding some part of myself. Like with Drew and letting him call me Mulan. And it's not just me. My mother with Michael. Stella with Lucas.

"Just . . . give me a moment," I say. My head is woozy.

"Mr. Nilsen is a busy man," Janelle says. "He has a hard stop at ten a.m."

But before I can respond, the elevator *dings* again and Edvin himself struts out. He's wearing a Patagonia vest over a plain black T-shirt and a Swiss watch encrusted in diamonds.

He gives me a perfunctory nod. "What's taking so long?"

Janelle tries to motion to the TV screen, but the story has already shifted to whatever recent dumb remark our president made about another world leader. I guess the Nexus scandal was only worth two minutes of airtime.

So she goes, "Char found out about the collaboration with Homeland Security."

Is that why Edvin pushed to close this deal so quickly? He probably knew this news was about to break and wanted me to sign before I heard.

He tilts his head. "So . . . ?"

"So it's *wrong*," I say, and then immediately cringe at how childish it sounds. If Khoi was here, he'd be more eloquent. He'd be able to nail exactly what is so gross about this. But Khoi isn't here, and my thoughts are too frantic and blobby to translate into words.

Edvin groans. "Are you serious, Char?"

"You know Hello World is for *helping* immigrants, right?"

He seems genuinely confused. "Those people are losers. *Losers!* You have nothing in common with them. You're a fighter. You're one of the good ones." And even though that is an absolutely disgusting thing for him to say, there's still some small, stupid part of me that perks up like, *He thinks you're special*!

Mom walks toward us. "What's happening?" she asks me in Chinese.

Edvin gives a once-over to her baggy jeans and graying hair, and for a brief moment I think I glimpse contempt in his eyes.

I don't answer her. Instead, I say, "Please, I need more time to think." It comes out so soft, like a little girl's voice.

"We don't *have* time. The press conference is happening now," he says.

Of course. The press conference.

Maybe that's why he's been so interested in me. So he can prop me up as good PR, prove that he doesn't hate all immigrants. *Only the bad ones that are ruining our country.*

It hurts because—because—well, I actually thought he believed in me. Because I figured he meant it when he said I was talented and smart and awesome.

I'm so fucking naive.

Mom straightens to her full height of five-nothing, an entire foot shorter than Edvin. "You heard my daughter. She want a moment." Her voice is strong, like it's made of bronze.

"Ma'am, I don't think you understand."

"I understand you fine," she says. "Sorry, but you going to wait."

Edvin scowls, and for a wild second I'm scared he's about to slap her. He's not somebody used to not getting what he wants. He's got all this brutal energy lurking beneath the Patagonia vest.

But the second passes and his face smooths out, placid. "Fine, but then we can no longer guarantee a spot in Nexus's incubator program for her. We have plenty of other incredible candidates."

Wait, no, I can't let this opportunity slip through my fingertips. I'm not ready to throw it away. I open my mouth to protest, to apologize, but then Mom says, "All good."

Edvin turns to me. "Char, don't do something you're going to regret." And then he strolls back to the elevator, flanked by Janelle.

When they're gone, I stare at Mom. "You just . . . you just stood up to a billionaire tech bro." Except I don't know how to say *billionaire tech bro* in Mandarin, exactly, so I think I end up saying *king of the computers*.

She waves a hand in the air like *It was nothing*, but her eyes flash with pride. "So why did you need more time?"

I flop down on the leather couch. "I don't know if I want to work with him anymore because his company . . ." Ugh. How to say this in Mandarin? "Uh, his company does bad things, but also, we really need the money and the opportunity, and . . ." I stop babbling when I see my mother shaking her head.

"*Baobei,* you don't need to worry about this."

"Huh?"

She sits beside me. "If you don't want to work with him, then don't."

"But we need the money. How are we going to survive?"

"I have some savings," she says. "In a bank account that Michael didn't know about, from before our marriage. And I'll find more work. Char, all you need to do is go to school and be a normal teenager."

"But . . ." I don't know what to say, but it feels like I need to push back. Come up with some plan. Before shit hits the fan. Because shit always hits the fan.

"And I got up early and used your laptop to check Facebook. One of my friends from graduate school replied to me this morning. She lives in Boston now. She said we can stay with her for the time being."

"Oh." Thank God, because I'm half sure Edvin Nilsen is never going to respond to another email of mine.

"Char, I haven't been a good mother to you."

The lie comes automatically. "You're fine."

"No, I didn't protect you," she says. "I was a shell of myself for many years. You suffered in ways no child should have to endure. And I'm sorry. I know I can never make it up to you."

Hearing her say that is like permission, somehow, to finally admit how painful it's been. My eyes tingle with the threat of tears. If I even try to speak, I think I might lose it, so all I do is nod and wait for the moment to pass.

"I have something to give you." She reaches into her handbag and fishes out a piece of yellowed paper. It's a handwritten letter, torn and tattered and taped together again.

Just like my heart, I think, and then am immediately mortified by how angsty-emo-band that thought is. I might as well start wearing raccoon eyeliner.

"Your biological father sent this last year. It's for you. I don't know how he found our address," she says. "When Michael saw it, he got mad and ripped it up. I rescued it from the garbage and fixed it as best as I could."

She brought this here from Oregon. She must've hidden it in her purse, all this time.

My throat is suddenly tight.

Gingerly, I take the letter from her as if it's a grenade. "Why couldn't he just write an email?"

"Maybe he did and it got deleted by Michael. He has all my passwords."

The paper is thin and worn, but the ink is still legible. It's written in Chinese, which I can't read. And like, okay, I get it. Dude's Chinese, he's going to write in the language he knows.

But this is the first contact he's tried to make with his American daughter, and he couldn't be bothered to use a translation app?

"Why didn't you give me this earlier?"

"I was scared he'd break your heart again. I wanted to wait until you were eighteen. But you've been forced to grow up more quickly than most teenagers. I think you're mature enough to decide for yourself what relationship you want to have with your father." She hesitates. "But be careful."

"Yeah, no sh—um, I know. Honestly, I don't think I'm even going to reach out to him." I'm tempted to ball up the letter and Kobe it into the nearest wastebasket. Although given how bad my aim is, I might end up hitting some unwitting bystander in the eye.

"Don't be rash. He's your father. And he regrets what happened and he wants to be part of your life."

I shrug. "Well, he's had a decade to fix that and he didn't." I try to say this casually, like I don't care, but the words come out unsteady.

"No love is perfect," she says. "But you don't need perfect. *Baobei*, don't shut everyone out of your life because you're in pain. You have to let people in. Even if they might hurt you." The way she says it, I'm not sure we're talking about my father anymore.

And somehow those are the words that break me open.

My body slackens. Mom holds me while I cry, really cry, this embarrassing, heaving falling-apart. My soul is wringing itself out and I don't know what will be left when it's done.

"Char, that boy loves you," she murmurs into my hair. "I've seen the way he looks at you. It's more than some teenage fling. You should let him love you."

"But . . . you with Baba, with Michael . . ." I can barely get the words out between sobs.

"The problem wasn't love itself," she says. "But love is only as good as the heart as it comes from. Michael had a cruel and volatile heart. Your father had a selfish and weak heart. But Khoi is so pure and good."

It feels like I'm drowning in a million different emotions. Over the years I've built this wall around my heart, brick by brick, so that nothing could leak through. So that I could protect the rest of myself from the poison that burns there. And now she's swinging a wrecking ball and demolishing everything. It's so unfair.

"Do you love him too?" she asks.

My first instinct is to dodge the question, the same way I did yesterday when he asked the same thing. But—no. I can't spend my entire life running away.

Do I love Khoi? What does it mean to love somebody? I like kissing him. I like touching him. Being with him feels like my entire being has dissolved into gold dust. Our last night together flashes through my mind—his bare skin on mine, his fingertips grazing me everywhere—and suddenly I'm too warm. Oh God, I really don't want to be thinking about this in front of my mother.

Anyway, there's lust and then there's love, and I'm not entirely sure what the difference is, but they aren't the same thing. I'm sure about that.

And this has to be deeper than sheer desire. This is a boy who flew across the country for me, faced down my terrifying stepdad. He saw how fucked up my family is, and he still didn't leave.

This is real.

Khoi makes me feel like I can be braver and better than I am. Like I can be myself in all my ugly, messy ways and he will still accept me. And I know that he will always have my back when the world is a hell storm.

Before I met him, I felt so alone and unworthy, like I was flailing in dark, choppy waters. Now I have a lighthouse. And the lighthouse is Khoi Astor.

The revelation reminds me of the first time I saw the Milky Way, on a family camping trip in seventh grade, before things got really bad with Michael. We were in eastern Oregon, the middle of nowhere, and the night sky brimmed with countless celestial objects. The edge of the galaxy, a bright arc of silver, filled me with astonishment.

But the stars had always been there, no? I simply hadn't been able to see them. They'd been washed out by artificial light, the light that comes from cities, the light that seems so important to us but is a mere speck compared to a star.

"Yes," I say. "I do love him."

I just haven't told him yet. And suddenly, now that I know, I want to race outside, find him, and blurt out my feelings. They feel too big to be contained.

"*Baobei*," she says, trying to hide a smile and completely failing at it. "I think you know what you need to do."

Chapter Thirty-Nine

But I can't rush to Khoi immediately. I have to slay the dragon that is the Boston public transportation system.

First the red line is delayed by twenty minutes. Then my bus transfer at Porter Square gets held up by a passenger's emotional support peacock that escapes its carrier. In retrospect, true love is probably worth calling an Uber for.

The Astors reside in Arlington, a suburb west of Cambridge. As I walk through the neighborhood, passing by these million-dollar homes on a sleepy street, I feel so out of place. Like a dandelion hiding in a field of daisies.

They're in an adorable brick town house. White-picket fence, garden gnomes. It's so quintessentially American.

I ring the doorbell. It sings through his house, shriller than I expected. Ugh. What if Khoi isn't the one to answer the door? What if it's his aunt or uncle? What if they think I'm not good enough for him? I'm suddenly struck by an urge to play ding-dong ditch.

But I force myself to keep my feet planted. I'm not going to run away anymore.

Seconds crawl by before the door opens.

When I see him, my breath catches.

Khoi looks better than he did yesterday. Healthier. Like he finally got a good night's sleep. His black hair is shiny and the color has returned to his face. He's beautiful, but of course, he always is.

He rubs his eyes like he's not sure his vision is working right. "Char? How did you find this place?"

"It's on your prescription labels." I hadn't meant to memorize the address, but somehow it had carved itself into my mind anyway. Like so many other Khoi-related facts.

We sit on the steps in the bright sun. There's so much to say but I don't know where to start. On the bus ride over I had this entire monologue I was trying out in my head, but now that he's here, it's completely dissolved on my tongue.

So what comes out isn't a gorgeous, heart-wrenching declaration of love. It's "I'm not going to sign with Edvin."

I wasn't totally sure what I was going to do until right this moment, but now that the words have left my mouth, it feels like the obvious choice. The only choice. I've already wasted too much of my life with trash dudes, forcing myself to tolerate their shit because I needed something from them. I don't want to spend another second doing that.

Khoi doesn't seem surprised.

"Yeah, I was wondering if you saw the news," he says. "My

uncle is pissed since the Nilsens are a major donor to his university. It's pretty terrible what Nexus is doing."

"Did you know about that before?"

He leans backward, shifting his weight onto his hands. "There were always whispers." I suddenly remember that Obi had mentioned something similar during the opening ceremony, which feels like a lifetime ago.

"Why didn't you tell me?"

He sighs. "You seemed to really look up to him. I didn't want to take that away from you if the rumors weren't confirmed."

"They're confirmed now. I realized he was using me as a PR stunt." I try to sound breezy about it, but it doesn't quite work.

"I'm so sorry, Char." He starts to reach for me but then he hesitates, like he isn't sure if he's allowed to do that anymore.

So I pull the guy into a hug, tucking my face against his shoulder. The scent of sandalwood soap wraps around me like a blanket.

"It was just kinda nice to have someone like Edvin believe in me, I guess," I say into his shirt. Embarrassingly, my voice cracks on the last syllable.

He strokes my hair, and there's a shiver down my back. "You don't need him to believe in you. You're amazing already. Look at everything you did this summer, on top of all the crap you had to deal with. The other campers didn't go through half the stuff you did. Like, I think Haru's greatest challenge was finding a dispensary that would accept his fake ID."

The words are nice but I don't know when I'm going to start truly, truly believing that in my bones. But Khoi makes me think that maybe I can get there someday.

I break away from the hug. I want to look him in the eyes when I say this next part.

He meets my gaze steadily.

"I love you," I say. "I'm sorry I didn't say it earlier. I was scared and everything was a dumpster fire, and it felt like I'd gotten fucked over already by too many people who were supposed to love me. But I love you. Of course I do."

He bites his lip. "You don't have to . . ."

"No, I mean it. Those assholes . . . they've already taken too much away from me, you know? My pain, that's between me and them. That's got nothing to do with you. I can't lose you because of their bullshit."

Maybe I'll never open that letter from my biological father. Maybe I'll read it once and repurpose it as kindling for a bonfire. Or maybe I'll reply to him—embrace my inner boomer and send something with an actual stamp. I don't know.

But here's what I do know. I can't look at every boy and see someone else's ghost.

"We must have a lot in common," Khoi says. "Because I love me too."

I shove him.

"Okay, okay! I also love you. But I said that yesterday!" He laughs, this bright, magnolia-yellow sound. "If you and your mom need a place to stay, you're free to take our guest room for as long as you want. I'm serious."

"We should be okay," I say, thinking of Mom's graduate school friend who offered to help. "But I'll let you know if things change. Thank you. That's really generous."

"Yeah. Of course. Just . . . whatever you need."

And I know exactly what I want from him. "Let's be together," I say before my brain gets in its own way. "Like, for real. I want to be your girlfriend."

He hesitates. "Char, you're in a vulnerable position right now."

"You're totally right," I say. "My life is uncertain and I have no freaking clue where I'll even be living next week. But I know I want you in it—all the mess, all the chaos."

"Char," he says again, pressing a hand to my cheek. His voice is like a promise. "If you're sure about me, it would be an honor to join your chaos."

My heart is giddy and wild and so, so full. "Khoi, you're the one thing I *am* sure about." And then I kiss him fiercely. He kisses me back and kisses me back and never pulls away. It feels like the truest thing in the world. It feels like home.

ACKNOWLEDGMENTS

As a teenager, I vaguely imagined books bursting fully formed from the minds of over-caffeinated authors, kind of like an Athena-from-Zeus situation, but with more espresso. Anyway, I am so fortunate to have been so wrong. There are many, many people who have helped *You Had Me at Hello World* become what it is today.

Thank you to Penny Moore, who believed in this book first and championed it all the way through, as well as the rest of Aevitas Creative Entertainment. Thank you to Deeba Zargarpur for taking such wonderful care of this story and helping me shape it into the best version of itself. Your vision and attention to detail have made me a much stronger writer. Thank you to Jen Ung for your transformative notes on Char's emotional journey. Thank you to Heedayah Lockman and Laura Eckes for the adorable cover, which I can't stop staring at. And thank you to the rest of the Simon & Schuster Books for Young Readers publishing team: Xenia Weakly, Brenna Sinnott, Hilary Zarycky, Kayley Hoffman, Brenna Franzitta, Morgan York, Sara Berko, Lindsey Ferris, Alex Santos, and Justin Chanda, who have worked tirelessly to bring Char and Khoi into the world. You are all marvelous.

I have been privileged to cross paths with many mentors who believed in me before I believed in myself. Thank you to my high school English teachers, Mrs. Hensley and Mrs. Brown, who fostered an early love of literature in me. To the MIT writing department, especially my professors Helen Elaine Lee and Junot Díaz, for a world-class education, and Edward Schiappa, too, for all your encouragement. To the MIT admissions blog team, especially Chris Peterson, for helping me figure out who I wanted to become over the course of many, many conversations. I couldn't have made this journey without all of you.

Like Char, I grew up in Oregon—but unlike her, I was tremendously blessed to grow up alongside fantastic people who hyped me up. Thank you to Marjorie Sheiman—I'm so glad that a summer camp production of *Annie* brought us together. To Tina Wu and Evangeline Liu for getting me through high school. To Alex King for reading my high school writing, even though it was mostly terrible. To Michelle Gouw for reading my middle school writing, which was probably even worse. To Aliris Tang and the rest of the Chinese American community from Portland. And finally to my best friend from high school, Alec Leng, for analyzing media with me, for listening to my numerous tangents, and for telling me exactly how bad the first draft of this book was. I'm glad you think it's better now.

MIT is a magical place because it is brimming with so many wonderful people. Steven Truong, I'm grateful that 8.01 brought us together, even if I learned zero physics. Sam Pauley, thank you for reading this manuscript way back in 2020 and for yapping with me about everything young adult novels. Michelle Xu, thank you for all your insight and kindness over the years, and for promising to be honest if my writing is garbage. Ivy

Li, you are so incisive and so well-read, and I'm honored that you were my first-ever editor, even if it was just for the college newspaper. Jude He, you are incredibly talented and endlessly inspiring, and also, thank you for drawing Char and gifting me my first-ever piece of fanart (!!). Cathy Ji, I am constantly in awe of your brilliance and compassion. Athena Sanchez and Maritza Gallegos, thank you for unconditionally cheering me on. Louis Wenjun Hou, sorry again for that weekend in Tokyo where I holed up in our Airbnb to panic revise. Ajay Arora, I appreciate the commiserating over the starving artist vs. software engineer path—we're on this struggle bus together. Tiffany Trinh and the rest of Tiffcord, thank you for all the memes and good times. Also, shout-out to Claire Cheng, Izzy Chong, Vincent Huang, Agni Kumar, Lani Lee, Nathan Liang, Sharon Lin, Kevin Ly, Faraz Masroor, Chris Xu, Yang Yan, Derek Yen, and Sulli Yost.

I write these acknowledgements from San Francisco, where I've been incredibly lucky to be surrounded by such an abundance of friendship. Akshaya Dinesh, no book could top your real-life hackathon romances, but I hope this one gets close. Bryan Wu, thank you for all the whimsical adventures, and here's to many more. Jenny Cai, Ivory Tang, and Langston Nashold (aka Palindrome House), I couldn't have asked for better roommates. Also, Shan Shan Huang, Cher Hu, Lyna Kim, Jackson Lee, Naomi Lee, Diane Li, Jyoti Rani, Uri Sejas, Michelle Teh, and Macy Toppan, thank you all for being in my life this past year as I've juggled both the adulting thing and the author thing. And, of course, Jeffrey Cheng, you have been so generous. This book benefited tremendously from your fanfic beta reading expertise. Thank you for believing in me so much.

Robert Cunningham, Sicong Shen, and the rest of my Las Vegas housemates, thank you for being much-needed bright spots during those pandemic months. The NYC crew: Kelly Zhang, who is proof that, sometimes, Facebook Marketplace does cough up incredible roommates—forever in awe of your cockroach-squashing skills. Daniel Zeng, thank you for the late-night Hell's Kitchen McDonald's runs. Alice Li, you are a ray of sunshine.

Thank you to M. Ezra Zhang, my first-ever writing friend; we've come a long way from our CTY days. To Jialu Bao for commiserating over the publishing-during-undergrad thing and all your wisdom. To Sheila Panyam for reading an early draft of this manuscript and all your insights. To Jasmine Cui and Jess Zhou for your moral support. To Linda Tong for the thought-provoking conversations. To the many writers who came before me and whose work shaped my understanding of literature. And to my first-ever readers from my seventh-grade fanfiction.net days. As a twelve-year-old, it meant the world to actually reach other people with my stories.

Gerald Hillenbrand, thank you for all your generosity over the years and welcoming me like a family member. Much of this book was drafted at your home. Chris Hillenbrand, I am so lucky to call you my best friend. To fully express my gratitude, it would take an entire novel—so I wrote this one. You are my lighthouse.

The biggest thank-you to my family. To Mom and Dad, thank you for instilling a love of books in me. Thank you for taking me to the library and sending me to writing camp and making me memorize poems as a kid, even though I forgot them all. I am so ridiculously privileged to have grown up with parents who appreciate the written word. To Kyler, thank you for always pushing me to be the best version of myself. I have the coolest little brother in the world. 感谢外祖母和祖母在我最忙碌的写作时光中提供的后勤支持.

And thank *you*, dear reader, for spending time with this book. It is always an honor.